THE KINGFISHER TREASURY OF

CLASSIC STORIES

KINGFISHER
An imprint of Kingfisher Publications Plc
New Penderel House, 283-288 High Holborn
London WC1V 7HZ
www.kingfisherpub.com

First published by Kingfisher 2002
2 4 6 8 10 9 7 5 3 1

Many of these stories were reproduced in
The Kingfisher Book of Classic Boy Stories (2000)
and *The Kingfisher Book of Classic Girl Stories* (1999).

A CIP catalogue record for this book is available from the British Library.

ISBN 0 7534 0663 2

Printed in China
1TR/0602/SF/*UD CG (CG)/140MA

THE KINGFISHER TREASURY OF

CLASSIC STORIES

Chosen by Rosemary Sandberg and Michael Morpurgo

KINGFISHER

Contents

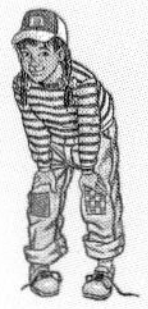

FOREWORD

A good story is a gift for life. It has magical powers to transport us to other times and places, into other lives, and to teach us about other people – and about ourselves. The best stories grip us and won't let us go, living in our imaginations long after the book is closed. The characters we meet become our friends, and forever after we smile at recollections of Winnie-the-Pooh stuck in the entrance to Rabbit's burrow, or draw courage from remembering the grit of Gilly Hopkins or the fortitude of Oliver Twist.

There is nothing to match the splendid feeling of losing yourself in a good book. Everyday concerns melt away as you run barefoot with Heidi in the Swiss Alps or do bloody battle alongside Beowulf against the monster, Grendel. As you read – or listen – the author is writing just for you. And you can live whatever life you choose: pirate, adventurer, junior witch or future king.

This treasury is bursting with wonderful stories – stories that have stood the test of time, cherished by generations. Alongside such classics as *Alice's Adventures in Wonderland*, *Treasure Island* and *Black Beauty* are more contemporary favourites such as *The Iron Man*, *The Worst Witch* and *Charlie and the Chocolate Factory* – modern classics that have already won their place in the hearts of children everywhere.

The stories have been chosen by two outstanding figures in the world of children's literature. Rosemary Sandberg and Michael Morpurgo each describe first discovering the real power of stories for themselves at around the age of seven. This was the age at which Rosemary first joined the library – "with my own ticket", she recalls gleefully – and at which Michael first went away to boarding school and craved an escape from "maths and semolina, and squeaky beds, and chilblains, and the smell of cabbage and shoe polish".

Each quickly discovered the comfort a good story can offer – the thrill and excitement of joining in a wild adventure, the solace of finding your own experiences reflected in the lives of others, the inspiration of characters with bolder spirits, greater freedoms.

This love of stories has stayed with them both throughout lives that have been devoted to bringing good books to children – Rosemary Sandberg as a distinguished publisher and agent, Michael Morpurgo as one of today's most acclaimed writers.

In this rich and inspirational collection, Rosemary and Michael have each chosen extracts from some of their favourite books, inviting us to share their passions in short introductions to each story. Chosen to capture the spirit of the books from which they come, the extracts offer tasters of some of the greatest children's stories. Some you may already know, others will be new discoveries that you will want to seek out in a library or bookshop to read more about the characters and places that have captured your imagination. Some stories are accompanied by their original illustrations; others are given fresh interpretations by some of our very best contemporary artists.

As you turn the pages of this book, you will visit exciting new worlds – and store up memories that will last a lifetime.

Introduction

Winnie-the-Pooh is Christopher Robin's bear. Pooh, who likes honey – a lot – and has friends called Eeyore, Piglet and Tigger, must be just about the most famous bear the world has ever known. No other bear gets himself stuck as often as Pooh – if he isn't getting his head stuck in a pot of honey, then he's getting himself stuck down a rabbit hole. "Silly old Bear!"

M. M.

WINNIE~THE~POOH

A. A. MILNE

In Which Pooh Goes Visiting and Gets into a Tight Place

Edward Bear, known to his friends as Winnie-the-Pooh, or Pooh for short, was walking through the Forest one day, humming proudly to himself. He had made up a little hum that very morning, as he was doing his Stoutness Exercises in front of the glass: *Tra-la-la, tra-la-la,* as he stretched up as high as he could go, and then *Tra-la-la, tra-la – oh, help! – la,* as he tried to reach his toes. After breakfast he had said it over and over to himself until he had learnt it off by heart, and now he was humming it right through, properly. It went like this:

Tra-la-la, tra-la-la,
Tra-la-la, tra-la-la,
Rum-tum-tiddle-um-tum.
Tiddle-iddle, tiddle-iddle,
Tiddle-iddle, tiddle-iddle,
Rum-tum-tum-tiddle-um.

Well, he was humming this hum to himself, and walking along gaily, wondering what everybody else was doing, and what it felt like, being somebody else, when suddenly he came to a sandy bank, and in the bank was a large hole.

"Aha!" said Pooh. (*Rum-tum-tiddle-um-tum.*) "If I know anything about anything, that hole means Rabbit," he said, "and Rabbit means Company," he said, "and Company means Food and Listening-to-Me-Humming and such like. *Rum-tum-tum-tiddle-um.*"

So he bent down, put his head into the hole, and called out:

"Is anybody at home?"

There was a sudden scuffling noise from inside the hole, and then silence.

"What I said was, 'Is anybody at home?'" called out Pooh very loudly.

"No!" said a voice; and then added, "You needn't shout so loud. I heard you quite well the first time."

"Bother!" said Pooh. "Isn't there anybody here at all?"

"Nobody."

Winnie-the-Pooh took his head out of the hole, and thought for a little, and he thought to himself, "There must be somebody there, because somebody must have *said* 'Nobody.'" So he put his head back in the hole, and said:

"Hallo, Rabbit, isn't that you?"

"No," said Rabbit, in a different sort of voice this time.

"But isn't that Rabbit's voice?"

"I don't *think* so," said Rabbit. "It isn't *meant* to be."

"Oh!" said Pooh.

He took his head out of the hole, and had another think, and then he put it back, and said:

"Well, could you very kindly tell me where Rabbit is?"

"He has gone to see his friend Pooh Bear, who is a great friend of his."

"But this *is* Me!" said Bear, very much surprised.

"What sort of Me?"

"Pooh Bear."

"Are you sure?" said Rabbit, still more surprised.

"Quite, quite sure," said Pooh.

"Oh, well, then, come in."

So Pooh pushed and pushed and pushed his way through the hole, and at last he got in.

"You were quite right," said Rabbit, looking at him all over. "It *is* you. Glad to see you."

"Who did you think it was?"

"Well, I wasn't sure. You know how it is in the Forest. One can't have *anybody* coming into one's house. One has to be *careful*. What about a mouthful of something?"

Pooh always liked a little something at eleven o'clock in the morning, and he was very glad to see Rabbit getting out the plates and mugs; and when Rabbit said, "Honey or condensed milk with your bread?" he was so excited that he said, "Both," and then, so as not to seem greedy, he added, "But don't bother about the bread, please." And for a long time after that he said nothing . . . until at last, humming to himself in a rather sticky voice, he got up, shook Rabbit lovingly by the paw, and said that he must be going on.

"Must you?" said Rabbit politely.

"Well," said Pooh, "I could stay a little longer if it – if you –" and he tried very hard to look in the direction of the larder.

"As a matter of fact," said Rabbit, "I was going out myself directly."

"Oh well, then, I'll be going on. Good-bye."

"Well, good-bye, if you're sure you won't have any more."

"*Is* there any more?" asked Pooh quickly.

Rabbit took the covers off the dishes, and said, "No, there wasn't."

"I thought not," said Pooh, nodding to himself. "Well, good-bye, I must be going on."

So he started to climb out of the hole. He pulled with his front paws, and pushed with his back paws, and in a little while his nose was out in the open again . . . and then his ears . . . and then his front paws . . . and then his shoulders . . . and then –

"Oh, help!" said Pooh. "I'd better go back."

"Oh, bother!" said Pooh. "I shall have to go on."

"I can't do either!" said Pooh. "Oh, help *and* bother!"

Now, by this time Rabbit wanted to go for a walk too, and finding the front door full, he went out by the back door, and came round to Pooh, and looked at him.

"Hallo, are you stuck?" he asked.

"N-no," said Pooh carelessly. "Just resting and thinking and humming to myself."

"Here, give us a paw."

Pooh Bear stretched out a paw, and Rabbit pulled and pulled and pulled . . .

"*Ow!*" cried Pooh. "You're hurting!"

"The fact is," said Rabbit, "you're stuck."

"It all comes," said Pooh crossly, "of not having front doors big enough."

"It all comes," said Rabbit sternly, "of eating too much. I thought at the time," said Rabbit, "only I didn't like to say anything," said Rabbit, "that one of us was eating too much," said Rabbit, "and I knew it wasn't *me*," he said. "Well, well, I shall go and fetch Christopher Robin."

Christopher Robin lived at the other end of the Forest, and when he came back with Rabbit, and saw the front half of Pooh, he said, "Silly old Bear," in such a loving voice that everybody felt quite hopeful again.

"I was just beginning to think," said Bear, sniffing slightly, "that Rabbit might never be able to use his front door again. And I should *hate* that," he said.

"So should I," said Rabbit.

"Use his front door again?" said Christopher Robin. "Of course he'll use his front door again."

"Good," said Rabbit.

"If we can't pull you out, Pooh, we might push you back."

Rabbit scratched his whiskers thoughtfully, and pointed out that, when once Pooh was pushed back, he was back, and of course nobody was more glad to see Pooh than *he* was, still there it was, some lived in trees and some lived underground, and –

"You mean I'd *never* get out?" said Pooh.

"I mean," said Rabbit, "that having got *so* far, it seems a pity to waste it."

Christopher Robin nodded.

"Then there's only one thing to be done," he said. "We shall have to wait for you to get thin again."

"How long does getting thin take?" asked Pooh anxiously.

"About a week, I should think."

"But I can't stay here for a *week*!"

"You can *stay* here all right, silly old Bear. It's getting you out which is so difficult."

"We'll read to you," said Rabbit cheerfully.

"And I hope it won't snow," he added. "And I say, old fellow, you're taking up a good deal of room in my house – *do* you mind if I use your back legs as a towel-horse? Because, I mean, there they are – doing nothing – and it would be very convenient just to hang the towels on them."

"A week!" said Pooh gloomily. "*What about meals?*"

"I'm afraid no meals," said Christopher Robin, "because of getting thin quicker. But we *will* read to you."

Bear began to sigh, and then found he couldn't because he was so tightly stuck; and a tear rolled down his eye, as he said:

"Then would you read a Sustaining Book, such as would help and comfort a Wedged Bear in Great Tightness?"

So for a week Christopher Robin read that sort of book at the North end of Pooh, and Rabbit hung his washing on the South end . . . and in between Bear felt himself getting slenderer and slenderer. And at the end of the week Christopher Robin said, "*Now!*"

So he took hold of Pooh's front paws and Rabbit took hold of Christopher Robin, and all Rabbit's friends and relations took hold of Rabbit, and they all pulled together . . .

And for a long time Pooh only said "*Ow!*" . . .

And "*Oh!*" . . .

And then, all of a sudden, he said "*Pop!*" just as if a cork were coming out of a bottle.

And Christopher Robin and Rabbit and all Rabbit's friends and relations went head-over-heels backwards . . . and on top of them came Winnie-the-Pooh – free!

So, with a nod of thanks to his friends, he went on with his walk through the forest, humming proudly to himself. But Christopher Robin looked after him lovingly, and said to himself, "Silly old Bear!"

Introduction

How peaceful life is on the river bank for new friends Mole and Rat. Ratty has introduced Mole to the pleasures of messing about in boats. Finding the perfect backwater at last, they stop for a scrumptious picnic. The calm is broken by the arrival of Otter, and briefly Badger. Ratty and Otter begin discussing the recent boating exploits of Toad when, in the distance, they glimpse a short, stout figure rolling about a good deal in his boat. It is Toad, of course. Mole is intrigued and wants to know much more about this curious rower. And here he gets his chance. During the following summer and winter months, this resourceful band of friends get up to all kinds of adventures and mishaps along the river bank and in the Wild Wood. While they laugh and squabble, Mole, Ratty, Badger and, most boisterously of all, the irrepressible Mr Toad, have the time of their lives.

R. S.

THE WIND IN THE WILLOWS

KENNETH GRAHAME

The Open Road

"But what I wanted to ask you was, won't you take me to call on Mr Toad? I've heard so much about him, and I do so want to make his acquaintance."

"Why, certainly," said the good-natured Rat, jumping to his feet and dismissing poetry from his mind for the day. "Get the boat out, and we'll paddle up there at once. It's never the wrong time to call on Toad. Early or late he's always the same fellow. Always good-tempered, always glad to see you, always sorry when you go!"

"He must be a very nice animal," observed the Mole, as he got into the boat and took the sculls, while the Rat settled himself comfortably in the stern.

"He is indeed the best of animals," replied Rat. "So simple, so good-natured, and so affectionate. Perhaps he's not very clever –

we can't all be geniuses; and it may be that he is both boastful and conceited. But he has got some great qualities, has Toady."

Rounding a bend in the river, they came in sight of a handsome, dignified old house of mellowed red brick, with well-kept lawns reaching down to the water's edge.

"There's Toad Hall," said the Rat; "and that creek on the left, where the notice-board says 'Private. No landing allowed', leads to his boat-house, where we'll leave the boat. The stables are over there to the right. That's the banqueting-hall you're looking at now – very old, that is. Toad is rather rich, you know, and this is really one of the nicest houses in these parts, though we never admit as much to Toad."

They glided up the creek, and the Mole shipped his sculls as they passed into the shadow of a large boat-house. Here they saw many handsome boats, slung from the cross-beams or hauled up on a slip, but none in the water; and the place had an unused and a deserted air.

The Rat looked around him. "I understand," said he. "Boating is played out. He's tired of it, and done with it. I wonder what new fad he has taken up now? Come along and let's look him up. We shall hear all about it quite soon enough."

They disembarked, and strolled across the gay flower-decked lawns in search of Toad, whom they presently happened upon resting in a wicker garden-chair, with a preoccupied expression of face, and a large map spread out on his knees.

"Hooray!" he cried, jumping up on seeing them, "this is splendid!" He shook the paws of both of them warmly, never waiting for an introduction to the Mole. "How *kind* of you!" he went on, dancing round them. "I was just going to send a boat down the river for you, Ratty, with strict orders that you were to be fetched up here at once, whatever you were doing. I want you badly – both of you. Now what will you take? Come inside and have something! You don't know how lucky it is, your turning up just now!"

"Let's sit quiet a bit, Toady!" said the Rat, throwing himself into an easy chair, while the Mole took another by the side of him and made some civil remark about Toad's "delightful residence".

"Finest house on the whole river," cried Toad boisterously. "Or anywhere else, for that matter," he could not help adding.

Here the Rat nudged the Mole. Unfortunately the Toad saw him do it, and turned very red. There was a moment's painful silence. Then Toad burst out laughing. "All right, Ratty," he said. "It's only my way, you know. And it's not such a very bad house, is it? You know you rather like it yourself. Now, look here. Let's be sensible. You are the very animals I wanted. You've got to help me. It's most important!"

"It's about your rowing, I suppose," said the Rat, with an innocent air. "You're getting on fairly well, though you splash a good bit still. With a great deal of patience, and any quantity of coaching, you may –"

"O, pooh! boating!" interrupted the Toad, in great disgust. "Silly boyish amusement. I've given that up *long* ago. Sheer waste of time, that's what it is. It makes me downright sorry to see you fellows, who ought to know better, spending all your energies in that aimless manner. No, I've discovered the real thing, the only genuine occupation for a lifetime. I propose to devote the remainder of mine to it, and can only regret the wasted years that lie behind me, squandered in trivialities. Come with me, dear Ratty, and your amiable friend also, if he will be so very good, just as far as the stable-yard, and you shall see what you shall see!"

He led the way to the stable-yard accordingly, the Rat following with a most mistrustful expression; and there, drawn out of the coach-house into the open, they saw a gipsy caravan, shining with newness, painted a canary-yellow picked out with green, and red wheels.

"There you are!" cried the Toad, straddling and expanding himself. "There's real life for you, embodied in that little cart. The open road, the dusty highway, the heath, the common, the hedgerows, the rolling downs! Camps, villages, towns, cities! Here today, up and off to somewhere else tomorrow! Travel, change, interest, excitement! The whole world before you, and a horizon that's always changing! And mind, this is the very finest cart of its

sort that was ever built, without any exception. Come inside and look at the arrangements. Planned 'em all myself, I did!"

The Mole was tremendously interested and excited, and followed him eagerly up the steps and into the interior of the caravan. The Rat only snorted and thrust his hands deep into his pockets, remaining where he was.

It was indeed very compact and comfortable. Little sleeping-bunks – a little table that folded up against the wall – a cooking-stove, lockers, bookshelves, a bird cage with a bird in it; and pots, pans, jugs and kettles of every size and variety.

"All complete!" said the Toad triumphantly, pulling open a locker. "You see – biscuits, potted lobster, sardines – everything you can possibly want. Soda-water here – baccy there – letter-paper, bacon, jam, cards and dominoes – you'll find," he continued, as they descended the steps again, "you'll find that nothing whatever has been forgotten, when we make our start this afternoon."

"I beg your pardon," said the Rat slowly, as he chewed a straw, "but did I overhear you say something about '*we*', and '*start*', and '*this afternoon*'?"

"Now, you dear good old Ratty," said Toad imploringly, "don't begin talking in that stiff and sniffy sort of way, because you know you've *got* to come. I can't possibly manage without you, so please consider it settled, and don't argue – it's the one thing I can't stand. You surely don't mean to stick to your dull fusty old river all your life, and just live in a hole in a bank, and *boat*? I want to show you the world! I'm going to make an *animal* of you, my boy!"

Introduction

Milly-Molly-Mandy lives with Father, Mother, Grandma and Grandpa, Aunty, Uncle and Toby the dog in a little white house with a thatched roof. She has short hair and short legs, but a very long name: Millicent Margaret Amanda, or Milly-Molly-Mandy for short and for everyday. She has all sorts of adventures with little-friend-Susan and Billy Blunt, and sometimes she likes playing on her own. One day she decides to give a party, so, with the help of her friends, she starts to plan. And somehow the guest list gets longer and longer . . .

R. S.

MILLY ~ MOLLY ~ MANDY

JOYCE LANKESTER BRISLEY

Milly~Molly~Mandy Gives a Party

Once upon a time Milly-Molly-Mandy had a plan. And when she had thought over the plan for a while she went to look in her money-box. And in the money-box were four pennies and a ha'penny, which Milly-Molly-Mandy did not think would be enough for her plan. So Milly-Molly-Mandy went off to talk it over with her little-friend-Susan down the road.

"Susan," said Milly-Molly-Mandy, "I've got a plan (only it's a great secret). I want to give a party in our barn to Farver and Muvver and Grandpa and Grandma and Uncle and Aunty. And I want to buy refreshments. And you and I will be waitresses. And if there's anything over we can eat it up afterwards."

Little-friend-Susan thought it a very good plan indeed.

"Will we wear caps?" she asked.

"Yes," said Milly-Molly-Mandy, "and aprons. Only I haven't got enough money for the refreshments, so I don't think there'll be any over. We must think."

So Milly-Molly-Mandy and little-friend-Susan sat down and thought hard.

"We must work and earn some," said Milly-Molly-Mandy.

"But how?" said little-friend-Susan.

"We might sell something," said Milly-Molly-Mandy.

"But what?" said little-friend-Susan.

So they had to think some more.

Presently Milly-Molly-Mandy said, "I've got pansies and marigolds in my garden."

And little-friend-Susan said, "I've got nasturtiums in mine."

"We could run errands for people," said Milly-Molly-Mandy.

"And clean brass," said little-friend-Susan.

That was a lovely idea, so Milly-Molly-Mandy fetched a pencil and paper and wrote out very carefully:

Millicent Margaret
Amanda & Susan & Co.
have bunches of flowers
for sale and clean brass
very cheap (we do not
spill the polish) and run
errands very cheap.

"What's 'and Co.'?" said little-friend-Susan.

"It's just business," said Milly-Molly-Mandy, "but perhaps we might ask Billy Blunt to be it. And he could be a waiter."

Then they hung the notice on the front gate, and waited just the other side of the hedge.

Several people passed, but nobody seemed to want anything. Then at last a motor-car came along with a lady and gentleman in it; and when they saw the nice white cottage with the thatched roof they stopped at the gate to ask if they could get some cream there.

Milly-Molly-Mandy said, "I'll go and ask Muvver," and took the little pot they held out. And when she came back with it full of cream the lady and gentleman had read the notice and were asking little-friend-Susan questions. As the lady paid for the cream she said they must certainly have some flowers. So they each bought a bunch. And then the gentleman said the round brass thing in front of his car needed cleaning very badly – could the firm do it straight away?

So Milly-Molly-Mandy said, "Yes, sir," and raced back to the cottage to give Mother the cream-money and to borrow the brass-polishing box. And then she cleaned the round brass thing in front of the car with one piece of cloth and little-friend-Susan rubbed it bright with another piece of cloth, and the lady and gentleman looked on and seemed very satisfied.

Then the gentleman asked, "How much?" and paid them two pence for the flowers and a penny for the polishing. Milly-Molly-Mandy wanted to do some more polishing for the money, but the gentleman said they couldn't stop. And then they said goodbye and went off, and the lady turned and waved, and Milly-Molly-Mandy and little-friend-Susan waved back until they were gone.

Milly-Molly-Mandy and little-friend-Susan felt very happy and pleased.

And now they had sevenpence-ha'penny for the refreshments. Father and Mother and Grandpa and Grandma and Uncle and

Aunty and Mrs Moggs, little-friend-Susan's mother, made seven.

Then who should look over the hedge but Mr Jakes, the Postman, on his way home from collecting letters from the letter-boxes. He had seen the notice on the gate.

"What's this? You trying to make a fortune?" said the Postman.

"Yes," said Milly-Molly-Mandy, "we've earned threepence!"

"My! And what do you plan to do with it?" said the Postman.

"We've got a secret!" said Milly-Molly-Mandy, with a little skip.

"Ah!" said the Postman. "I guess it's a nice one, too!"

Milly-Molly-Mandy looked at little-friend-Susan, and then she looked at the Postman. He was a nice Postman. "You won't tell if we tell you?" she asked.

"Try me!" said the Postman promptly. So Milly-Molly-Mandy told him they were planning to give a party to Father and Mother and Grandpa and Grandma and Uncle and Aunty and Mrs Moggs.

"They're in luck, they are!" said the Postman. "Nobody asks me to parties."

Milly-Molly-Mandy looked at little-friend-Susan again, and then she looked at the Postman. He was a very nice Postman. Then she said, "Supposing you were invited, would you come?"

"You try me!" said the Postman promptly again. And then he hitched up his letter-bag and went on.

"Farver and Muvver and Grandpa and Grandma and Uncle and Aunty and Mrs Moggs and the Postman. We've got to earn some more," said Milly-Molly-Mandy. "Let's go down to the village and ask Billy Blunt to be 'and Co.', and p'r'aps he'll have an idea."

Billy Blunt was in the road outside the corn-shop, mending the handles of his box on wheels. He had made it nearly all himself, and it was a very nice one, painted green like the water-butt and the lawn roller. He thought "and Co." was rather a funny name, but he said he would be it all right, and offered to make them a box with a slit in it, where they could keep their earnings. And he put in four farthings out of his collection. (Billy Blunt was collecting farthings – he had nineteen in an empty bird-seed bag.)

So now they had eightpence-ha'penny for the refreshments.

On Monday morning, on their way home to dinner, Milly-Molly-Mandy and little-friend-Susan passed Mrs Jakes, the Postman's wife, at her door, getting a breath of fresh air before dishing up her dinner. And Mrs Jakes said, "Good morning! How's the firm of Millicent Margaret Amanda, Susan and Co. getting on?"

Milly-Molly-Mandy said, "Very well, thank you!"

"My husband's told me about your brass-cleaning," said Mrs Jakes. "I've got a whole mantelshelf full that wants doing!"

Milly-Molly-Mandy and little-friend-Susan were very pleased, and arranged to come in directly after school was over in the afternoon and clean it.

And they cleaned a mug and three candlesticks and two lamps – one big and one little – and a tray and a warming-pan, and they didn't spill or waste any of the polish. Mrs Jakes seemed very satisfied, and gave them each a penny and a piece of cake.

So now they had tenpence-ha'penny for refreshments.

But when they got outside Milly-Molly-Mandy said, "Farver and Muvver and Grandpa and Grandma and Uncle and Aunty and Mrs Moggs and the Postman and Mrs Postman – I wonder if we've earned enough, Susan?"

As they turned home they passed the forge, and of course they had to stop a moment at the doorway, as usual, to watch the fire roaring, and Mr Rudge the Blacksmith banging with his hammer on the anvil.

Little-friend-Susan was just a bit nervous of the Blacksmith – he was so big, and his face was so dirty it made his teeth look very white and his eyes very twinkly when he smiled at them. But Milly-Molly-Mandy knew he was nice and clean under the dirt, which he couldn't help while he worked. So she smiled back.

And the Blacksmith said, "Hello!"

And Milly-Molly-Mandy said, "Hello!"

Then the Blacksmith beckoned with his finger and said, "Come here!"

Milly-Molly-Mandy gave a little jump, and little-friend-Susan pulled at her hand, but Milly-Molly-Mandy knew he was really just a nice man under the dirt, so she went up to him.

And the Blacksmith said, "Look what I've got here!" And he showed them a tiny little horseshoe, just like a proper one, only smaller, which he had made for them to keep. Milly-Molly-Mandy and little-friend-Susan were pleased!

Milly-Molly-Mandy thanked him very much. And then she looked at the Blacksmith and said, "If you were invited to a party, would you come?"

And the Blacksmith looked at Milly-Molly-Mandy with twinkly eyes and said he'd come quite fast – so long as it wasn't before five o'clock on Saturday, when he was playing cricket with his team in the meadow.

When they got outside again Milly-Molly-Mandy said, "Farver and Muvver and Grandpa and Grandma and Uncle and Aunty and Mrs Moggs and the Postman and Mrs Postman and the Blacksmith. We'll ask them for half past five, and we ought to earn some more money, Susan!"

Just then they met Billy Blunt coming along, pulling his box on wheels with a bundle in it. And Billy Blunt grinned and said,

"I'm fetching Mrs Bloss's washing, for the firm!" Milly-Molly-Mandy and little-friend-Susan were pleased!

When Saturday morning came all the invitations had been given out, and the firm of Millicent Margaret Amanda, Susan and Co. was very busy putting things tidy in the barn, and covering up things which couldn't be moved with lots of green branches which Grandpa was trimming from the hedges.

And when half past five came Milly-Molly-Mandy and little-friend-Susan, with clean hands and paper caps and aprons, waited by the barn door to welcome the guests. And each gentleman received a marigold buttonhole, and each lady a pansy.

Everybody arrived in good time, except the Blacksmith, who was just a little bit late – he looked so clean and pink in his white cricket flannels, Milly-Molly-Mandy hardly knew him – and Billy Blunt. But Billy Blunt came lugging a gramophone and two records which he had borrowed from a bigger boy at school. (He never told, but he had given the boy all the rest of his collection of farthings – fifteen of them, which makes threepence-three-farthings – in exchange.)

Then Billy Blunt, who didn't want to dance, looked after the gramophone, while Father and Mother and Grandpa and Grandma and Uncle and Aunty and Mrs Moggs and the Postman and Mrs Postman and the Blacksmith and Milly-Molly-Mandy and little-friend-Susan danced together in the old barn till the dust flew. And Milly-Molly-Mandy danced a lot with the Blacksmith as well as with everybody else, and so did little-friend-Susan.

They did enjoy themselves!

And then there were refreshments – raspberry drops and aniseed balls on saucers trimmed with little flowers; and late blackberries on leaf plates; and sherbet drinks, which Billy Blunt prepared while Milly-Molly-Mandy and little-friend-Susan stood by to tell people just the very moment to drink, when it was fizzing properly. (It was exciting!) And a jelly which Milly-Molly-Mandy and little-friend-Susan had made themselves from a packet, only it had to be eaten rather like soup, as it wouldn't stand up properly.

But Father and Mother and Grandpa and Grandma and Uncle and Aunty and Mrs Moggs and the Postman and Mrs Postman and the Blacksmith all said they had never enjoyed a jelly so much.

And the Blacksmith, in a big voice, proposed a vote of thanks to the firm for the delightful party and refreshments, and everybody else said "Hear! Hear!" and clapped. And Milly-Molly-Mandy and little-friend-Susan joined in the clapping too, which wasn't quite proper, but they were so happy they couldn't help it!

And then all the guests went home.

And when the firm came to clear up the refreshments they found there was only one aniseed ball left. But placed among the empty saucers and glasses on the bench were a small basket of pears and a bag of mixed sweets with a ticket "For the Waiter and Waitresses" on it!

Introduction

Ramona Quimby never thinks of herself as a pest, but her over-enthusiastic antics always seem to land her in trouble. When you are the youngest in the family and the youngest person in the street, you have to make a great big noisy fuss just to get noticed. But now that she is going to school, Ramona tries quite hard to be good. At rest time she wants to be the wake-up fairy so she gives a little snore to show what a good rester she is . . . but when the other children start to snore and to giggle, her friend Howie says, "Ramona started it!". That isn't her fault, now is it? When Hallowe'en comes round, everyone dresses up for the school parade. Howie wants to be a pirate, but ends up having to wear his sister's old cat costume – with a broken tail. Ramona decides to be the baddest witch in the parade, in a scary, flabby mask. Now she can be as naughty as she likes.

R. S.

RAMONA THE PEST

BEVERLY CLEARY

The Baddest Witch in the World

When they were in sight of the playground, Ramona saw that it was already swarming with both the morning and the afternoon kindergartens in their Hallowe'en costumes. Poor Miss Binny, dressed like Mother Goose, now had the responsibility of sixty-eight boys and girls. "Run along, Ramona," said Mrs Quimby, when they had crossed the street. "Howie's mother and I will go around to the big playground and try to find a seat on a bench before they are all taken."

Ramona ran screaming on to the playground. "Yah! Yah! I'm the baddest witch in the world!" Nobody paid any attention, because everyone else was screaming, too. The noise was glorious. Ramona yelled and screamed and shrieked and chased anyone who would run. She chased tramps and ghosts and ballerinas. Sometimes other witches in masks exactly like hers chased her, and then she would

turn around and chase the witches right back. She tried to chase Howie, but he would not run. He just stood beside the fence holding his broken tail and missing all the fun.

Ramona discovered dear little Davy in a skimpy pirate costume from the toy store. She could tell he was Davy by his thin legs. At last! She pounced and kissed him through her rubber mask. Davy looked startled, but he had the presence of mind to make a gagging noise while Ramona raced away, satisfied that she finally had managed to catch and kiss Davy.

Then Ramona saw Susan getting out of her mother's car. As she might have guessed, Susan was dressed as an old-fashioned girl with a long skirt, an apron, and pantalettes. "I'm the baddest witch in the world!" yelled Ramona, and ran after Susan, whose curls bobbed daintily about her shoulders in a way that could not be disguised. Ramona was unable to resist. After weeks of longing she tweaked one of Susan's curls, and yelled "*Boing!*" through her rubber mask.

"You stop that," said Susan, and smoothed her curls.

"Yah! Yah! I'm the baddest witch in the world!" Ramona was carried away. She tweaked another curl and yelled another muffled "*Boing!*"

A clown laughed and joined Ramona. He too tweaked a curl and yelled, "*Boing!*"

The old-fashioned girl stamped her foot. "You stop that!" she said angrily.

"*Boing! Boing!*" Others joined the game. Susan tried to run away, but no matter which way she ran there was someone eager to stretch a curl and yell, "*Boing!*" Susan ran to Miss Binny. "Miss Binny! Miss Binny!" she cried. "They're teasing me! They're pulling my hair and boinging me!"

"Who's teasing you?" asked Miss Binny.

"Everybody," said Susan tearfully. "A witch started it."

"Which witch?" asked Miss Binny.

Susan looked around. "I don't know which witch," she said, "but it was a bad witch."

That's me, the baddest witch in the world, thought Ramona. At the same time she was a little surprised. That others really would not know that she was behind her mask had never occurred to her.

"Never mind, Susan," said Miss Binny. "You stay near me, and no one will tease you."

Which witch, thought Ramona, liking the sound of the words. Which witch, which witch. As the words ran through her thoughts Ramona began to wonder if Miss Binny could guess who she was. She ran up to her teacher and shouted in her muffled voice, "Hello, Miss Binny! I'm going to get you, Miss Binny!"

"Ooh, what a scary witch!" said Miss Binny, rather absent-mindedly, Ramona thought. Plainly Miss Binny was not really

frightened, and with so many witches running around she had not recognized Ramona.

No, Miss Binny was not the one who was frightened. Ramona was. Miss Binny did not know who this witch was. Nobody knew who Ramona was, and if nobody knew who she was, she wasn't anybody.

"Get out of the way, old witch!" Eric R. yelled at Ramona. He did not say, "Get out of the way, Ramona."

Ramona could not remember a time when there was not someone near who knew who she was. Even last Hallowe'en, when she dressed up as a ghost and went trick-or-treating with Beezus and the older boys and girls, everyone seemed to know who she was. "I can guess who this little ghost is," the neighbours said, as they dropped a miniature candy bar or a handful of peanuts into her paper bag. And now, with so many witches running around and still more witches on the big playground, no one knew who she was.

"Davy, guess who I am!" yelled Ramona. Surely Davy would know.

"You're just another old witch," answered Davy.

The feeling was the scariest one Ramona had ever experienced. She felt lost inside her costume. She wondered if her mother would know which witch was which, and the thought that her own mother might not know her frightened Ramona even more. What if her mother forgot her? What if everyone in the whole world forgot her? With that terrifying thought, Ramona snatched off her mask, and although its ugliness was no longer the most frightening thing about it, she rolled it up so she would not have to look at it.

How cool the air felt outside that dreadful mask! Ramona no longer wanted to be the baddest witch in the world. She wanted to be Ramona Geraldine Quimby and be sure that Miss Binny and everyone on the playground knew her. Around her the ghosts and tramps and pirates raced and shouted, but Ramona stood near the door of the kindergarten quietly watching.

Davy raced up to her and yelled, "Yah! You can't catch me!"

"I don't want to catch you," Ramona informed him.

Davy looked surprised and a little disappointed, but he ran off on his thin little legs, shouting, "Yo-ho-ho and a bottle of rum!"

Joey yelled after him, "You're not really a pirate. You're just Mush Pot Davy!"

Miss Binny was trying to herd her sixty-eight charges into a double line. Two mothers who felt sorry for the teacher were helping round up the kindergarten to start the Hallowe'en parade, but as always there were some children who would rather run around than do what they were supposed to do. For once Ramona was not one of them. On the big playground someone started to play a marching record through a loudspeaker. The Hallowe'en parade that Ramona had looked forward to since she was in nursery school was about to begin.

"Come along, children," said Miss Binny. Seeing Ramona standing alone, she said, "Come on, Ramona."

It was a great relief to Ramona to hear Miss Binny speak her name, to hear her teacher say "Ramona" when she was looking at her. But as much as Ramona longed to prance along to the marching music with the rest of her class, she did not move to join them.

"Put on your mask, Ramona, and get in line," said Miss Binny, guiding a ghost and a gypsy into place.

Ramona wanted to obey her teacher, but at the same time she was afraid of losing herself behind that scary mask. The line of kindergarteners, all of them wearing masks except Howie with his

pipe-cleaner whiskers, was less straggly now, and everyone was eager to start the parade. If Ramona did not do something quickly she would be left behind, and she could not let such a thing happen, not when she had waited so many years to be in a Hallowe'en parade.

Ramona took only a moment to decide what to do. She ran to her cupboard inside the kindergarten building and snatched a crayon from her box. Then she grabbed a piece of paper from the supply cupboard. Outside she could hear the many feet of the morning and afternoon kindergartens marching off to the big playground. There was no time for Ramona's best printing, but that was all right. This job was not seat work to be supervised by Miss Binny. As fast as she could Ramona printed her name, and then she could not resist adding with a flourish her last initial, complete with ears and whiskers.

Now the whole world would know who she was! She was Ramona Quimby, the only girl in the world with ears and whiskers on her last initial. Ramona pulled on her rubber mask, clapped her pointed hat on top of it, snapped the elastic under her chin and ran after her class as it marched on to the big playground. She did not care if she was last in line and had to march beside gloomy old Howie, still lugging his broken tail.

Around the playground marched the kindergarten followed by the first grade and all the other grades while mothers and little brothers and sisters watched. Ramona felt very grown-up

remembering how last year she had been a little sister sitting on a bench watching for her big sister Beezus to march by and hoping for a left-over doughnut.

"Yah! Yah! I'm the baddest witch in the world!" Ramona chanted, as she held up her sign for all to see. Around the playground she marched towards her mother, who was waiting on the bench. Her mother saw her, pointed her out to Mrs Kemp, and waved. Ramona beamed inside her stuffy mask. Her mother recognized her!

Poor little Willa Jean in her stroller could not read, so Ramona called out to her, "It's me, Willa Jean. I'm Ramona, the baddest witch in the world!"

Willa Jean in her rabbit mask understood. She laughed and slapped her hands on the tray of her stroller.

Ramona saw Henry's dog Ribsy trotting along, supervising the parade. "Yah! Ribsy! I'm going to get you, Ribsy!" she threatened, as she marched past.

Ribsy gave a short bark, and Ramona was sure that even Ribsy knew who she was as she marched off to collect her doughnut and apple juice.

Introduction

Mr and Mrs Darling have gone out, leaving their three children, John, Michael and Wendy, safely tucked up in bed – or so they think. Nana the dog senses something is wrong up in the nursery. She barks and barks before running off to raise the alarm. But by the time Mr and Mrs Darling get home, it's too late. From the street they can see the nursery lights are on and the children are flying through the air, round and round – and not three children but four. Peter Pan is taking the children to Neverland. Fly off with them for the greatest adventure of your life.

M. M.

PETER PAN

J. M. BARRIE

The Flight

"Second to the right, and straight on till morning."

That, Peter had told Wendy, was the way to the Neverland; but even birds, carrying maps and consulting them at windy corners, could not have sighted it with these instructions. Peter, you see, just said anything that came into his head.

At first his companions trusted him implicitly, and so great were the delights of flying that they wasted time circling round church spires or any other tall objects on the way that took their fancy.

John and Michael raced, Michael getting a start.

They recalled with contempt that not so long ago they had thought themselves fine fellows for being able to fly round a room.

Not so long ago. But how long ago? They were flying over the sea before this thought began to disturb Wendy seriously. John thought it was their second sea and their third night.

Sometimes it was dark and sometimes light, and now they were very cold and again too warm. Did they really feel hungry

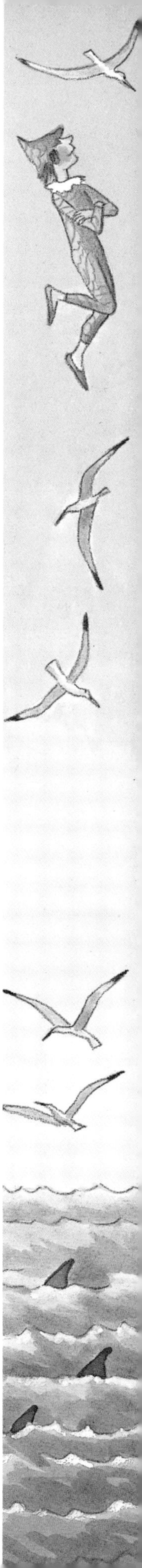

at times, or were they merely pretending because Peter had such a jolly new way of feeding them? His way was to pursue birds who had food in their mouths suitable for humans and snatch it from them; then the birds would follow and snatch it back; and they would all go chasing each other gaily for miles, parting at last with mutual expressions of good-will. But Wendy noticed with gentle concern that Peter did not seem to know that this was rather an odd way of getting your bread and butter, nor even that there are other ways.

Certainly they did not pretend to be sleepy, they were sleepy; and that was a danger, for the moment they popped off, down they fell. The awful thing was that Peter thought this funny.

"There he goes again!" he would cry gleefully, as Michael suddenly dropped like a stone.

"Save him, save him!" cried Wendy, looking with horror at the cruel sea far below. Eventually Peter would dive through the air, and catch Michael just before he could strike the sea, and it was lovely the way he did it; but he always waited till the last moment, and you felt it was his cleverness that interested him and not the saving of human life. Also he was fond of variety, and the sport that engrossed him one moment would suddenly cease to engage him, so there was always the possibility that the next time you fell he would let you go.

He could sleep in the air without falling, by merely lying on his back and floating, but this was, partly at least, because he was so light that if you got behind him and blew he went faster.

"Do be more polite to him," Wendy whispered to John, when they were playing "Follow my Leader".

"Then tell him to stop showing off," said John.

When playing Follow my Leader, Peter would fly close to the water and touch each shark's tail in passing, just as in the street

you may run your finger along an iron railing. They could not follow him in this with much success, so perhaps it was rather like showing off, especially as he kept looking behind to see how many tails they missed.

"You must be nice to him," Wendy impressed on her brothers. "What would we do if he were to leave us?"

"We could go back," Michael said.

"How could we ever find our way back without him?"

"Well, then, we could go on," said John.

"That is the awful thing, John. We should have to go on, for we don't know how to stop."

This was true; Peter had forgotten to show them how to stop.

John said that if the worst came to the worst, all they had to do was to go straight on, for the world was round, and so in time they must come back to their own window.

"And who is to get food for us, John?"

"I nipped a bit out of that eagle's mouth pretty neatly, Wendy."

"After the twentieth try," Wendy reminded him. "And even though we became good at picking up food, see how we bump against clouds and things if he is not near to give us a hand."

Indeed they were constantly bumping. They could now fly strongly, though they still kicked far too much; but if they saw a cloud in front of them, the more they tried to avoid it, the more certainly did they bump into it. If Nana had been with them she would have had a bandage round Michael's forehead by this time.

Peter was not with them for the moment, and they felt rather lonely up there by themselves. He could go so much faster than they that he would suddenly shoot out of sight, to have some adventure in which they had no share. He would come down laughing over something fearfully funny he had been saying to a star, but he had already forgotten what it was, or he would

come up with mermaid scales still sticking to him, and yet not be able to say for certain what had been happening. It was really rather irritating to children who had never seen a mermaid.

"And if he forgets them so quickly," Wendy argued, "how can we expect that he will go on remembering us?"

Indeed, sometimes when he returned he did not remember them, at least not well. Wendy was sure of it. She saw recognition come into his eyes as he was about to pass them the time of day and go on; once even she had to tell him her name.

"I'm Wendy," she said agitatedly.

He was very sorry. "I say, Wendy," he whispered to her, "always if you see me forgetting you, just keep on saying 'I'm Wendy', and then I'll remember."

Of course this was rather unsatisfactory. However, to make amends he showed them how to lie out flat on a strong wind that was going their way, and this was such a pleasant change that they tried it several times and found they could sleep thus with security. Indeed they would have slept longer, but Peter tired quickly of sleeping, and soon he would cry in his captain voice, "We get off here." So with occasional tiffs, but on the whole rollicking, they drew near the Neverland; for after many moons they did reach it, and, what is more, they had been going pretty straight all the time, not perhaps so much owing to the guidance of Peter or Tink as because the island was out looking for them. It is only thus that anyone may sight those magic shores.

"There it is," said Peter calmly.

"Where, where?"

"Where all the arrows are pointing."

Indeed a million golden arrows were pointing out the island to the children, all directed by their friend the sun, who wanted them to be sure of their way before leaving them for the night.

Wendy and John and Michael stood on tiptoe in the air to get their first sight of the island. Strange to say, they all recognized it at once, and until fear fell upon them they hailed it, not as something long dreamt of and seen at last, but as a familiar friend to whom they were returning home for the holidays.

"John, there's the lagoon."

"Wendy, look at the turtles burying their eggs in the sand."

"I say, John, I see your flamingo with the broken leg."

"Look, Michael, there's your cave."

"John, what's that in the brushwood?"

"It's a wolf with her whelps. Wendy, I do believe that's your little whelp."

"There's my boat, John, with her sides stove in."

"No, it isn't. Why, we burned your boat."

"That's her, at any rate. I say, John, I see the smoke of the redskin camp."

"Where? Show me, and I'll tell you by the way the smoke curls whether they are on the war-path."

"There, just across the Mysterious River."

"I see now. Yes, they are on the war-path right enough."

Peter was a little annoyed with them for knowing so much; but if he wanted to lord it over them his triumph was at hand, for have I not told you that anon fear fell upon them?

It came as the arrows went, leaving the island in gloom.

In the old days at home the Neverland had always begun to look a little dark and threatening by bedtime. Then unexplored patches arose in it and spread; black shadows moved about in them; the roar of the beasts of prey was quite different now, and above all, you lost the certainty that you would win. You were quite glad that the night-lights were on. You even liked Nana to say that this was just the mantelpiece over here, and that the

Neverland was all make-believe.

Of course the Neverland had been make-believe in those days; but it was real now, and there were no night-lights, and it was getting darker every moment, and where was Nana?

They had been flying apart, but they huddled close to Peter now. His careless manner had gone at last, his eyes were sparkling, a tingle went through them every time they touched his body. They were now over the fearsome island, flying so low that sometimes a tree grazed their face. Nothing horrid was visible in the air, yet their progress had become slow and laboured, exactly as if they were pushing their way through hostile forces. Sometimes they hung in the air until Peter had beaten on it with his fists.

"They don't want us to land," he explained.

"Who are they?" Wendy whispered, shuddering.

But he could not or would not say. Tinker Bell had been asleep on his shoulder, but now he wakened her and sent her on in front.

Sometimes he poised himself in the air, listening intently with his hand to his ear, and again he would stare down with eyes so bright that they seemed to bore two holes to earth. Having done these things, he went on again.

His courage was almost appalling. "Do you want an adventure now," he said casually to John, "or would you like to have your tea first?"

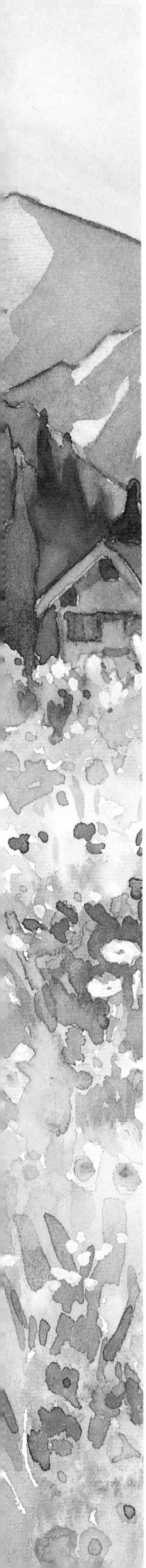

Introduction

Heidi is only five, and she has lived with her Aunt Detie since her mother died. But now that Detie has a job in far-off Frankfurt, the little girl goes to live with her grandfather in his hut in the Swiss Alps. Up in the high pastures, Heidi meets young Peter, the goatherd. Like everyone in the small village of Dörfli, Peter knows Heidi's grandfather as "Uncle Alp". When Detie leaves her with the old man, it does not take Heidi long to settle into her new life. She delights in her freedom, running wild with the goats, climbing a ladder to sleep in the hay-loft on a bed of fresh, sweet-smelling hay, and spending carefree days in the meadows with Peter and the goats.

R. S.

HEIDI

JOHANNA SPYRI

A Day with the Goats

Heidi was awakened next morning by a shrill whistle and as she opened her eyes a beam of sunlight came through the hole in the wall, making the hay shine like gold. At first she could not think where she was, then she heard her grandfather's deep voice outside and remembered joyfully that she had come to live in the mountains. Now she jumped out of bed, full of excitement at all the new experiences awaiting her. She dressed herself as quickly as possible, then climbed down the ladder and hurried outside. Peter was waiting there with his herd and her grandfather was just bringing Daisy and Dusky from their stall. She went to say good morning to them all.

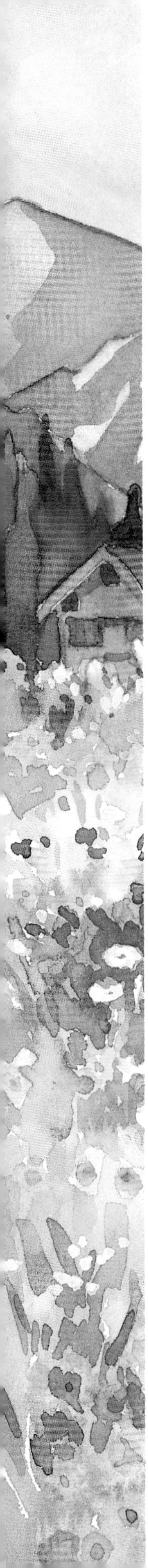

"Do you want to go up to the pasture with Peter?" asked the old man. This idea clearly delighted her. "You must have a wash first, or the sun will laugh to see you so dirty."

He pointed to a tub full of water, standing in the sun beside the door, and Heidi went over to it at once and began to splash about. Uncle Alp went indoors, calling to Peter, "Come here, General of the goats, and bring your knapsack with you." Peter held out the little bag which contained his meagre lunch, and watched with big eyes as the old man put in a piece of bread and a piece of cheese, both twice as big as his own.

"Take this mug, too, and fill it for her twice at dinner-time. She doesn't know how to drink straight from the goat as you do. She'll stay with you all day, and mind you look after her and see that she doesn't fall down the ravine."

Heidi came running in. "The sun can't laugh at me now," she said. Her grandfather smilingly agreed. In her desire to please the sun, she had rubbed her face with the hard towel until she looked like a boiled lobster.

"When you come home tonight, you'll have to go right inside the tub like a fish, for you'll get black feet running about with the goats. Now off you go."

It was very beautiful on the mountain that morning. The night wind had blown all the clouds away and the sky was deep blue. The sun shone brilliantly on the green pasture land and the flowers which were blooming everywhere. There were primroses, blue gentian, and dainty yellow rock-roses. Heidi rushed to and fro, wild with excitement at the sight of them. She quite forgot Peter and the goats, and kept stopping to gather flowers and put them in her apron. She wanted to take them home to stick among the hay in her bedroom, to make it look like a meadow.

Peter needed eyes all round his head. It was more than one pair could do to keep watch on Heidi as well as the goats, for they too were running about in all directions. He had to whistle and shout and swing his stick in the air to bring the wandering animals together.

"Where have you got to now, Heidi?" he called once, rather crossly.

"Here," came her voice from behind a little hillock some distance back. It was covered with primroses which had a most delicious scent. Heidi had never smelt anything so lovely before and had sat down among them to enjoy it to the full.

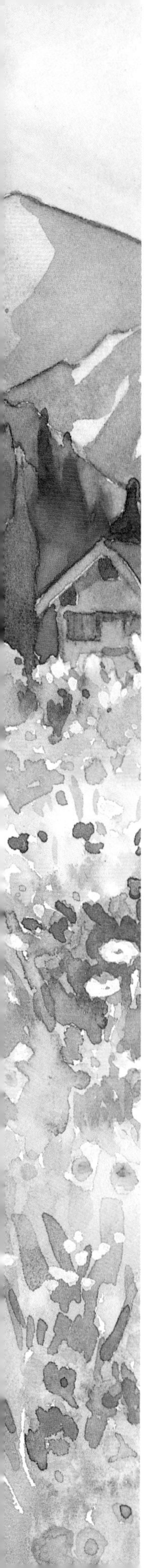

"Come on," called Peter. "Uncle said I wasn't to let you fall over the ravine."

"Where's that?" she called, without moving.

"Right up above. We've still a long way to go, so do come on. Hear the old hawk croaking away up there?"

Heidi jumped up at this last remark and ran to him with her apron full of flowers.

"You've got enough now," he said, as they started to climb again. "Don't pick any more, otherwise you'll always be lagging behind, and besides, if you keep on, there won't be any left for tomorrow."

Heidi saw the sense of this, and anyway her apron was almost full. She kept close to Peter after that, and the goats went on in a more orderly fashion too, for now they could smell the fragrant herbs they loved which grew on their grazing ground, and were anxious to reach them.

Peter usually took up his quarters for the day at the very foot of a rocky mountain peak. On the steep slopes above, there were only a few bushes and stunted fir trees, and the summit itself was just bare rock. On one side was the sheer drop over the ravine which Uncle Alp had spoken of. When they reached this place Peter took off his knapsack and laid it, for safety, in a little hollow, for there were sometimes strong gusts of wind and he had no wish to see his precious food go bowling down the mountain. Then he lay down in the sun to rest after the strenuous climb. Heidi put her apronful of flowers in the same little hollow. Then she sat down beside Peter and looked around her. The valley below was bathed in sunlight. In front of them a snow-clad mountain stood out against the blue sky and to the left of this was a huge mass of rock, with jagged twin peaks. Everything was very still. Only a gentle breeze set the blue and yellow flowers nodding on their slender stems.

Peter fell asleep and the goats climbed about among the bushes. Heidi sat quite still, enjoying it all. She gazed so intently at the mountain peaks that soon they seemed to her to have faces and to be looking like old friends. Suddenly she heard a loud noise. Looking up, she saw an enormous bird, circling overhead with outstretched wings and croaking harshly as it flew. "Peter, Peter, wake up!" she cried. "Here's the hawk." Peter sat up and together they watched as the great bird soared higher and higher into the sky and finally disappeared over the grey peaks.

"Where's it gone to?" asked Heidi, who had never seen a bird as big as that before and had watched its flight with great interest.

"Home to its nest," replied Peter.

"Does it live right up there? How wonderful! Why does it make such a noise?"

"Because it has to," explained Peter briefly.

"Let's climb up and see where it lives," she proposed.

"Oh, no, we won't! Even the goats can't climb as high as that, and don't forget Uncle told me to look after you," he said with marked disapproval. To Heidi's surprise he began whistling and shouting, but the goats recognized the familiar sounds and came towards him from all directions, though some lingered to nibble a tasty blade of grass, while others butted one another playfully. Heidi jumped up and ran among them, delighted to see them so obviously enjoying themselves. She spoke to each one, and every one was different and easily distinguishable from the others.

Meanwhile, Peter opened his bag and spread its contents out in a square on the ground, two large portions for Heidi and two smaller ones for himself. Then he filled the mug with milk from Daisy and placed it in the middle of the square. He called to Heidi, but she was slower to come than the goats had been. She was so busy with her new playmates that she had ears and eyes

for nothing else. He went on calling till his voice re-echoed from the rocks and at last she appeared. When she saw the meal laid out so invitingly, she skipped up and down with pleasure.

"Stop jigging about," said Peter, "it's dinner-time. Sit down and begin."

"Is the milk for me?"

"Yes, and those huge pieces of bread and cheese. I'll get you another mugful from Daisy when you've drunk that one. Then I'll have a drink myself."

"Where will you get yours from?" she inquired.

"From my own goat, Spot. Now start eating."

She drank the milk, but ate only a small piece of bread and passed the rest over to Peter, with the cheese. "You can have that," she said. "I've had enough." He looked at her in amazement for he had never in his life had any food to give away. At first he hesitated, thinking she must be joking, but she went on holding it out to him and finally put it on his knee. This convinced him that she really meant what she said, so he took it, nodded his thanks and settled down to enjoy the feast. Heidi meanwhile sat watching the goats.

"What are they all called, Peter?" she asked presently.

Peter did not know a great deal, but this was a question he could answer without difficulty. He told her all the names, pointing to each animal in turn. She listened attentively and soon knew one from the other. Each had little tricks by which it could easily be recognized by anyone looking at them closely, as she was doing. Big Turk had strong horns, and was always trying to butt the others, so they kept out of his way as much as possible. The only one to answer him back was a frisky little kid called Finch, with sharp little horns, and Turk was generally too astonished at such impudence to make a fight of it. Heidi was

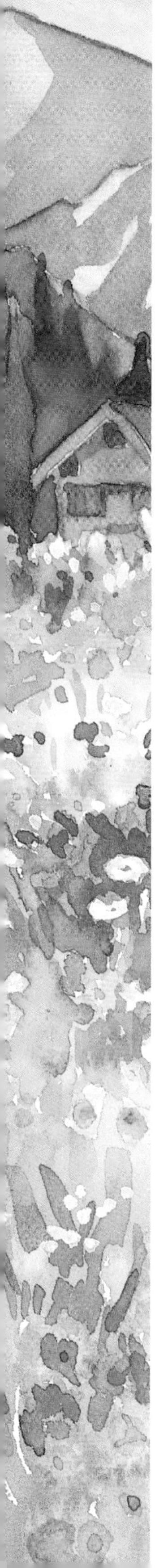

particularly attracted to a little white goat called Snowflake, which was bleating most pitifully. She had tried earlier to comfort it. Now she ran up to it again, put her arm around its neck, and asked fondly, "What's the matter, Snowflake? What are you crying for?" At that, the goat nestled against her and stopped bleating.

Peter had not yet finished his meal, but he called out between mouthfuls, "She's crying because her mother doesn't come up here any more. She's been sold to someone in Mayenfeld."

"Where's her grandmother then?"

"Hasn't got one."

"Or her grandfather?"

"Hasn't one."

"Poor Snowflake," said Heidi, hugging the little animal again. "Don't cry any more. I shall be up here every day now, and you can always come to me if you feel lonely." Snowflake rubbed her head on the little girl's shoulder, and seemed to be comforted.

Peter had now finished eating and came up to Heidi, who was making fresh discoveries all the time. She noticed that Daisy and Dusky seemed more independent than the other goats and carried themselves with a sort of dignity. They led the way as the herd went up to the bushes again. Some of them stopped here and there to sample a tasty herb, others went straight up, leaping over any small obstacles in their path. Turk was up to his tricks as usual, but Daisy and Dusky ignored him completely and were soon nibbling daintily at the leaves of the two thickest bushes. Heidi watched them for some time. Then she turned to Peter, who was lying full-length on the grass.

"Daisy and Dusky are the prettiest of all the goats," she said.

"I know. That's Uncle – he keeps them very clean and gives them salt and he has a fine stall for them," he replied. Then he suddenly jumped up and ran after his herd, with Heidi close behind, anxious not to miss anything. He had noticed that inquisitive little Finch was right at the edge of the ravine, where the ground fell away so steeply that if it went any farther, it might go over and would certainly break its legs. Peter stretched out his hands to catch hold of the little kid, but he slipped and fell, though he managed to grasp one of its legs, and Finch, highly indignant at such treatment, struggled wildly to get away. "Heidi, come here," called Peter, "come and help."

He couldn't get up unless he let go of Finch's leg, which he was nearly pulling out of its socket already. Heidi saw at once what to do and pulled up a handful of grass, which she held under Finch's nose.

"Come on, don't be silly," she said. "You don't want to fall down there and hurt yourself."

At that the little goat turned round and ate the grass from her hand, and Peter was able to get up. He took hold of the cord, on which a little bell was hung round Finch's neck. Heidi took hold of it too, on the other side, and together they brought the runaway safely back to the herd. Then Peter took up his stick to give it a good beating, and, seeing what was coming, Finch tried to get out of the way.

"Don't beat him," pleaded Heidi. "See how frightened he is."

"He deserves it," Peter replied, raising his arm, but she caught hold of him and exclaimed, "No, you're not to! It will hurt him. Leave him alone!" She looked at him so fiercely that he was astonished and dropped the stick.

"I won't beat him if you'll give me some of your cheese again tomorrow," he said, feeling he ought to have some compensation after the fright the little goat had given him.

"You can have it all, tomorrow and every day," promised Heidi. "I shan't want it. And I'll give you some of my bread as well, but

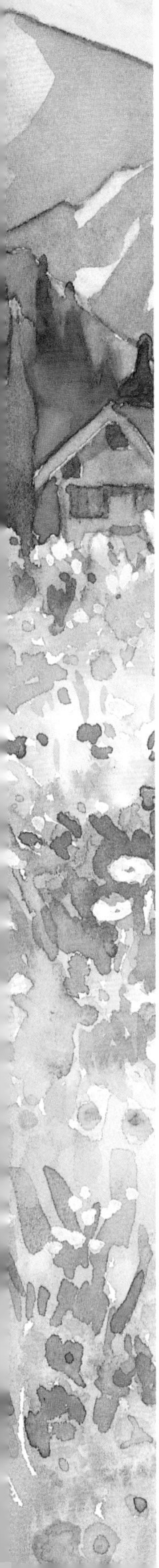

then you must never beat Finch or Snowflake or any of them."

"It's all the same to me," said Peter, which was his way of saying that he promised. He let Finch go and he bounded back to the herd.

It was getting late and the setting sun spread a wonderful golden glow over the grass and the flowers, and the high peaks shone and sparkled. Heidi sat for a while, quietly enjoying the beautiful scene, then all at once she jumped up, crying, "Peter, Peter! A fire, a fire! The mountains are on fire and the snow and the sky too. Look, the trees and the rocks are all burning, even up there by the hawk's nest. Everything's on fire!"

"It's always like this in the evening," Peter said calmly, whittling away at his stick. "It's not a fire."

"What is it then?" she cried, rushing about to look at the wonderful sight from all sides. "What is it, Peter?"

"It just happens," he said.

"Oh, just see, the mountains have got all rosy red! Look at the one with the snow on top. What are their names, Peter?"

"Mountains don't have names," he answered.

"How pretty the rosy snow looks, and the red rocks. Oh dear," she added, after a pause, "now the colour's going and everything's turning grey. Oh, it's all over." She sat down, looking as upset as if it was indeed the end of everything.

"It'll be the same again tomorrow," explained Peter. "Now it's time to go home." He whistled and called the goats together and they started the downward journey.

"Is it always like this up here?" asked Heidi hopefully.

"Usually."

"Will it be the same tomorrow?"

"Yes, it will," he assured her.

With this she was content and as she had so much to think

about, she didn't say another word till they reached the hut and saw her grandfather sitting under the fir trees, on the seat he had fixed there so that he could watch for the return of his animals. The little girl ran towards him, followed by Daisy and Dusky, and Peter called, "Goodnight, Heidi. Come again tomorrow." She ran back to say goodbye and promised to go with him the next day.

Introduction

Geppetto, the old village woodcarver, wants to make a puppet, a boy puppet. But he gets more than he bargained for. He makes it so well that his puppet becomes a virtual boy. Once made, Geppetto soon finds out that his Pinocchio, like most boys, has a mind of his own. And like any other boy, he gets himself into all sorts of trouble. Luckily he meets a good fairy, who often helps him out. Here's Pinocchio saying and doing anything he can to avoid taking his medicine. When I was a boy I used to make a lot of fuss about taking my medicine – I still do – but I was an angel compared to Pinocchio!

M. M.

PINOCCHIO

CARLO COLLODI

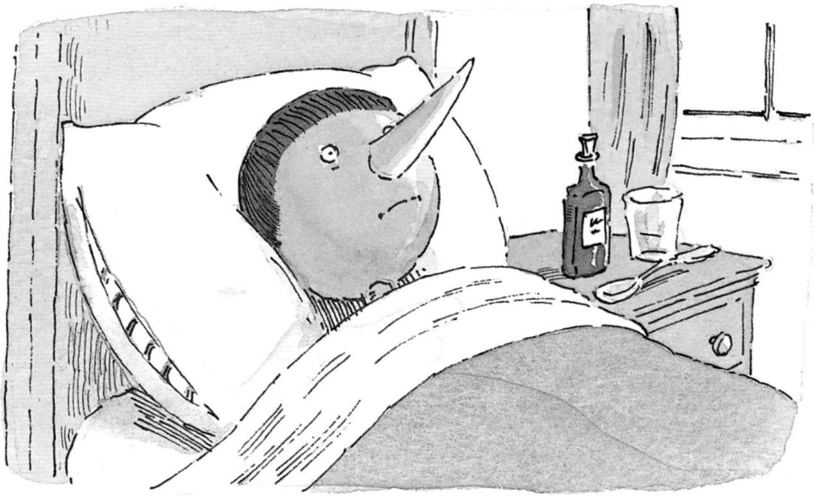

As soon as the three doctors had left the room, the fairy came to Pinocchio. She touched his forehead with her hand, and felt that he had a dangerous fever.

Thereupon she dissolved some white powder in half a glass of water and, holding it to his lips, said lovingly, "Drink this, and in a few days you will be better."

Pinocchio looked at the glass, made a sour face, and asked in a complaining voice, "Is it sweet, or bitter?"

"It is bitter, but it will do you good."

"If it's bitter I won't drink it."

"Listen to me, and drink it!"

"I don't like anything bitter."

"If you drink it, I shall give you a lump of sugar, to take the taste out of your mouth."

"Where is the lump of sugar?"

"Here it is," said the fairy, taking one out of a golden sugar basin.

"First I want the lump of sugar, and then I'll drink the horrid bitter water."

"You promise to drink it?"

"Yes."

The fairy gave him the sugar, and Pinocchio crunched and swallowed it in a second, saying as he licked his lips, "It would be fine if sugar were medicine. I'd take it every day."

"Now keep your promise, and drink these few drops of water. They will bring back your health."

Pinocchio took the glass in his hand unwillingly. He brought it to his nose, and held it to his lips, then again to his nose, and at last he said, "It's too bitter! It's too bitter! I can't drink it."

"How can you tell, when you haven't even tasted it!"

"Oh, I know it is! I know from its smell. Give me another lump of sugar, and then I'll drink it."

So the fairy, with all the patience of a good mother, put another lump of sugar in his mouth, and then she offered him the glass again.

"I can't drink it like that," said the puppet, making hundreds of grimaces.

"Why can't you?"

"Because that pillow on my feet annoys me."

The fairy removed the pillow.

'It's no use. I can't drink it like that, either."

"What is the matter now?"

"The door bothers me; it's half open."

The fairy went and shut the door.

"The fact is," cried Pinocchio, bursting into tears, "I won't drink that bitter water – no, no, no . . ."

"My child, you will be sorry."

"I don't care."

"You are very ill."

"I don't care."

"This fever will send you to the other world in a few hours."

"I don't care."

"Are you not afraid to die?"

"Not a bit! I'd rather die than drink that horrid medicine!"

At that moment the door of the room opened, and four rabbits as black as ink came in, carrying a little black coffin on their shoulders.

"What do you want of me?" shouted Pinocchio, sitting up in his bed in terror.

"We have come to take you away," said the biggest rabbit.

"To take me away! But I'm not dead yet!"

"No, not quite yet, but you have only a few minutes to live, because you refused the medicine that would have made you well."

"O fairy, kind fairy," cried the puppet, "give me the glass at once; hurry, for Heaven's sake, for I don't want to die! No, I will not die!"

He took the glass in both hands, and emptied it at a draught.

"Ah, well!" said the rabbits. "This time we have made a journey for nothing." And taking the little coffin on their shoulders they left the room, murmuring and grumbling between their teeth.

A few minutes later Pinocchio jumped out of bed quite well; for you must know that wooden marionettes have the privilege of being ill very seldom and of getting well very quickly.

When the fairy saw him running and rushing about the room as gay and lively as a young rooster, she said, "So my medicine really did you good?"

"I should say so! It brought me back to life."

"Then, for Heaven's sake, why was it so hard to make you drink it?"

"I think because we boys are all like that. We fear the medicine more than the sickness."

"Shame on you! Boys should know that the right medicine, taken in time, might save them from a serious illness, perhaps even from death."

"Oh, another time I won't make so much fuss. I'll remember those black rabbits with the coffin on their shoulders, and take the glass at once, and down it will go!"

"Now, come here, and tell me how it happened that you fell into the hands of assassins."

"It was like this: the Showman, Fire-eater, gave me some gold pieces and said, 'Here, take these to your father.' But on the road I met the fox and the cat, two very decent people, and they said, 'Would you like to change these pieces into a thousand – yes, into two thousand – gold pieces? Come with us, and we will take you to the Field of Miracles.' So I said, 'Let us go!' And they said, 'Let's stop at the Red Crab Inn, and continue our way after midnight.' And when I woke up they were not there, because they had left already. Then I started after them in the dark, and I couldn't tell you how dark it was. And so I met two assassins in coal sacks, who said to me, 'Hand over your money!' And I said, 'I haven't any', because I had hidden the four gold pieces in my mouth. One of the assassins tried to put his hand in my mouth, and I bit it off; but what I spat out wasn't a hand, but a cat's paw. And the assassins ran after me, and I ran and ran until they caught me, and hung me by the neck to a tree in the wood, saying, 'We'll come back tomorrow, and then you will be dead, and your mouth will be open, and we'll get the money hidden under your tongue.'"

"Where are the four gold pieces now?" asked the fairy.

"I've lost them," answered Pinocchio. But he told a lie, for he had them in his pocket. No sooner had he told this lie than his nose, which was already very long, became two inches longer.

"Where did you lose them?"

"In the wood near by."

At this second lie, his nose became still longer.

"If you lost them near here," said the fairy, "we can search for them; for everything lost in that wood can easily be found."

"Oh! Now I remember everything," replied the puppet, greatly confused. "I didn't lose the money. I swallowed it when I was drinking your medicine."

At this third lie, his nose grew so long that poor Pinocchio could not move in any direction. If he turned one way, his nose hit the bed or the window panes; if he turned the other, it struck the walls or the door; if he raised his head a little, there was danger of putting his nose into the fairy's eyes.

The fairy looked at him, and laughed.

"What are you laughing at?" asked the puppet, much

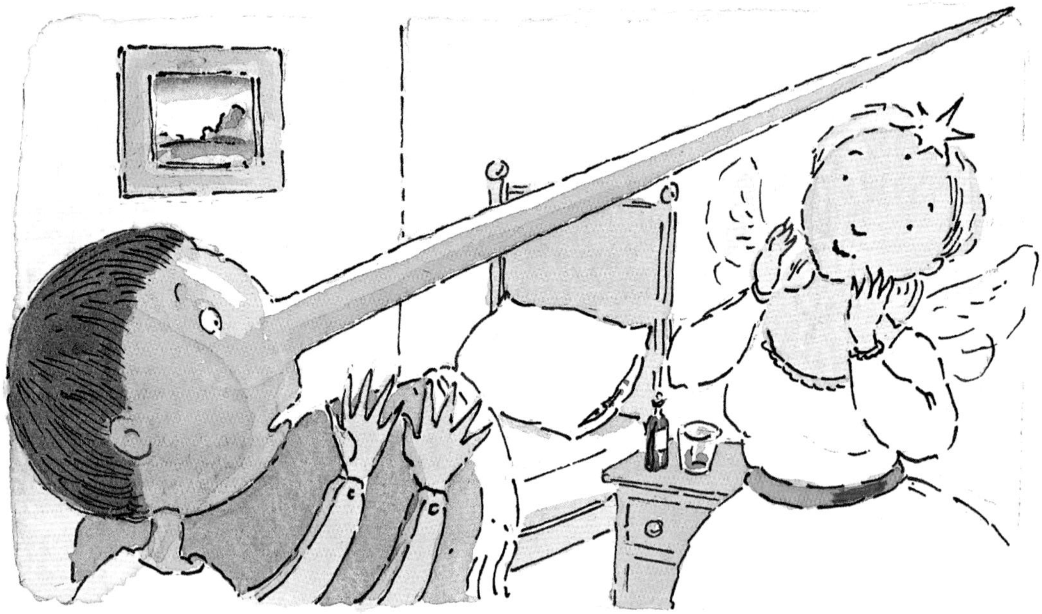

embarrassed and worried about his nose, which was growing to such a size.

"I am laughing at the lies you have told."

"How did you know I was telling lies?"

"Lies, my dear boy, can easily be recognized. There are two kinds of them: those with short legs, and those with long noses. Your kind have long noses."

Pinocchio wanted to hide his face for shame. He tried to run out of the room, but he could not, for his nose was so long that he could not go through the door.

Introduction

I expect you've always thought that being a witch comes naturally. Not so, as Mildred Hubble quickly finds out. After only two days at Miss Cackle's Academy for Witches, she crashes her broomstick against the wall. Try as she might to ride it, she always seems to topple off. And have you ever heard of a witch who is scared of the dark? Well, Mildred is! But she is at least inventive and, when her cat cannot balance on her broomstick, she pops it in her satchel for the ride, much to her teacher Miss Hardbroom's fury. Tomorrow all the first-year witches are to have a potion test. What will Mildred make of that?

R. S.

THE WORST WITCH

JILL MURPHY

The Potion Test

It was the morning of the potion test, and the girls were filing into the potion lab, each hoping she had learned the right spell, except for Ethel, who knew everything and never worried about such matters.

"Come along, girls! Two to a cauldron!" barked Miss Hardbroom. "Today we shall make a laughter potion. No textbooks to be used – put that book away this *instant,* Mildred! Work quietly, and when you have finished you may take a small sip of the mixture to make sure it is correctly made. You may begin."

Maud and Mildred were sharing a cauldron, of course, but unfortunately neither of them had learned that particular spell.

"I think I can remember it vaguely," whispered Maud. "Bits of it, anyway." She began to sort through the ingredients which had been laid out on each workbench.

When everything was stirred together in the cauldron, the bubbling liquid was bright pink. Mildred stared at it doubtfully.

"I'm sure it should be green," she said. "In fact I'm sure we should have put in a handful of pondweed-gathered-at-midnight."

"Are you *sure*?" asked Maud.

"Yes . . ." replied Mildred, not very definitely.

"*Absolutely* sure?" Maud asked again. "You know what happened last time."

"I'm *quite* sure," insisted Mildred. "Anyway, there's a handful of pondweed laid out on each bench. I'm positive we're supposed to put it in."

"Oh, all right," said Maud. "Go on, then. It can't do any harm."

Mildred grabbed the pondweed and dropped it into the mixture. They took turns at stirring it for a few minutes until it began to turn dark green.

"What a horrid colour," said Maud.

"Are you ready, girls?" asked Miss Hardbroom, rapping on her desk. "You should have been ready minutes ago. A laughter potion should be made quickly for use in an emergency."

Ethel was still working on the bench in front of Mildred, who stood on tiptoe to sneak a look at the colour of Ethel's potion. To her horror, it was bright pink.

"Oh, no," Mildred thought, with a sinking feeling. "I wonder what potion we've made?"

Miss Hardbroom banged on the desk again.

"We shall now test the potion," she commanded. "Not too much, please. We don't want anyone hysterical."

Each pupil took a test-tubeful of liquid and drank a little. At once shrieks of laughter rang through the room, especially from Ethel's bench where they had made the best potion of all and were laughing so much that tears rolled down their cheeks. The only two girls who weren't laughing were Mildred and Maud.

"Oh, dear," said Maud. "I feel most peculiar. Why aren't we laughing, Mil?"

"I have to tell you," confessed Mildred, "I think –" But before she had time to say any more, the two girls had disappeared!

"Cauldron number two!" snapped Miss Hardbroom. "You seem to have made the wrong spell."

"It was my fault," said Mildred's voice from behind the cauldron.

"That I do not doubt," Miss Hardbroom said sourly. "You had both better sit down until you reappear, and then, Mildred, perhaps a trip to Miss Cackle's office would do you some good. You can explain why I sent you."

Everyone had left the room by the time the two young witches finally began to reappear. This was a very slow process, with first the head and then the rest of the body becoming gradually visible.

"I'm sorry," said Mildred's head and shoulders.

"That's all right," said Maud's head. "I just wish you'd *think* a bit more. We had the right potion to start with."

"Sorry," mumbled Mildred again, then she began to laugh. "Hey, Maud, you do look funny with just your head showing!"

At once they both began to laugh, and soon they were best friends again.

"I suppose I'd better go and see Old Cackle now," said Mildred, when she had completely reappeared.

"I'll come with you to the door," offered Maud.

Miss Cackle was small and very fat, with short grey hair and green horn-rimmed glasses which she usually wore pushed up on top of her head. She was the exact opposite of Miss Hardbroom, being absent-minded in appearance and rather gentle by nature. The girls were not in the least bit afraid of her, whereas

Miss Hardbroom could reduce any of them to a miserable heap with just one word. Miss Cackle used a different technique. By always being friendly and pleased to see a pupil in her office, she made them feel embarrassed if they had something unpleasant to tell her, as Mildred nearly always had.

Mildred knocked at Miss Cackle's door, hoping she would be out. She wasn't.

"Come in!" called the familiar voice from inside.

Mildred opened the door and went in. Miss Cackle, glasses on her nose for once, was busily writing in a huge register. She looked up and peered over her spectacles.

"Ah, Mildred," she said pleasantly. "Come and sit down while I finish filling in this register."

Mildred closed the door and sat by Miss Cackle's desk.

"I wish she wasn't so pleased to see me," she thought.

Miss Cackle slammed the register shut and pushed her glasses on to the top of her head.

"Now, Mildred, what can I do for you?"

Mildred twisted her fingers together.

"Well, actually, Miss Cackle," she began slowly. "Miss Hardbroom sent me to see you because I made the wrong potion again."

The smile faded from the headmistress's face and she sighed, as if with deep disappointment. Mildred felt about an inch high.

"Really, Mildred," Miss Cackle said in a tired voice, "I have run out of things to say to you. Week after week you come here, sent by every member of staff in the school, and my words just seem to go straight in one ear and out of the other. You will never get the Witches' Higher Certificate if this appalling conduct continues. You must be the worst witch in the entire school. Whenever there's any trouble you are nearly always to be found at the bottom of it, and it's just not good enough, my dear. Now, what have you to say for yourself this time?"

"I don't really know, Miss Cackle," Mildred said humbly. "Everything I do just seems to go wrong, that's all. I don't mean to do it."

"Well, that's no excuse, is it?" said Miss Cackle. "Everyone else manages to live without causing an uproar wherever they go. You must pull yourself together, Mildred. I don't want to hear any more bad reports about you, do you understand?"

"Yes, Miss Cackle," said Mildred, in as sorry a voice as she could manage.

"Run along, then," said the headmistress, "and remember what I have said to you."

Maud was waiting in the corridor, eager to know what had been said, when her friend came out of the office.

"She's nice really," Mildred said. "Just told me all the usual things. She hates telling people off. I'll have to try to be better from now on. Come on, let's go and give the kittens another broomstick lesson."

Introduction

Mary, Laura and Baby Carrie live with their parents, Black Susan the cat, and Jack the bulldog, in a log house deep in the woods of Wisconsin in Midwest America. The little girls spend their days helping Ma to churn butter and prepare the wild beasts Pa has hunted for dinner, and tending vegetables in the garden. In the wintertime, they keep all snug and cosy warm inside the little house, playing games of pretend in the attic, making paper dolls and listening to Pa's wonderful stories about when he was a boy. And the most thrilling time of all? Why, Christmas, of course!

R. S.

Little House in the Big Woods

Christmas

Christmas was coming.

The little log house was almost buried in snow. Great drifts were banked against the walls and windows, and in the morning when Pa opened the door, there was a wall of snow as high as Laura's head. Pa took the shovel and shovelled it away, and then he shovelled a path to the barn, where the horses and cows were snug and warm in their stalls.

The days were clear and bright. Laura and Mary stood on chairs by the window and looked out across the glittering snow at the glittering trees. Snow was piled all along their bare, dark branches, and it sparkled in the sunshine. Icicles hung from the eaves of the house to the snow-banks, great icicles as large at the top as Laura's arm. They were like glass and full of sharp lights.

Pa's breath hung in the air like smoke, when he came along

the path from the barn. He breathed it out in clouds and it froze in white frost on his moustache and beard.

When he came in, stamping the snow from his boots, and caught Laura up in a bear's hug against his cold, big coat, his moustache was beaded with little drops of melting frost.

Every night he was busy, working on a large piece of board and two small pieces. He whittled them with his knife, he rubbed them with sandpaper and with the palm of his hand, until when Laura touched them they felt soft and smooth as silk.

Then with his sharp jack-knife he worked at them, cutting the edges of the large one into little peaks and towers, with a large star curved on the very tallest point. He cut little holes through the wood. He cut the holes in shapes of windows, and little stars, and crescent moons, and circles. All around them he carved tiny leaves, and flowers, and birds.

One of the little boards he shaped in a lovely curve, and around its edges he carved leaves and flowers and stars, and through it he cut crescent moons and curlicues.

Around the edges of the smallest board he carved a tiny flowering vine.

He made the tiniest shavings, cutting very slowly and carefully, making whatever he thought would be pretty.

At last he had the pieces finished and one night he fitted them together. When this was done, the large piece was a beautifully carved back for a smooth little shelf across its middle. The large star was at the very top of it. The curved piece supported the shelf underneath, and it was carved beautifully, too. And the little vine ran around the edge of the shelf.

Pa had made this bracket for a Christmas present for Ma. He hung it carefully against the log wall between the windows, and Ma stood her little china woman on the shelf.

The little china woman had a china bonnet on her head, and china curls hung against her china neck. Her china dress was laced across in front, and she wore a pale pink china apron and little gilt china shoes. She was beautiful, standing on the shelf with flowers and leaves and birds and moons carved all around her, and the large star at the very top.

Ma was busy all day long, cooking good things for Christmas. She baked salt-rising bread and rye'n'Injun bread, and Swedish crackers, and a huge pan of baked beans, with salt pork and molasses. She baked vinegar pies and dried-apple pies, and filled a big jar with cookies, and she let Laura and Mary lick the cake spoon.

One morning she boiled molasses and sugar together until they made a thick syrup, and Pa brought in two pans of clean, white snow from outdoors. Laura and Mary each had a pan, and Pa and Ma showed them how to pour the dark syrup in little streams on to the snow.

They made circles, and curlicues, and squiggledy things, and these hardened at once and were candy. Laura and Mary might eat one piece each, but the rest was saved for Christmas Day.

All this was done because Aunt Eliza and Uncle Peter and the cousins, Peter and Alice and Ella, were coming to spend Christmas.

The day before Christmas they came. Laura and Mary heard the gay ringing of sleigh bells, growing louder every moment, and then the big bobsled came out of the woods and drove up to the gate. Aunt Eliza and Uncle Peter and the cousins were in it, all covered up, under blankets and robes and buffalo skins.

They were wrapped up in so many coats and mufflers and veils and shawls that they looked like big, shapeless bundles.

When they all came in, the little house was full and running over. Black Susan ran out and hid in the barn, but Jack leaped in circles through the snow, barking as though he would never stop. Now there were cousins to play with!

As soon as Aunt Eliza had unwrapped them, Peter and Alice and Ella and Laura and Mary began to run and shout. At last Aunt Eliza told them to be quiet. Then Alice said:

"I'll tell you what let's do. Let's make pictures."

Alice said they must go outdoors to do it, and Ma thought it was too cold for Laura to play outdoors. But when she saw how disappointed Laura was, she said she might go, after all, for a little while. She put on Laura's coat and mittens and the warm cape with the hood, and wrapped a muffler around her neck, and let her go.

Laura had never had so much fun. All morning she played outdoors in the snow with Alice and Ella and Peter and Mary, making pictures. The way they did it was this:

Each one by herself climbed up on a stump, and then all at once, holding their arms out wide, they fell off the stumps into the soft, deep snow. They fell flat on their faces. Then they tried to get up without spoiling the marks they made when they fell. If they did it well, there in the snow were five holes, shaped almost exactly like four little girls and a boy, arms and legs and all. They called these their pictures.

They played so hard all day that when night came they were too excited to sleep. But they must sleep, or Santa Claus would not come. So they hung their stockings by the fireplace, and said their prayers, and went to bed – Alice and Ella and Mary and Laura all in one big bed on the floor.

Peter had the trundle-bed. Aunt Eliza and Uncle Peter were going to sleep in the big bed, and another bed was made on the attic floor for Pa and Ma. The buffalo robes and all the blankets had been brought in from Uncle Peter's sled, so there were enough covers for everybody.

. . .

They lay there whispering till Ma said: "Charles, those children never will get to sleep unless you play for them." So Pa got his fiddle.

The room was still and warm and full of firelight. Ma's shadow, and Aunt Eliza's and Uncle Peter's were big and quivering on the walls in the flickering firelight, and Pa's fiddle sang merrily to itself.

It sang "Money Musk" and "The Red Heifer", "The Devil's Dream", and "Arkansas Traveller". And Laura went to sleep while Pa and the fiddle were both softly singing:

"My darling Nelly Gray, they have taken you away,
And I'll never see my darling any more . . ."

In the morning they all woke up almost at the same moment. They looked at their stockings, and something was in them. Santa Claus had been there. Alice and Ella and Laura in their red flannel nightgowns and Peter in his red flannel nightshirt, all ran shouting to see what he had brought.

In each stocking there was a pair of bright red mittens and there was a long flat stick of red-and-white-striped, peppermint candy, all beautifully notched along the side.

They were all so happy they could hardly speak at first. They just looked with shining eyes at those lovely Christmas presents. But Laura was happiest of all. Laura had a rag doll.

She was a beautiful doll. She had a face of white cloth with black button eyes. A black pencil had made her eyebrows, and her cheeks and her mouth were red with the ink made from pokeberries. Her hair was black yarn that had been knitted and ravelled, so that it was curly.

She had little red flannel stockings and little black cloth gaiters for shoes, and her dress was pretty pink and blue calico.

She was so beautiful that Laura could not say a word. She just held her tight and forgot everything else. She did not know that everyone was looking at her, till Aunt Eliza said:

"Did you ever see such big eyes!"

The other girls were not jealous because Laura had mittens, and candy, *and* a doll, because Laura was the littlest girl, except Baby Carrie and Aunt Eliza's little baby, Dolly Varden. The babies were too small for dolls. They were so small they did not even know about Santa Claus. They just put their fingers in their mouths and wriggled because of all the excitement.

Laura sat down on the edge of the bed and held her doll. She loved her red mittens and she loved the candy, but she loved her doll best of all. She named her Charlotte.

Then they all looked at each other's mittens, and tried on their own, and Peter bit a large piece out of his stick of candy, but Alice and Ella and Mary and Laura licked theirs, to make it last longer.

"Well, well!" Uncle Peter said. "Isn't there even one stocking with nothing but a switch in it? My, my, have you all been such good children?"

But they didn't believe Santa Claus could, really, have given any of them nothing but a switch. That happened to some children, but it couldn't happen to them. It was so hard to be good all the time, every day, for a whole year.

"You mustn't tease the children, Peter," Aunt Eliza said.

Ma said, "Laura, aren't you going to let the other girls hold your doll?" She meant, "Little girls must not be so selfish."

So Laura let Mary take the beautiful doll, and then Alice held her a minute, and then Ella. They smoothed the pretty dress and admired the red flannel stockings and the gaiters, and the curly woollen hair. But Laura was glad when at last Charlotte was safe in her arms again.

Pa and Uncle Peter had each a pair of new, warm mittens, knitted

in little squares of red and white. Ma and Aunt Eliza had made them.

Aunt Eliza had brought Ma a large red apple stuck full of cloves. How good it smelled! And it would not spoil, for so many cloves would keep it sound and sweet.

Ma gave Aunt Eliza a little needle-book she had made, with bits of silk for covers and soft white flannel leaves into which to stick the needles. The flannel would keep the needles from rusting.

They all admired Ma's beautiful bracket, and Aunt Eliza said that Uncle Peter had made one for her – of course, with different carving.

Santa Claus had not given them anything at all. Santa Claus did not give grown people presents, but that was not because they had not been good. Pa and Ma were good. It was because they were grown up, and grown people must give each other presents.

Then all the presents must be laid away for a little while. Peter went out with Pa and Uncle Peter to do the chores, and Alice and Ella helped Aunt Eliza make the beds, and Laura and Mary set the table, while Ma got breakfast.

For breakfast there were pancakes, and Ma made a pancake man for each one of the children. Ma called each one in turn to bring her plate, and each could stand by the stove and watch, while with the spoonful of batter Ma put on the arms and the legs and the head. It was exciting to watch her turn the whole little man over, quickly and carefully, on a hot griddle. When it was done, she put it smoking-hot on the plate.

Peter ate the head off his man, right away. But Alice and Ella and Mary and Laura ate theirs slowly in little bits, first the arms and legs and then the middle, saving the head for last.

Today the weather was so cold that they could not play outdoors, but there were the new mittens to admire, and the candy to lick. And they all sat on the floor together and looked at the pictures in the Bible, and the pictures of all kinds of animals and birds in Pa's big green book. Laura kept Charlotte in her arms the whole time.

Then there was the Christmas dinner. Alice and Ella and Peter and Mary and Laura did not say a word at table, for they knew that children should be seen and not heard. But they did not need to ask for second helpings. Ma and Aunt Eliza kept their plates full and let them eat all the good things they could hold.

"Christmas comes but once a year," said Aunt Eliza.

Dinner was early, because Aunt Eliza, Uncle Peter and the cousins had such a long way to go.

"Best the horses can do," Uncle Peter said, "we'll hardly make it home before dark."

So as soon as they had eaten dinner, Uncle Peter and Pa went to put the horses to the sled, while Ma and Aunt Eliza wrapped up the cousins.

They pulled heavy woollen stockings over the woollen stockings and the shoes they were already wearing. They put on mittens and coats and warm hoods and shawls, and wrapped mufflers around their necks and thick woollen veils over their faces. Ma slipped piping-hot baked potatoes into their pockets to keep their fingers warm and Aunt Eliza's flat-irons were hot on the stove, ready to put at their feet in the sled. The blankets and the quilts and the buffalo robes were warmed, too.

So they all got into the big bobsled, cosy and warm, and Pa tucked the last robe well in around them.

"Goodbye! Goodbye!" they called, and off they went, the horses trotting gaily and the sleigh bells ringing.

In just a little while the merry sound of the bells was gone, and Christmas was over. But what a happy Christmas it had been!

Introduction

It is cold, bitter cold. Everything that Charlie Bucket tastes seems to be made of ice and the wind is like a knife on his cheek. Indoors, the Bucket family huddle together for warmth. All they can afford are thin cabbagey meals three times a day. Every day on his way to school Charlie passes Willy Wonka's chocolate factory and smells the chocolate on the air, taking deep swallowing breaths as though he were trying to eat the smell itself. If only he can get lucky and win one of the five golden tickets – then he will win a tour of the chocolate factory and enough sweets and chocolate to last the rest of his life. Miracles do happen.

M. M.

Charlie and the Chocolate Factory

Roald Dahl

The Miracle

The cruel weather went on and on.

And every day, Charlie Bucket grew thinner and thinner. His face became frighteningly white and pinched. The skin was drawn so tightly over the cheeks that you could see the shapes of the bones underneath. It seemed doubtful whether he could go on much longer like this without becoming dangerously ill.

And now, very calmly, with that curious wisdom that seems to come so often to small children in times of hardship, he began to make little changes here and there in some of the things that he did, so as to save his strength. In the mornings, he left the house ten minutes earlier so that he could walk slowly to school, without ever having to run. He sat quietly in the classroom during break, resting himself, while the others rushed outdoors and threw snowballs and wrestled in the snow. Everything he did now, he did slowly and carefully, to prevent exhaustion.

Then one afternoon, walking back home with the icy wind in his face (and incidentally feeling hungrier than he had ever felt before), his eye was caught suddenly by something silvery lying in the gutter, in the snow. Charlie stepped off the kerb and bent down to examine it. Part of it was buried under the snow, but he saw at once what it was.

It was a fifty-pence piece!

Quickly he looked around him.

Had somebody just dropped it?

No – that was impossible because of the way part of it was buried.

Several people went hurrying past him on the pavement, their chins sunk deep in the collars of their coats, their feet crunching in the snow. None of them was searching for any money; none of them was taking the slightest notice of the small boy crouching in the gutter.

Then was it *his*, this fifty pence?

Could he *have* it?

Carefully, Charlie pulled it out from under the snow. It was damp and dirty, but otherwise perfect.

A WHOLE fifty pence!

He held it tightly between his shivering fingers, gazing down at it. It meant one thing to him at that moment, only *one* thing. It meant FOOD.

Automatically, Charlie turned and began moving towards the nearest shop. It was only ten paces away . . . it was a newspaper and stationery shop, the kind that sells almost everything, including sweets and cigars . . . and what he would *do*, he whispered quickly to himself . . . he would buy one luscious bar of chocolate and eat it *all* up, every bit of it, right then and there . . . and the rest of the money he would take straight back home and give to his mother.

Charlie entered the shop and laid the damp fifty pence on the counter.

"One Wonka's Whipple-Scrumptious Fudgemallow Delight," he said, remembering how much he had loved the one he had on his birthday.

The man behind the counter looked fat and well-fed. He had big lips and fat cheeks and a very fat neck. The fat around his neck bulged out all around the top of his collar like a rubber ring. He turned and reached behind him for the chocolate bar, then he turned back again and handed it to Charlie. Charlie grabbed it and quickly tore off the wrapper and took an enormous bite. Then he took another . . . and another . . . and oh, the joy of being able to cram large pieces of something sweet and solid into one's mouth! The sheer blissful joy of being able to fill one's mouth with rich solid food!

"You look like you wanted that one, sonny," the shopkeeper said pleasantly.

Charlie nodded, his mouth bulging with chocolate.

The shopkeeper put Charlie's change on the counter. "Take it easy," he said. "It'll give you a tummy-ache if you swallow it like that without chewing."

Charlie went on wolfing the chocolate. He couldn't stop. And in less than half a minute, the whole thing had disappeared down his throat. He was quite out of breath, but he felt marvellously, extraordinarily happy. He reached out a hand to take the change. Then he paused. His eyes were just above the level of the counter. They were staring at the silver coins lying there. The coins were all five-penny pieces. There were nine of them altogether. Surely it wouldn't matter if he spent just one more . . .

"I think," he said quietly, "I think . . . I'll have just one more of those chocolate bars. The same kind as before, please."

"Why not?" the fat shopkeeper said, reaching behind him again and taking another Whipple-Scrumptious Fudgemallow Delight from the shelf. He laid it on the counter.

Charlie picked it up and tore off the wrapper . . . and *suddenly* . . . from underneath the wrapper . . . there came a brilliant flash of gold.

Charlie's heart stood still.

"It's a Golden Ticket!" screamed the shopkeeper, leaping about a foot in the air. "You've got a Golden Ticket! You've found the last Golden Ticket! Hey, would you believe it! Come and look at this, everybody! The kid's found Wonka's last Golden Ticket! There it is! It's right here in his hands!"

It seemed as though the shopkeeper might be going to have a fit. "In my shop, too!" he yelled. "He found it right here in my own little shop! Somebody call the newspapers quick and let them know! Watch out now, sonny! Don't tear it as you unwrap it!

That thing's precious!"

In a few seconds, there was a crowd of about twenty people clustering around Charlie, and many more were pushing their way in from the street. Everybody wanted to get a look at the Golden Ticket and at the lucky finder.

"Where is it?" somebody shouted. "Hold it up so all of us can see it!"

"There it is, there!" someone else shouted. "He's holding it in his hands! See the gold shining!"

"How did *he* manage to find it, I'd like to know?" a large boy shouted angrily. "*Twenty* bars a day I've been buying for weeks and weeks!"

"Think of all the free stuff he'll be getting too!" another boy said enviously. "A lifetime supply!"

"He'll need it, the skinny little shrimp!" a girl said, laughing.

Charlie hadn't moved. He hadn't even unwrapped the Golden Ticket from around the chocolate. He was standing very still, holding it tightly with both hands while the crowd pushed and shouted all around him. He felt quite dizzy. There was a peculiar floating sensation coming over him, as though he were floating up in the air like a balloon. His feet didn't seem to be touching the ground at all. He could hear his heart thumping away loudly somewhere in his throat.

At that point, he became aware of a hand resting lightly on his shoulder, and when he looked up, he saw a tall man standing over him. "Listen," the man whispered. "I'll buy it from you. I'll give you fifty pounds. How about it, eh? And I'll give you a new bicycle as well. Okay?"

"Are you *crazy*?" shouted a woman who was standing equally close. "Why, I'd give him *two hundred* pounds for that ticket! You want to sell that ticket for two hundred pounds, young man?"

"That's *quite* enough of that!" the fat shopkeeper shouted, pushing his way through the crowd and taking Charlie firmly by the arm. "Leave the kid alone, will you! Make way there! Let him out!" And to Charlie, as he led him to the door, he whispered, "Don't you let *anybody* have it! Take it straight home, quickly, before you lose it! Run all the way and don't stop till you get there, you understand?"

Charlie nodded.

"You know something," the fat shopkeeper said, pausing a moment and smiling at Charlie, "I have a feeling you needed a break like this. I'm awfully glad you got it. Good luck to you, sonny."

"Thank you," Charlie said, and off he went, running through

the snow as fast as his legs would go. And as he flew past Mr Willy Wonka's factory, he turned and waved at it and sang out, "I'll be seeing you! I'll be seeing you soon!" And five minutes later he arrived at his own home.

Charlie burst through the front door, shouting, "*Mother! Mother! Mother!*"

Mrs Bucket was in the old grandparents' room, serving them their evening soup.

"*Mother!*" yelled Charlie, rushing in on them like a hurricane. "Look! I've got it! Look, Mother, look! The last Golden Ticket! It's mine! I found some money in the street and I bought two bars of chocolate and the second one had the Golden Ticket and there were *crowds* of people all around me wanting to see it and the shopkeeper rescued me and I ran all the way home and here I am! *IT'S THE FIFTH GOLDEN TICKET, MOTHER, AND I'VE FOUND IT!*"

Introduction

We all sing "We're off to see the Wizard, the wonderful Wizard of Oz . . .", but how many of us know about Dorothy's adventure into the magical land of Oz with her little dog, Toto? It all begins when a rampaging cyclone sweeps across the flat plains of Kansas, whirls her little wooden house high into the air and sets it down in the middle of a strange country of marvellous beauty. All Dorothy can think about is finding her way back home to Kansas, to be with Aunt Em and Uncle Harry. Four funny little people called Munchkins approach her and suggest that the Wizard of Oz might help, so off she sets, following the road of yellow brick, to his palace in the Emerald City. On the way she is joined by the Scarecrow, who longs for brains, the Tin Woodman, who wants a heart, and the Cowardly Lion, who wishes he were brave. Perhaps the Wizard will be able to help them, too? They have all manner of mysterious adventures along the yellow-brick road, but as they come near to the Emerald City, the fulfilment of their dreams seems still far away.

R. S.

THE WIZARD OF OZ

L. FRANK BAUM

The Guardian of the Gates

"We must journey on until we find the road of yellow brick again," said Dorothy; "and then we can keep on to the Emerald City."

So, the Lion being fully refreshed, and feeling quite himself again, they all started upon the journey, greatly enjoying the walk through the soft, fresh grass; and it was not long before they reached the road of yellow brick and turned again towards the Emerald City where the great Oz dwelt.

The road was smooth and well paved, now, and the country about was beautiful, so that the travellers rejoiced in leaving the forest far behind, and with it the many dangers they had met in its gloomy shades. Once more they could see fences built beside the road; but these were painted green, and when they came to a small house, in which a farmer evidently lived, that also was painted green. They passed by several of these houses during the afternoon, and sometimes people came to the doors and looked at them as if they would like to ask questions; but no one came near

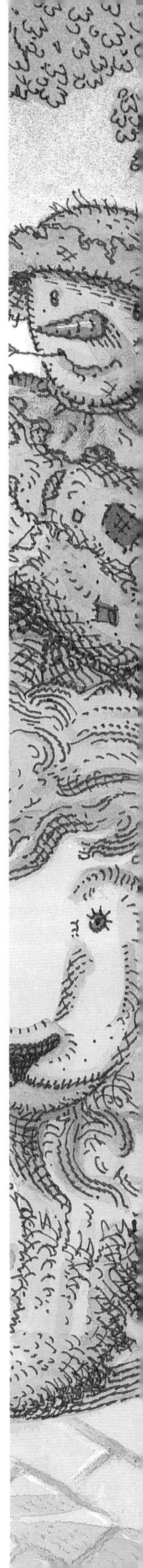

them nor spoke to them because of the great Lion, of which they were much afraid. The people were all dressed in clothing of a lovely emerald-green colour and wore peaked hats like those of the Munchkins.

"This must be the Land of Oz," said Dorothy, "and we are surely getting near the Emerald City."

"Yes," answered the Scarecrow. "Everything is green here, while in the country of the Munchkins blue was the favourite colour. But the people do not seem to be as friendly as the Munchkins and I'm afraid we shall be unable to find a place to pass the night."

"I should like something to eat besides fruit," said the girl, "and I'm sure Toto is nearly starved. Let us stop at the next house and talk to the people."

So, when they came to a good-sized farmhouse, Dorothy walked boldly up to the door and knocked.

A woman opened it just far enough to look out, and said, "What do you want, child, and why is that great Lion with you?"

"We wish to pass the night with you, if you will allow us," answered Dorothy; "and the Lion is my friend and comrade, and would not hurt you for the world."

"Is he tame?" asked the woman, opening the door a little wider.

"Oh, yes," said the girl, "and he is a great coward, too; so that he will be more afraid of you than you are of him."

"Well," said the woman, after thinking it over and taking another peep at the Lion, "if that is the case you may come in, and I will give you some supper and a place to sleep."

So they entered the house, where there were, besides the woman, two children and a man. The man had hurt his leg, and was lying on the couch in a corner. They seemed greatly surprised to see so strange a company, and while the woman was busy laying the table the man asked:

"Where are you all going?"

"To the Emerald City," said Dorothy, "to see the Great Oz."

"Oh, indeed!" exclaimed the man. "Are you sure that Oz will see you?"

"Why not?" she replied.

"Why, it is said that he never lets anyone come into his presence. I have been to the Emerald City many times, and it is a beautiful and wonderful place; but I have never been permitted to see the Great Oz, nor do I know of any living person who has seen him."

"Does he never go out?" asked the Scarecrow.

"Never. He sits day after day in the great throne room of his palace, and even those who wait upon him do not see him face to face."

"What is he like?" asked the girl.

"That is hard to tell," said the man thoughtfully. "You see, Oz is a great Wizard, and can take on any form he wishes. So that some say he looks like a bird; and some say he looks like an elephant; and some say he looks like a cat. To others he appears as a beautiful fairy, or a brownie, or in any form that pleases him. But who the real Oz is, when he is in his own form, no living person can tell."

"That is very strange," said Dorothy; "but we must try, in some way, to see him, or we shall have made our journey for nothing."

"Why do you wish to see the terrible Oz?" asked the man.

"I want him to give me some brains," said the Scarecrow eagerly.

"Oh, Oz could do that easily enough," declared the man. "He has more brains than he needs."

"And I want him to give me a heart," said the Tin Woodman.

"That will not trouble him," continued the man, "for Oz has a large collection of hearts, of all sizes and shapes."

"And I want him to give me courage," said the Cowardly Lion.

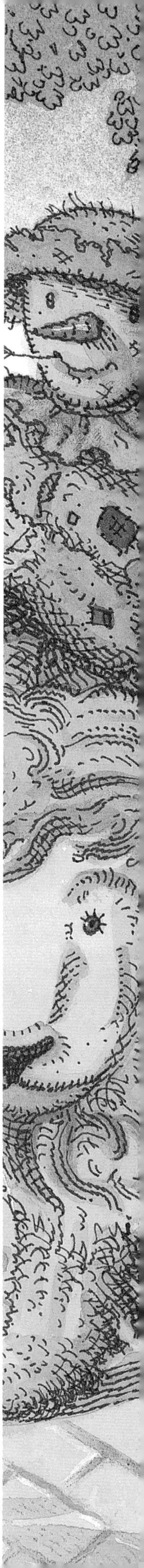

"Oz keeps a great pot of courage in his throne room," said the man, "which he has covered with a golden plate, to keep it from running over. He will be glad to give you some."

"And I want him to send me back to Kansas," said Dorothy.

"Where is Kansas?" asked the man, with surprise.

"I don't know," replied Dorothy sorrowfully, "but it is my home, and I'm sure it's somewhere."

"Very likely. Well, Oz can do anything; so I suppose he will find Kansas for you. But first you must get to see him, and that will be a hard task; for the Great Wizard does not like to see anyone, and he usually has his own way. But what do you want?" he continued, speaking to Toto. Toto only wagged his tail; for, strange to say, he could not speak.

The woman now called to them that supper was ready, so they gathered around the table and Dorothy ate some delicious porridge and a dish of scrambled eggs and a plate of nice white bread, and enjoyed her meal. The Lion ate some of the porridge, but did not care for it, saying it was made from oats and oats were food for horses, not for lions. The Scarecrow and the Tin Woodman ate nothing at all. Toto ate a little of everything, and was glad to get a good supper again.

The woman now gave Dorothy a bed to sleep in, and Toto lay down beside her, while the Lion guarded the door of her room so she might not be disturbed. The Scarecrow and the Tin Woodman stood up in a corner and kept quiet all night, although of course they could not sleep.

The next morning, as soon as the sun was up, they started on their way, and soon saw a beautiful green glow in the sky just before them.

"That must be the Emerald City," said Dorothy.

As they walked on, the green glow became brighter and

brighter, and it seemed that at last they were nearing the end of their travels. Yet it was afternoon before they came to the great wall that surrounded the City. It was high, and thick, and of a bright green colour.

In front of them, and at the end of the road of yellow brick, was a big gate, all studded with emeralds that glittered so in the sun that even the painted eyes of the Scarecrow were dazzled by their brilliancy.

There was a bell beside the gate, and Dorothy pushed the button and heard a silvery tinkle sound within. Then the big gate swung slowly open, and they all passed through and found themselves in a high arched room, the walls of which glistened with countless emeralds.

Before them stood a little man about the same size as the Munchkins. He was clothed all in green, from his head to his feet, and even his skin was of a greenish tint. At his side was a large green box.

When he saw Dorothy and her companions the man asked, "What do you wish in the Emerald City?"

"We came here to see the Great Oz," said Dorothy.

The man was so surprised at this answer that he sat down to think it over.

"It has been many years since anyone asked me to see Oz," he said, shaking his head in perplexity. "He is powerful and terrible, and if you come on an idle or foolish errand to bother the wise reflections of the Great Wizard, he might be angry and destroy you all in an instant."

"But it is not a foolish errand, nor an idle one," replied the Scarecrow; "it is important. And we have been told that Oz is a good Wizard."

"So he is," said the green man; "and he rules the Emerald City wisely and well. But to those who are not honest, or who approach him from curiosity, he is most terrible, and few have ever dared ask to see his face. I am the Guardian of the Gates, and since you demand to see the Great Oz I must take you to his palace. But first you must put on the spectacles."

"Why?" asked Dorothy.

"Because if you did not wear spectacles the brightness and the glory of the Emerald City would blind you. Even those who live in the City must wear spectacles night and day. They are all locked on, for Oz so ordered it when the City was first built, and I have the only key that will unlock them."

He opened the big box, and Dorothy saw that it was filled with spectacles of every size and shape. All of them had green glasses in them. The Guardian of the Gates found a pair that would just fit Dorothy and put them over her eyes. There were two golden bands fastened to them that passed around the back of her head, where they were locked together by a little key that was at the end of a chain the Guardian of the Gates wore around his neck. When they were on, Dorothy could not take them off had she wished, but of course she did not wish to be blinded by the glare of the Emerald City, so she said nothing.

Then the green man fitted spectacles for the Scarecrow and the Tin Woodman and the Lion, and even little Toto; and all were locked fast with the key.

Then the Guardian of the Gates put on his own glasses and told them he was ready to show them to the palace. Taking a big golden key from a peg on the wall, he opened another gate, and they all followed him through the portal into the streets of the Emerald City.

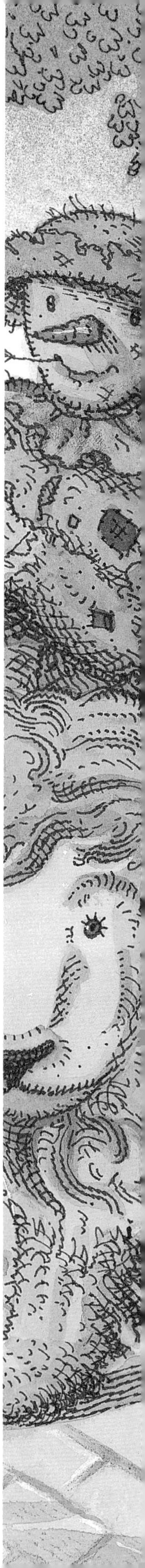

Introduction

An only child, Bertie grows up with his mother and father on a remote farm on the South African veld. He spends all his days safely behind the high compound fence around his garden. From here he can watch the animals as they come to the waterhole. One day he sees a lioness and her cub coming down to drink. To his astonishment the cub is white, pure white. Day after day, Bertie waits for them to come again, but they don't. Then comes the dreadful news that the lioness has been shot on the farm. Bertie longs for the orphaned cub to come back. But days pass and there is no sign of him. He has almost given up hope . . .

M. M.

THE BUTTERFLY LION

MICHAEL MORPURGO

Bertie and the Lion

One morning, a week or so later, Bertie was woken by a chorus of urgent neighing. He jumped out of his bed and ran to the window. A herd of zebras was scattering away from the waterhole, chased by a couple of hyenas. Then he saw more hyenas, three of them, standing stock still, noses pointing, eyes fixed on the waterhole. It was only now that Bertie saw the lion cub. But this one wasn't white at all. He was covered in mud, with his back to the waterhole, and he was waving a pathetic paw at the hyenas who were beginning to circle. The lion cub had nowhere to run to, and the hyenas were sidling ever closer.

Bertie was downstairs in a flash, leaping off the veranda and racing barefoot across the compound, shouting at the top of his voice. He threw open the gate and charged down the hill towards the waterhole, yelling and screaming and waving his arms like a wild thing. Startled at this sudden intrusion, the hyenas turned tail and ran, but not far. Once within range Bertie hurled a broadside of pebbles at them, and they ran off again, but again not far.

Then he was at the waterhole and between the lion cub and the hyenas, shouting at them to go away. They didn't. They stood and watched, uncertain for a while. Then they began to circle again, closer, closer . . .

That was when the shot rang out. The hyenas bolted into the long grass, and were gone. When Bertie turned round he saw his mother in her nightgown, rifle in hand, running towards him down the hill. He had never seen her run before. Between them they gathered up the mud-matted cub and brought him home. He was too weak to struggle, though he tried. As soon as they had given him some warm milk, they dunked him in the bath to wash him. As the first of the mud came off, Bertie saw he was white underneath.

"You see!" he cried triumphantly. "He *is* white! He *is*. I told you, didn't I? He's my white lion!" His mother still could not bring herself to believe it. Five baths later, she had to.

They sat him down by the stove in a washing basket and fed him again, all the milk he could drink, and he drank the lot. Then he lay down and slept. He was still asleep when Bertie's father got back at lunch time. They told him how it had all happened.

"Please, Father. I want to keep him," Bertie said.

"And so do I," said his mother. "We both do." And she spoke as Bertie had never heard her speak before, her voice strong, determined.

Bertie's father didn't seem to know quite how to reply. He just said: "We'll talk about it later," and then he walked out.

They did talk about it later when Bertie was supposed to be in bed. He wasn't, though. He heard them arguing. He was outside the sitting-room door, watching, listening. His father was pacing up and down.

"He'll grow up, you know," he was saying. "You can't keep a grown lion, you know that."

"And *you* know we can't just throw him to the hyenas," replied his mother. "He needs us, and maybe we need him. He'll be someone for Bertie to play with for a while." And then she added sadly: "After all, it's not as if he's going to have any brothers and sisters, is it?"

At this, Bertie's father went over to her and kissed her gently on the forehead. It was the only time Bertie had ever seen him kiss her.

"All right then," he said. "All right. You can keep your lion."

So the white lion cub came to live amongst them in the farmhouse. He slept at the end of Bertie's bed. Wherever Bertie went, the lion cub went too – even to the bathroom, where he would watch Bertie have his bath and lick his legs dry afterwards. They were never apart. It was Bertie who saw to the feeding –

milk four times a day from one of his father's beer bottles – until later on when the lion cub lapped from a soup bowl. There was impala meat whenever he wanted it, and as he grew – and he grew fast – he wanted more and more of it.

For the first time in his life Bertie was totally happy. The lion cub was all the brothers and sisters he could ever want, all the friends he could ever need. The two of them would sit side by side on the sofa out on the veranda and watch the great red sun go down over Africa, and Bertie would read him *Peter and the Wolf*, and at the end he would always promise him that he would never let him go off to a zoo and live behind bars like the wolf in the story. And the lion cub would look up at Bertie with his trusting amber eyes.

"Why don't you give him a name?" his mother asked one day.

"Because he doesn't need one," replied Bertie. "He's a lion, not a person. Lions don't need names."

Bertie's mother was always wonderfully patient with the lion, no matter how much mess he made, how many cushions he pounced on and ripped apart, no matter how much crockery he smashed. None of it seemed to upset her. And strangely, she was hardly ever ill these days. There was a spring to her step, and her laughter pealed around the house. His father was less happy about it. "Lions," he'd mutter on, "should not live in houses. You should keep him outside in the compound." But they never did. For both mother and son, the lion had brought new life to their days, life and laughter.

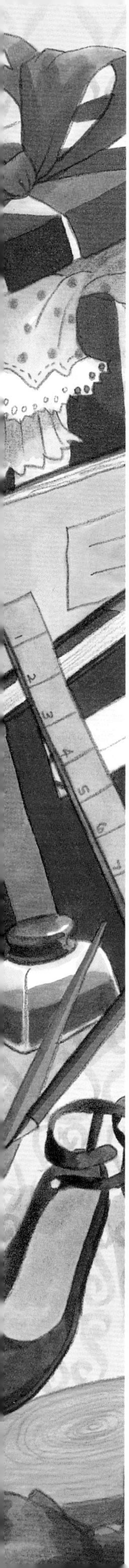

Introduction

Coming to a boarding school in England from her home in India is a big leap for Sara Crewe. She is only seven but already she feels as if she has lived a long, long time. Driving through the gloomy London streets with her father, they arrive at the dull red-brick building that is to be her home. MISS MINCHIN Select Seminary for Young Ladies *reads the sign, and Sara's heart sinks. It is not school that Sara fears, for she is always sitting with her nose in a book, and lessons for her are not a problem. But saying goodbye to her beloved father as he sets off for their beautiful home back in Bombay – that is the hardest thing of all. However, with her new doll, Emily, at her side, she goes into battle, determined to make her father proud of her.*

R. S.

A Little Princess

Frances Hodgson Burnett

A French Lesson

When Sara entered the schoolroom the next morning everybody looked at her with wide, interested eyes. By that time every pupil – from Lavinia Herbert, who was nearly thirteen and felt quite grown up, to Lottie Legh, who was only just four and the baby of the school – had heard a great deal about her. They knew very certainly that she was Miss Minchin's show pupil and was considered a credit to the establishment. One or two of them had even caught a glimpse of her French maid, Mariette, who had arrived the evening before. Lavinia had managed to pass Sara's room when the door was open, and had seen Mariette opening a box which had arrived late from some ship.

"It was full of petticoats with lace frills on them – frills and frills," she whispered to her friend Jessie as she bent over her geography. "I saw her shaking them out. I heard Miss Minchin say to Miss Amelia that her clothes were so grand that they were

ridiculous for a child. My mamma says that children should be dressed simply. She has got one of those petticoats on now. I saw it when she sat down."

"She has silk stockings on!" whispered Jessie, bending over her geography also. "And what little feet! I never saw such little feet."

"Oh," sniffed Lavinia spitefully, "that is the way her slippers are made. My mamma says that even big feet can be made to look small if you have a clever shoemaker. I don't think she is pretty at all. Her eyes are such a queer colour."

"She isn't pretty as other pretty people are," said Jessie, stealing a glance across the room, "but she makes you want to look at her again. She has tremendously long eyelashes, but her eyes are almost green."

Sara was sitting quietly in her seat, waiting to be told what to do. She had been placed near Miss Minchin's desk. She was not abashed at all by the many pairs of eyes watching her. She was interested, and looked back quietly at the children who looked at her. She wondered what they were thinking of, and if they liked Miss Minchin, and if they cared for their lessons, and if any of them had a papa at all like her own. She had had a long talk with Emily about her papa that morning.

"He is on the sea now, Emily," she had said. "We must be very great friends to each other and tell each other things. Emily, look at me. You have the nicest eyes I ever saw – but I wish you could speak."

She was a child full of imaginings and whimsical thoughts, and one of her fancies was that there would be a great deal of comfort in even pretending that Emily was alive and really heard and understood. After Mariette had dressed her in her dark-blue school-room frock and tied her hair with a dark-blue ribbon, she went to Emily, who sat in a chair of her own, and gave her a book.

"You can read that while I am downstairs," she said; and seeing Mariette looking at her curiously, she spoke to her with a serious little face.

"What I believe about dolls," she said, "is that they can do things they will not let us know about. Perhaps, really, Emily can read and talk and walk, but she will only do it when people are out of the room. That is her secret. You see, if people knew that dolls could do things, they would make them work. So, perhaps they have promised each other to keep it a secret. If you stay in the room, Emily will just sit there and stare; but if you go out, she will begin to read, perhaps, or go and look out of the window. Then if she heard either of us coming, she would just run back and jump into her chair and pretend she had been there all the time."

"*Comme elle est drôle!*" Mariette said to herself, and when she went downstairs she told the head housemaid about it. But she had already begun to like this odd little girl who had such an

intelligent small face and such perfect manners. She had taken care of children before who were not so polite. Sara was a very fine little person, and had a gentle, appreciative way of saying: "If you please, Mariette," "Thank you, Mariette," which was very charming. Mariette told the head housemaid that she thanked her as if she was thanking a lady.

"*Elle a l'air d'une princesse, cette petite,*" she said. Indeed, she was very much pleased with her new little mistress and liked her place greatly.

After Sara had sat in her seat in the schoolroom for a few minutes, being looked at by the pupils, Miss Minchin rapped in a dignified manner upon her desk.

"Young ladies," she said, "I wish to introduce you to your new companion." All the little girls rose in their places, and Sara rose also. "I shall expect you all to be very agreeable to Miss Crewe; she has just come to us from a great distance – in fact, from India. As soon as lessons are over you must make each other's acquaintance."

The pupils bowed ceremoniously, and Sara made a little curtsy, and then they sat down and looked at each other again.

"Sara," said Miss Minchin in her schoolroom manner, "come here to me."

She had taken a book from the desk and was turning over its leaves. Sara went to her politely.

"As your papa has engaged a French maid for you," she began, "I conclude that he wishes you to make a special study of the French language."

Sara felt a little awkward.

"I think he engaged her," she said, "because he – he thought I would like her, Miss Minchin."

"I am afraid," said Miss Minchin, with a slightly sour smile, "that you have been a very spoiled little girl and always imagine that things are done because you like them. My impression is that your papa wished you to learn French."

If Sara had been older or less punctilious about being quite polite to people, she could have explained herself in a very few words. But, as it was, she felt a flush rising on her cheeks. Miss Minchin was a very severe and imposing person, and she seemed so absolutely sure that Sara knew nothing whatever of French that she felt as if it would be almost rude to correct her. The truth was that Sara could not remember the time when she had not seemed to know French. Her father had often spoken it to her when she had been a baby. Her mother had been a Frenchwoman, and Captain Crewe had loved her language, so it happened that Sara had always heard and been familiar with it.

"I – I have never really learned French, but – but –" she began, trying shyly to make herself clear.

One of Miss Minchin's chief secret annoyances was that she did not speak French herself, and was desirous of concealing the irritating fact. She, therefore, had no intention of discussing the matter and laying herself open to innocent questioning by a new little pupil.

"That is enough," she said with polite tartness. "If you have not learned, you must begin at once. The French master, Monsieur Dufarge, will be here in a few minutes. Take this book and look at it until he arrives."

Sara's cheeks felt warm. She went back to her seat and opened the book. She looked at the first page with a grave face. She knew it would be rude to smile, and she was very determined not to be rude. But it was very odd to find herself expected to study a page which told her that "*le père*" meant "the father", and "*la mère*" meant "the mother".

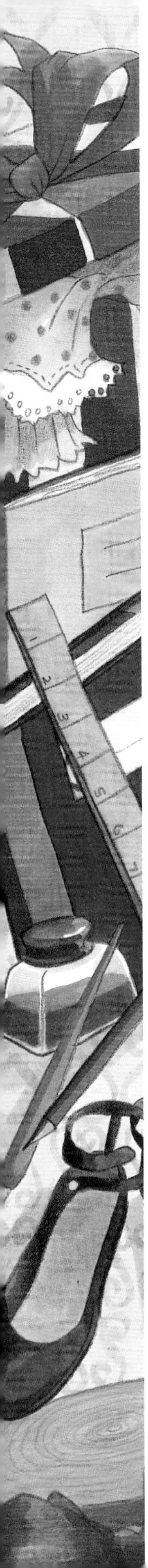

Miss Minchin glanced towards her scrutinizingly.

"You look rather cross, Sara," she said. "I am sorry you do not like the idea of learning French."

"I am very fond of it," answered Sara, thinking she would try again; "but –"

"You must not say 'but' when you are told to do things," said Miss Minchin. "Look at your book again."

And Sara did so, and did not smile, even when she found that "*le fils*" meant "the son", and "*le frère*" meant "the brother".

"When Monsieur Dufarge comes," she thought, "I can make him understand."

Monsieur Dufarge arrived very shortly afterwards. He was a very nice, intelligent, middle-aged Frenchman, and he looked interested when his eyes fell upon Sara trying politely to seem absorbed in her little book of phrases.

"Is this a new pupil for me, madame?" he said to Miss Minchin. "I hope that is my good fortune."

"Her papa – Captain Crewe – is very anxious that she should begin the language. But I am afraid she has a childish prejudice against it. She does not seem to wish to learn," said Miss Minchin.

"I am sorry of that, mademoiselle," he said kindly to Sara. "Perhaps, when we begin to study together, I may show you that it is a charming tongue."

Little Sara rose in her seat. She was beginning to feel rather desperate, as if she were almost in disgrace. She looked up into Monsieur Dufarge's face with her big, green-grey eyes, and they were quite innocently appealing. She began to explain quite simply in pretty and fluent French. Madame had not understood. She had not learned French exactly – not out of books – but her papa and other people had always spoken it to her, and she had read it and written it as she had read and written English. Her papa loved it, and she loved it because he did. Her dear mamma, who had died when she was born, had been French. She would be glad to learn anything monsieur would teach her, but what she had tried to explain to madame was that she already knew the words in this book – and she held out the little book of phrases.

When she began to speak Miss Minchin started quite violently and sat staring at her over her eye-glasses, almost indignantly, until she had finished. Monsieur Dufarge began to smile, and his smile was one of great pleasure. To hear this pretty childish voice speaking his own language so simply and charmingly made him feel almost as if he were in his native land – which in dark, foggy days in London sometimes seemed worlds away. When she had finished, he took the phrase-book from her, with a look almost affectionate. But he spoke to Miss Minchin.

"Ah, madame," he said, "there is not much I can teach her. She has not *learned* French; she *is* French. Her accent is exquisite."

"You ought to have told me," exclaimed Miss Minchin, much mortified, turning on Sara.

"I – I tried," said Sara. "I – I suppose I did not begin right."

Miss Minchin knew she had tried, and that it had not been her fault that she was not allowed to explain. And when she saw that the pupils had been listening, and that Lavinia and Jessie were giggling behind their French grammars, she felt infuriated.

"Silence, young ladies!" she said severely, rapping upon the desk. "Silence at once!"

And she began from that minute to feel rather a grudge against her show pupil.

Introduction

This wonderful book begins with these words:
"The Iron Man came to the top of the cliff.
How far had he walked? Nobody knows.
Where had he come from? Nobody knows.
How was he made? Nobody knows."
The Iron Man falls, shattering himself on the rocks below. Bit by bit he pieces himself together, all except for one ear which he cannot find. Maybe the sea has washed it away. He goes down to the sea to look – down, down until the water covers him completely. But we haven't seen the last of the Iron Man. In fact, the story's just beginning.

M. M.

THE IRON MAN

TED HUGHES

The Return of the Iron Man

From farm to farm, over the soft soil of the fields, went giant footprints, each one the size of a single bed.

The farmers, in a frightened, silent, amazed crowd, followed the footprints. And at every farm the footprints visited, all the metal machinery had disappeared.

Finally, the footprints led back up to the top of the cliff, where the little boy had seen the Iron Man appear the night before, when he was fishing. The footprints led right to the cliff-top.

And all the way down the cliff were torn marks on the rocks, where a huge iron body had slid down. Below, the tide was in. The grey, empty, moving tide. The Iron Man had gone back into the sea.

SO

The furious farmers began to shout. The Iron Man had stolen all their machinery. Had he eaten it? Anyway, he had taken it.

It had gone. So what if he came again? What would he take next time? Cows? Houses? People?

They would have to do something.

They couldn't call in the police or the Army, because nobody would believe them about this Iron Monster. They would have to do something for themselves.

So, what did they do?

At the bottom of the hill, below where the Iron Man had come over the high cliff, they dug a deep, enormous hole. A hole wider than a house, and as deep as three trees one on top of the other. It was a colossal hole. A stupendous hole! And the sides of it were sheer as walls.

They pushed all the earth off to one side.

They covered the hole with branches and the branches they covered with straw and the straw with soil, so when they finished the hole looked like a freshly-ploughed field.

Now, on the side of the hole opposite the slope up to the top of the cliff, they put an old rusty lorry. That was the bait. Now they reckoned the Iron Man would come over the top of the cliff out of the sea, and he'd see the old lorry which was painted red, and he'd come down to get it to chew it up and eat it. But on his way to the lorry he'd be crossing the hole, and the moment he stepped with his great weight on to that soil held up only with straw and branches, he would crash through into the hole and would never get out. They'd find him there in the hole. Then they'd bring the few bulldozers and earth-movers that he hadn't already eaten, and they'd push the pile of earth in on top of him, and bury him for ever in the hole. They were certain now that they'd get him.

Next morning, in great excitement, all the farmers gathered together to go along to examine their trap. They came carefully closer, expecting to see his hands tearing at the edge of the pit. They came carefully closer.

The red lorry stood just as they had left it. The soil lay just as they had left it, undisturbed. Everything was just as they had left it. The Iron Man had not come.

Nor did he come that day.

Next morning, all the farmers came again. Still, everything lay just as they had left it.

And so it went on, day after day. Still the Iron Man never came.

Now the farmers began to wonder if he would ever come again. They began to wonder if he had ever come at all. They began to make up explanations of what had happened to their machinery. Nobody likes to believe in an Iron Monster that eats tractors and cars.

Soon, the farmer who owned the red lorry they were using as bait decided that he needed it, and he took it away. So there lay the beautiful deep trap, without any bait. Grass began to grow on the loose soil.

The farmers talked of filling the hole in. After all, you can't leave a giant pit like that, somebody might fall in. Some stranger coming along might just walk over it and fall in.

But they didn't want to fill it in. It had been such hard work digging it. Besides they all had a sneaking fear that the Iron Man might come again, and that the hole was their only weapon against him.

At last they put up a little notice: "DANGER: KEEP OFF", to warn people away, and they left it at that.

Now the little boy Hogarth had an idea. He thought he could use that hole, to trap a fox. He found a dead hen one day, and threw it out on to the loose soil over the trap. Then towards

evening, he climbed a tree nearby, and waited. A long time he waited. A star came out. He could hear the sea.

Then – there, standing at the edge of the hole, was a fox. A big, red fox, looking towards the dead hen. Hogarth stopped breathing. And the fox stood without moving – sniff, sniff, sniff, out towards the hen. But he did not step out on to the trap. Slowly, he walked around the wide patch of raw soil till he got back to where he'd started, sniffing all the time out towards the bird. But he did not step out on to the trap. Was he too smart to walk out there where it was not safe?

But at that moment he stopped sniffing. He turned his head and looked towards the top of the cliff. Hogarth, wondering what the fox had seen, looked towards the top of the cliff.

There, enormous in the blue evening sky, stood the Iron Man, on the brink of the cliff, gazing inland.

In a moment, the fox had vanished.

Now what?

Hogarth carefully quietly hardly breathing climbed slowly down the tree. He must get home and tell his father. But at the bottom of the tree he stopped. He could no longer see the Iron Man against the twilight sky. Had he gone back over the cliff into the sea? Or was he coming down the hill, in the darkness under that high skyline, towards Hogarth and the farms?

Then Hogarth understood what was happening. He could hear a strange tearing and creaking sound. The Iron Man was pulling up the barbed-wire fence that led down the hill. And soon Hogarth could see him, as he came nearer, tearing the wire from the fence posts, rolling it up like spaghetti and eating it. The Iron Man was eating the barbed fencing wire.

But if he went along the fence, eating as he moved, he wouldn't come anywhere near the trap, which was out in the middle of the field. He could spend the whole night wandering about the countryside along the fences, rolling up the wire and eating it, and never would any fence bring him near the trap.

But Hogarth had an idea. In his pocket, among other things, he had a long nail and a knife. He took these out. Did he dare? His idea frightened him. In the silent dusk, he tapped the nail and the knife blade together.

Clink, Clink, Clink!

At the sound of the metal, the Iron Man's hands became still. After a few seconds, he slowly turned his head and the headlamp eyes shone towards Hogarth.

Again, Clink, Clink, Clink! went the nail on the knife.

Slowly, the Iron Man took three strides towards Hogarth, and again stopped. It was now quite dark. The headlamps shone red. Hogarth pressed close to the tree-trunk. Between him and the Iron Man lay the wide lid of the trap.

Clink, Clink, Clink! again he tapped the nail on the knife.

And now the Iron Man was coming. Hogarth could feel the earth shaking under the weight of his footsteps. Was it too late to run? Hogarth stared at the Iron Man, looming, searching towards him for the taste of the metal that had made that inviting sound.

Clink, Clink, Clink! went the nail on the knife. And CRASSSHHH!

The Iron Man vanished.

He was in the pit. The Iron Man had fallen into the pit. Hogarth went close. The earth was shaking as the Iron Man struggled underground. Hogarth peered over the torn edge of the great pit. Far below, two deep red headlamps glared up at him from the pitch blackness. He could hear the Iron Man's insides grinding down there and it sounded like a big lorry grinding its gears on a steep hill. Hogarth set off. He ran, he ran, home – home with the great news. And as he passed the cottages on the way, and as he turned down the lane towards his father's farm, he was shouting "The Iron Man's in the trap!" and "We've caught the Iron Giant!"

Introduction

There are not many girls whose name has gone into everyday language: to call someone a Pollyanna means she is endlessly optimistic, always looking on the very brightest side of things. When the orphaned Pollyanna goes to stay with her stern aunt Miss Polly Harrington, she is full of excitement, although Miss Polly's maid, Nancy, and the gardener's son, Timothy, both worry about how she will settle in to her new home. But Pollyanna's joy and enthusiasm are such that when she arrives, she does not notice Miss Polly's chilly greeting and rejoices in the gladness of her luck at being in the big white house with the green shutters. Pollyanna is given an attic room, where there are no screens to keep out insects when the windows are open. One particularly hot night, Aunt Polly insists that the windows be kept closed to keep out flies – but Pollyanna has the answer to keeping cool.

R. S.

POLLYANNA

ELEANOR H. PORTER

Pollyanna and Punishments

At half past eight Pollyanna went up to bed. The screens had not yet come, and the close little room was like an oven. With longing eyes Pollyanna looked at the two fast-closed windows – but she did not raise them. She undressed, folded her clothes neatly, said her prayers, blew out her candle and climbed into bed.

Just how long she lay in sleepless misery, tossing from side to side of the hot little cot, she did not know; but it seemed to her that it must have been hours before she finally slipped out of bed, felt her way across the room and opened her door.

Out in the main attic all was velvet blackness save where the moon flung a path of silver halfway across the floor from the east dormer window. With a resolute ignoring of that fearsome darkness to the right and to the left, Pollyanna drew a quick breath and pattered straight into that silvery path, and on to the window.

She had hoped, vaguely, that this window might have a screen, but it did not. Outside, however, there was a wide world of fairy-like beauty, and there was, too, she knew, fresh, sweet air that would feel so good to hot cheeks and hands!

As she stepped nearer and peered longingly out, she saw something else; she saw, only a little way below the window, the wide, flat tin roof of Miss Polly's sun-parlour built over the *porte-cochère*. The sight filled her with longing. If only, now, she were out there!

Fearfully she looked behind her. Back there, somewhere, were her hot little room and her still hotter bed; but between her and them lay a horrid desert of blackness across which one must feel one's way with outstretched, shrinking arms; while before her, out on the sun-parlour roof, were the moonlight and the cool, sweet night air.

If only her bed were out there! And folks did sleep out-of-doors. Joel Hartley at home, who was so sick with consumption, *had* to sleep out-of-doors.

Suddenly Pollyanna remembered that she had seen near this attic window a row of long white bags hanging from nails. Nancy had said they contained the winter clothing, put away for the summer. A little fearfully now, Pollyanna felt her way to these bags, selected a nice fat soft one (it contained Miss Polly's sealskin coat) for a bed; and a thinner one to be doubled up for a pillow, and still another (which was so thin it seemed almost empty) for a covering. Thus equipped, Pollyanna in high glee pattered to the moonlit window again, raised the sash, stuffed the burden through to the roof below, then let herself down after it, closing the window carefully behind her – Pollyanna had not forgotten those flies with their marvellous feet that carried things.

How deliciously cool it was! Pollyanna quite danced up and down with delight, drawing in long, full breaths of the refreshing air. The tin roof under her feet crackled with little resounding snaps that Pollyanna rather liked. She walked, indeed, two or three times back and forth from end to end – it gave her such a pleasant sensation of airy space after her hot little room; and the roof was so broad and flat that she had no fear of falling off. Finally, with a sigh of content, she curled herself up on the sealskin-coat mattress, arranged one bag for a pillow and the other for a covering, and settled herself to sleep.

"I'm so glad now that the screens didn't come," she murmured, blinking up at the stars; "else I couldn't have had this!"

Downstairs in Miss Polly's room next to the sun-parlour, Miss Polly herself was hurrying into dressing-gown and slippers, her face white and frightened. A minute before she had been telephoning in a shaking voice to Timothy.

"Come up quick! – you and your father. Bring lanterns. Somebody is on the roof of the sun-parlour. He must have climbed up the rose-trellis or somewhere, and of course he can get right into the house through the east window in the attic. I have locked the attic door down here – but hurry, quick!"

Some time later, Pollyanna, just dropping off to sleep, was startled by a lantern flash, and a trio of amazed ejaculations. She opened her eyes to find Timothy at the top of a ladder near her, Old Tom just getting through the window, and her aunt peering out at her from behind him.

"Pollyanna, what does this mean?" cried Aunt Polly then.

Pollyanna blinked sleepy eyes and sat up.

"Why, Mr Tom – Aunt Polly!" she stammered. "Don't look so scared! It isn't that I've got the consumption, you know, like Joel Hartley. It's only that I was so hot – in there. But I shut the window, Aunt Polly, so the flies couldn't carry those germ-things in."

Timothy disappeared suddenly down the ladder. Old Tom, with almost equal precipitation, handed his lantern to Miss Polly, and followed his son. Miss Polly bit her lip hard – until the men were gone, then she said sternly:

"Pollyanna, hand those things to me at once and come in here. Of all the extraordinary children!" she ejaculated a little later, as, with Pollyanna by her side, and the lantern in her hand, she turned back into the attic.

To Pollyanna the air was all the more stifling after that cool breath of the out-of-doors: but she did not complain. She only drew a long, quivering sigh.

At the top of the stairs Miss Polly jerked out crisply:

"For the rest of the night, Pollyanna, you are to sleep in my bed with me. The screens will be here tomorrow, but until then I consider it my duty to keep you where you are."

Pollyanna drew in her breath.

"With you? – in your bed?" she cried rapturously. "Oh, Aunt Polly, Aunt Polly, how perfectly lovely of you! And when I've so wanted to sleep with someone some time – someone that belonged to me, you know; not a Ladies' Aider. I've *had* them. My! I reckon I am glad now those screens didn't come! Wouldn't you be?"

There was no reply. Miss Polly was stalking on ahead. Miss Polly, to tell the truth, was feeling curiously helpless. For the third time since Pollyanna's arrival, Miss Polly was punishing Pollyanna – and for the third time she was being confronted with the amazing fact that her punishment was being taken as a special reward of merit. No wonder Miss Polly was feeling curiously helpless.

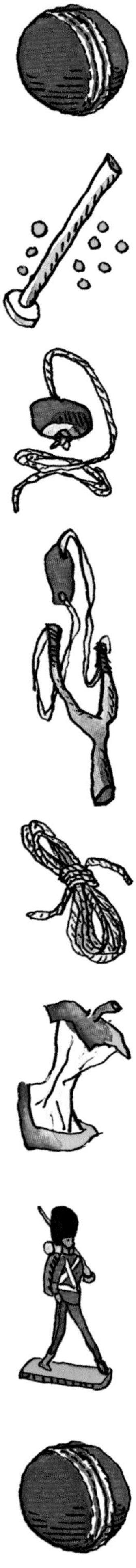

Introduction

William Brown is a rogue – there's never been anyone like him. What is terrific about him is that he gets himself into all sorts of scrapes and always comes out smiling. He says just what he thinks, just what he feels. If he gets an idea in his head, it's always the best idea he's ever had and he simply goes for it. And when things don't work out as he planned there is always trouble, big trouble. But does William mind? Does William care? Of course not. He picks himself up and goes on being himself, being just William. That's why we love him.

M. M.

JUST WILLIAM

RICHMAL CROMPTON

The Fall of the Idol

William was bored. He sat at his desk in the sunny schoolroom and gazed dispassionately at a row of figures on the blackboard.

"It isn't *sense*," he murmured scornfully.

Miss Drew was also bored, but, unlike William, she tried to hide the fact.

"If the interest on a hundred pounds for one year is five pounds," she said wearily, then, "William Brown, do sit up and don't look so stupid!"

William changed his position from that of lolling over one side of his desk to that of lolling over the other, and began to justify himself.

"Well, I can't unner*stand* any of it. It's enough to make anyone look stupid when he can't unner*stand* any of it. I can't think why people go on givin' people bits of money for givin' 'em lots of money and go on an' on doin' it. It dun't seem sense. Anyone's a mug for givin' anyone a hundred pounds just 'cause he says he'll go on givin' him five pounds and go on stickin' to his hundred pounds. How's he to *know* he will? Well," he warmed to his subject, "what's to stop him not givin' any five pounds once he's got hold of the hundred pounds an' goin' on stickin' to the hundred pounds—"

Miss Drew checked him by a slim, upraised hand.

"William," she said patiently, "just listen to me. Now suppose," her eyes roved round the room and settled on a small red-haired boy, "suppose that Eric wanted a hundred pounds for something and you lent it to him—"

"I wun't lend Eric a hundred pounds," he said firmly, "'cause I ha'n't got it. I've only got 3½d., an' I wun't lend that to Eric, 'cause I'm not such a mug, 'cause I lent him my mouth-organ once an' he bit a bit off an'—"

Miss Drew interrupted sharply. Teaching on a hot afternoon is rather trying.

"You'd better stay in after school, William, and I'll explain."

William scowled, emitted his monosyllable of scornful disdain "Huh!" and relapsed into gloom.

He brightened, however, on remembering a lizard he had caught on the way to school, and drew it from its hiding-place in his pocket. But the lizard had abandoned the unequal struggle for existence among the stones, top, penknife, bits of putty, and other small objects that inhabited William's pocket. The housing problem had been too much for it.

William in disgust shrouded the remains in blotting-paper, and disposed of it in his neighbour's inkpot. The neighbour protested and an enlivening scrimmage ensued.

Finally the lizard was dropped down the neck of an inveterate enemy of William's in the next row, and was extracted only with the help of obliging friends. Threats of vengeance followed, couched in blood-curdling terms, and written on blotting-paper.

Meanwhile Miss Drew explained Simple Practice to a small but earnest coterie of admirers in the front row. And William, in the back row, whiled away the hours for which his father paid the education authorities a substantial sum.

But his turn was to come.

At the end of afternoon school one by one the class departed, leaving William only nonchalantly chewing an india-rubber and glaring at Miss Drew.

"Now, William."

Miss Drew was severely patient.

William went up to the platform and stood by her desk.

"You see, if someone borrows a hundred pounds from someone else—"

She wrote down the figures on a piece of paper, bending low over her desk. The sun poured in through the window, showing the little golden curls in the nape of her neck. She lifted to William eyes that were stern and frowning, but blue as blue above flushed cheeks.

"Don't you *see*, William?" she said.

There was a faint perfume about her, and William the devil-may-care pirate and robber-chief, the stern despiser of all things effeminate, felt the first dart of the malicious blind god. He blushed and simpered.

"Yes, I see all about it now," he assured her. "You've explained it all plain now. I cudn't unner*stand* it before. It's a bit soft – in't it – anyway, to go lending hundred pounds about just 'cause someone says they'll give you five pounds next year. Some folks is mugs. But I do unner*stand* now. I cudn't unnerstand it before."

"You'd have found it simpler if you hadn't played with dead lizards all the time," she said wearily, closing her books.

William gasped.

He went home her devoted slave. Certain members of the class always deposited dainty bouquets on her desk in the morning. William was determined to outshine the rest. He went into the garden with a large basket and a pair of scissors the next morning before he set out for school.

It happened that no one was about. He went first to the hothouse. It was a riot of colour. He worked there with a thoroughness and concentration worthy of a nobler cause. He came out staggering beneath a piled-up basket of hothouse blooms. The hothouse itself was bare and desolate. Hearing a sound in the back garden he hastily decided to delay no longer, but to set out to school at once. He set out as unostentatiously as possible.

Miss Drew, entering her class-room, was aghast to see instead of the usual small array of buttonholes on her desk, a mass of already withering hothouse flowers completely covering her desk and chair.

William was a boy who never did things by halves.

"Good Heavens!" she cried in consternation.

William blushed with pleasure.

He changed his seat to one in the front row. All that morning he sat, his eyes fixed on her earnestly, dreaming of moments in which he rescued her from robbers and pirates (here he was somewhat inconsistent with his own favourite role of robber-chief and pirate), and bore her fainting in his strong arms to safety. Then she clung to him in love and gratitude, and they were married at once by the Archbishops of Canterbury and York.

William would have no half-measures. They were to be married by the Archbishops of Canterbury and York, or else the Pope. He wasn't sure that he wouldn't rather have the Pope. He would wear his black pirate suit with the skull and crossbones. No, that would not do—

"What have I just been saying, William?" said Miss Drew.

William coughed and gazed at her soulfully.

"'Bout lendin' money?" he said, hopefully.

"William!" she snapped. "This isn't an arithmetic lesson. I'm trying to teach you about the Armada."

"Oh, *that*!" said William brightly and ingratiatingly. "Oh, yes."

"Tell me something about it."

"I don't *know* anything – not jus' yet—"

"I've been *telling* you about it. I do wish you'd listen," she said despairingly.

William relapsed into silence, nonplussed, but by no means cowed.

When he reached home that evening he found that the garden was the scene of excitement and hubbub. One policeman was measuring the panes of glass in the conservatory door, and another was on his knees examining the beds near. His grown-up sister, Ethel, was standing at the front door.

"Every single flower has been stolen from the conservatory some time this morning," she said excitedly. "We've only just been able to get the police. William, did you see anyone about when you went to school this morning?"

William pondered deeply. His most guileless and innocent expression came to his face.

"No," he said at last. "No, Ethel, I didn't see nobody."

William coughed and discreetly withdrew.

That evening he settled down at the library table, spreading out his books around him, a determined frown upon his small face.

His father was sitting in an armchair by the window reading the evening paper.

"Father," said William suddenly, "s'pose I came to you an' said you was to give me a hundred pounds an' I'd give you five pounds next year an' so on, would you give it me?"

"I should not, my son," said his father firmly.

William sighed.

"I knew there was something wrong with it," he said.

Mr Brown returned to the leading article, but not for long.

"Father, what was the date of the Armada?"

"Good Heavens! How should I know? I wasn't there."

William sighed.

"Well, I'm tryin' to write about it and why it failed an'— why did it fail?"

Mr Brown groaned, gathered up his paper, and retired to the dining-room.

He had almost finished the leading article when William appeared, his arms full of books, and sat down quietly at the table.

"Father, what's the French for 'my aunt is walking in the garden'?"

"What on earth are you doing?" said Mr Brown irritably.

"I'm doing my home-lessons," said William virtuously.

"I never even knew you had the things to do."

"No," William admitted gently, "I don't generally take much bother over them, but I'm goin' to now – 'cause Miss Drew" – he blushed slightly and paused – "'cause Miss Drew" – he blushed more deeply and began to stammer, "'c-cause Miss Drew" – he was almost apoplectic.

Mr Brown quietly gathered up his paper and crept out to the veranda, where his wife sat with the week's mending.

"William's gone raving mad in the dining-room," he said pleasantly, as he sat down. "Takes the form of a wild thirst for knowledge, and a babbling of a Miss Drawing, or Drew, or something. He's best left alone."

Mrs Brown merely smiled placidly over the mending.

Mr Brown had finished one leading article and begun another before William appeared again. He stood in the doorway frowning and stern.

"Father, what's the capital of Holland?"

"Good Heavens!" said his father. "Buy him an encyclopedia. Anything, anything. What does he think I am? What—"

"I'd better set apart a special room for his home-work," said Mrs Brown soothingly, "now that he's beginning to take such an interest."

"A room!" echoed his father bitterly. "He wants a whole house."

Miss Drew was surprised and touched by William's earnestness and attention the next day. At the end of the afternoon school he kindly offered to carry her books home for her. He waved aside all protests. He marched home by her side discoursing pleasantly, his small freckled face beaming devotion.

"I like pirates, don't you, Miss Drew? An' robbers an' things like that? Miss Drew, would you like to be married to a robber?"

He was trying to reconcile his old beloved dream of his future estate with the new one of becoming Miss Drew's husband.

"No," she said firmly.

His heart sank.

"Nor a pirate?" he said sadly.

"No."

"They're quite nice really – pirates," he assured her.

"I think not."

"Well," he said resignedly, "we'll jus' have to go huntin' wild animals and things. That'll be all right."

"Who?" she said, bewildered.

"Well – jus' you wait," he said darkly.

Then: "Would you rather be married by the Archbishop of York or the Pope?"

"The Archbishop, I think," she said gravely.

He nodded.

"All right."

Introduction

Have you ever wanted to do extraordinary things and to say the first thing that comes into your head, no matter how impossibly silly? Well, for nine-year-old Pippi with her red hair and her curious clothes, anything and everything is possible. A thoroughly independent spirit, Pippi lives alone in a cottage in Sweden with her horse and a monkey, and has the wildest adventures imaginable. Here she is, with her friends Tommy and Annika, on her first ever visit to the circus.

R. S.

PIPPI LONGSTOCKING

ASTRID LINDGREN

Pippi Goes to the Circus

There was a crowd of people outside the circus tent, and in front of the ticket window stood a long queue. By and by it was Pippi's turn. She stuck her head through the window, looked hard at the dear old lady who sat there, and said, "How much does it cost to look at *you*?"

The old lady was from a foreign country, so she didn't understand what Pippi meant. She answered, "Liddle girl, it is costink vive crones the front rows and dree crones the back rows and wan crones the zdandinkroom."

"I see," said Pippi. "But you must promise that you'll walk on the rope too."

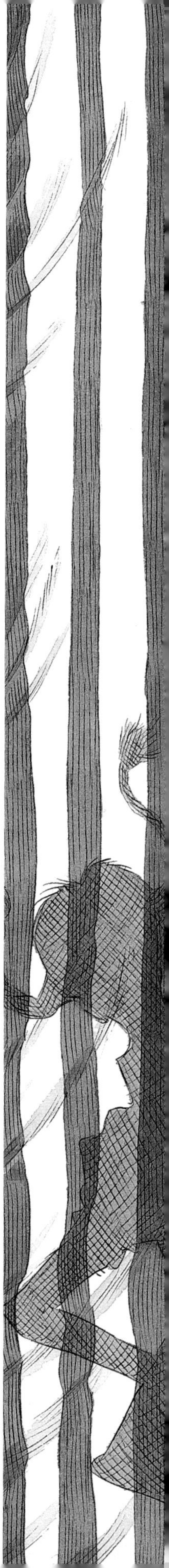

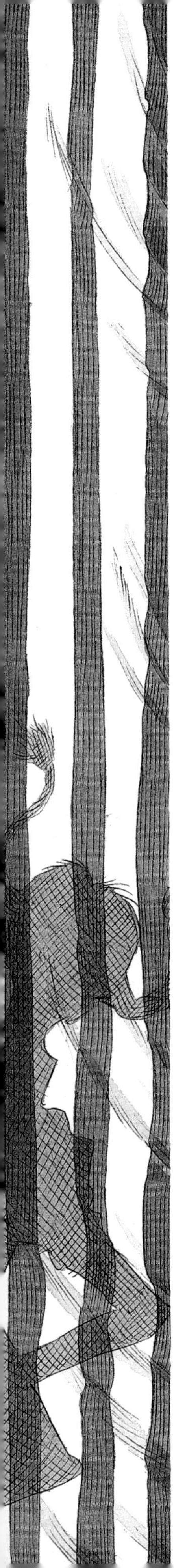

Now Tommy stepped in and said that Pippi would have a ticket for the back rows. Pippi gave a gold piece to the old lady and she looked suspiciously at it. She bit it, too, to see if it were real. At last she was convinced that it really was gold, and Pippi got her ticket. She got a great many silver coins in change as well.

"What do I want with all that nasty little white money?" said Pippi crossly. "Keep it. I'll look at you twice instead. From the zdandinkroom."

So, as Pippi absolutely didn't want any money back, the lady changed her ticket for a front row one, and gave Tommy and Annika front row tickets as well, without their having to add any money of their own. In this way, Pippi and Tommy and Annika came to sit on some very fine red chairs by the ringside. Tommy and Annika turned round several times in order to wave to their schoolmates, who sat much farther away.

"*This* is a queer hut," said Pippi, looking about her with wonder. "But they've spilled sawdust on the floor, I see. Not that I'm fussy, but it *does* look a bit untidy."

Tommy explained to Pippi that there was always sawdust in circus rings for the horses to run on.

On a platform sat the circus musicians, and they suddenly began to play a rousing march. Pippi clapped her hands wildly and jumped up and down in her chair with delight.

"Does it cost something to listen, too, or can you do that free?" she wondered.

Just then the curtain was pulled back from the artistes' entrance, and the ringmaster, dressed in black and with a whip in his hand, came running in, and with him there came ten white horses with red plumes on their heads.

The ringmaster cracked his whip, and the horses cantered round the ring. Then he cracked his whip again, and they all stood with their front legs up on the railing which circled the ring. One of the horses had stopped just in front of the children. Annika didn't like having a horse so close to her, so she crouched back in her chair as far as she could. But Pippi leaned forward, lifted up the horse's front leg, and said, "How's yourself? My horse sends his regards to you. It's *his* birthday too today, though he has bows on his tail instead of his head."

As luck would have it, Pippi let go of the horse's foot before the ringmaster cracked his whip the next time, because then all the horses jumped down from the railing and began to canter again.

When the act was finished, the ringmaster bowed beautifully, and the horses trotted out. A second later the curtain opened again for a coal-black horse, and on his back stood a beautiful lady dressed in green silk tights. Her name was Miss Carmencita, it said in the programme.

The horse trotted round in the sawdust, and Miss Carmencita stood there calmly and smiled. But then something happened. Just as the horse passed Pippi's place, something came whistling through the air. It was none other than Pippi herself. There she suddenly stood on the horse's back behind Miss Carmencita. At first, Miss Carmencita was so astonished that she nearly fell off the horse. Then she became angry. She began to hit behind herself with her hands in order to get Pippi to jump off. But she couldn't manage it.

"Calm down a little," said Pippi. "You're not the only one who's going to have fun. There are others who've paid *their* money too, believe it or not!"

Then Miss Carmencita wanted to jump off herself, but she couldn't do that either, for Pippi had a steady hold round her waist. The people in the circus couldn't help laughing. It looked so silly, they thought, to see the beautiful Miss Carmencita held

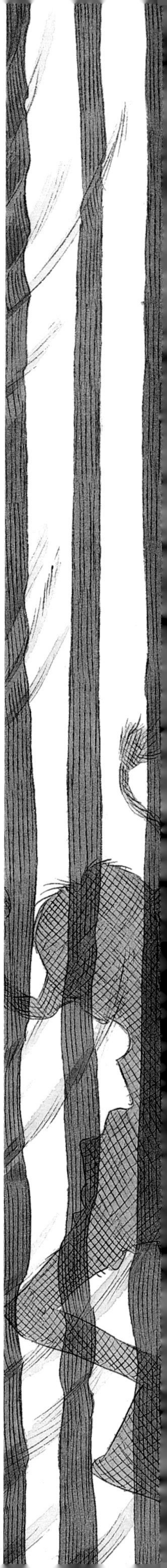

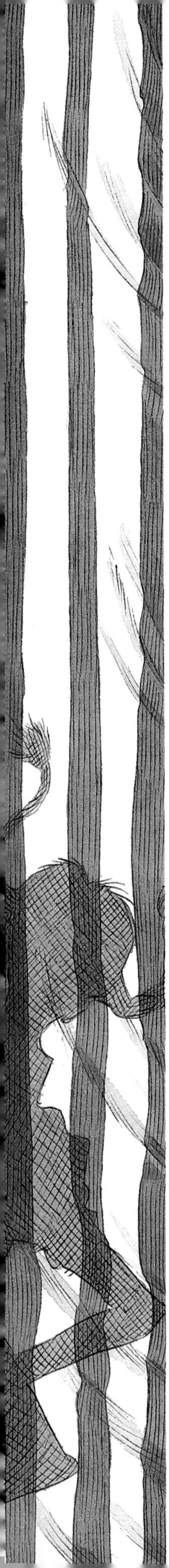

fast by a little red-headed scamp who stood on the horse's back in her big shoes looking as if she'd never done anything *but* perform in a circus.

But the ringmaster didn't laugh. He made a sign to his red-coated attendants to run forward and stop the horse.

"Is the act over already?" said Pippi, disappointed. "Just now when we were having such fun!"

"Derrible child," hissed the ringmaster between his teeth, "go avay!"

Pippi looked sorrowfully at him. "Well, but, now," she said, "why are you so angry with me? I thought everyone was supposed to have a nice time here."

She jumped down from the horse, and went and sat down in her place. But now two big attendants came to throw her out. They took hold of her and tried to lift her.

It was no use. Pippi just sat still, and it simply wasn't possible to move her from the spot, though they tugged as hard as they could. So they shrugged their shoulders and went away.

In the meantime the next act had begun. It was Miss Elvira, who was to walk the tightrope. She wore a pink tulle dress and carried a pink parasol in her hand. With small neat steps she ran out on to the rope. She swung her legs and did all manner of tricks. It was very pretty indeed. She proved too that she could go backwards on the thin rope. But when she came back to the little platform at the end of the line and turned round, Pippi was standing there.

"What was it you said?" said Pippi, delighted to see Miss Elvira's surprised expression.

Miss Elvira didn't say anything at all, but jumped down from the rope and threw her arms around the neck of the ringmaster, who was her father. Again he sent for his attendants to throw

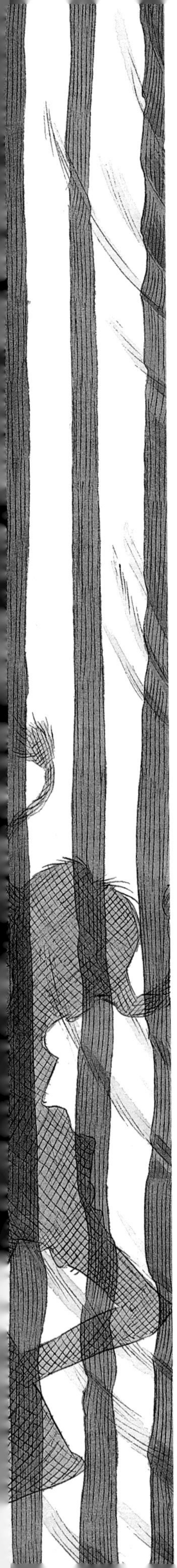

Pippi out. This time he sent for five. But all the people in the circus shouted, "Let her be! We want to see the little redhead!"

And they stamped their feet and clapped their hands.

Pippi ran out on the line. And Miss Elvira's tricks were nothing compared to what Pippi could do. When she came to the middle of the rope, she stretched one leg straight up into the air, and her big shoe spread out like a roof over her head. She waggled her foot a little, to scratch behind her ear.

The ringmaster was not the least bit pleased that Pippi was performing in his circus. He wanted to be rid of her. So he sneaked forward and loosened the mechanism which held the line tight, and he was sure that Pippi would fall off.

But she didn't. She began to swing the rope instead. Back and forth swayed the line, faster and faster swung Pippi, and then – suddenly – she took a leap into the air and landed right on the ringmaster. He was so frightened that he began to run.

"This horse is even more fun," said Pippi. "But why haven't you any tassels in your hair?"

Now Pippi thought it was time to turn back to Tommy and Annika. She climbed off the ringmaster and went and sat down, and then the next act was about to begin. There was a moment's delay, because the ringmaster first had to go out and drink a glass of water and comb his hair. But after that he came in, bowed to the audience, and said, "Ladies and chantlemen! In ze next moment you vill zee vun of ze vunders uff all time, ze zdrongest man in ze vorld, Mighty Adolf, who nobody has effer beaten yet. And here he is, ladies and chantlemen. Mighty Adolf!"

A gigantic man stepped into the ring. He was dressed in scarlet tights, and he had a leopard skin round his stomach. He bowed to the audience, and looked very self-satisfied indeed.

"Just *look* at which mossels!" said the ringmaster, squeezing

Mighty Adolf's arm where the muscles bulged like bowls under the skin.

"And now, ladies and chantlemen, I giff you a grrreat offer! Weech of you dares to try a wrestling match with Mighty Adolf, who dares to try to beat ze vorld's zdrongest man? A hundred crowns I pay to the vun who can beat Mighty Adolf. A hundred crowns, consider it, ladies and chantlemen! Step right up! Who'll giff it a try?"

Nobody came forward.

"What did he say?" asked Pippi. "And why is he speaking Arabian?"

"He said that the person who can beat that great big man over there will get a hundred crowns," said Tommy.

"I can do it," said Pippi. "But I think it would be a shame to beat him, 'cause he looks such a nice man."

"But you could *never* do it," said Annika. "Why, that's the strongest man in the world!"

"Man, yes," said Pippi. "But I'm the strongest *girl* in the world, don't forget."

In the meanwhile, Mighty Adolf was lifting dumb-bells and bending thick iron bars to show how strong he was.

"Now, now, goot people!" shouted the ringmaster. "Is there rilly nobody who should like to vin a hundred crowns? Must I rilly keep them for myself?" he said, waving a hundred-crown note.

"No, I rilly don't think you must," said Pippi, climbing over the railing to the ring.

"Go! Disappear! I don't vant I should zee you," the ringmaster hissed.

"Why are you always so unfriendly?" said Pippi reproachfully. "I only want to fight with Mighty Adolf."

"Zis is no time for chokes," said the ringmaster. "Go avay,

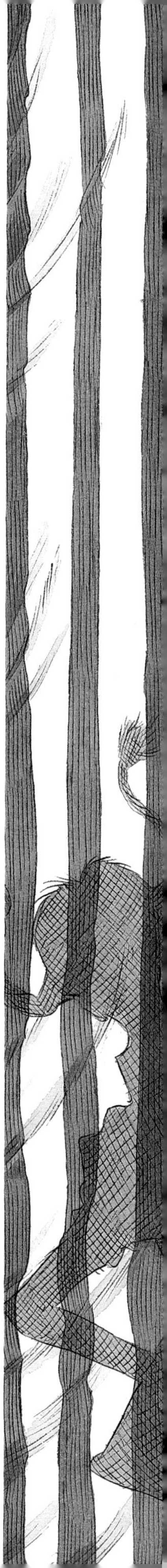

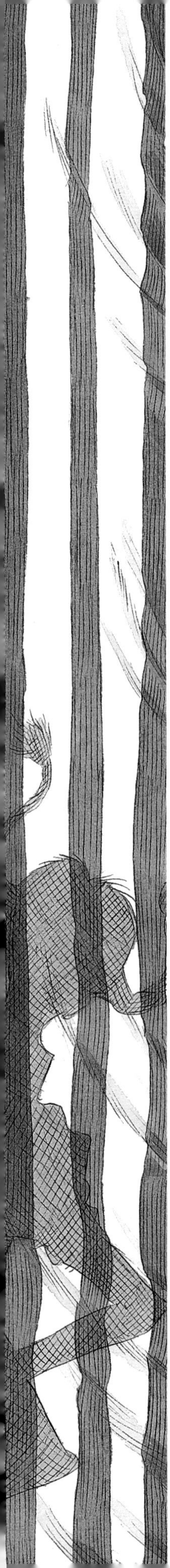

before Mighty Adolf hears your impertinence!"

But Pippi went right past the ringmaster and over to Mighty Adolf. She took his big hand in hers and shook it heartily.

"Now, shall we have a bit of a wrestle, you and I?" she said.

Mighty Adolf looked at her and didn't understand a thing.

"In one minute I'm going to begin," said Pippi.

And she did. She grappled properly with Mighty Adolf, and before anyone knew how it had happened, she'd laid him flat on the mat. Mighty Adolf scrambled up, quite red in the face.

"Hurrah for Pippi!" shouted Tommy and Annika. All the people at the circus heard this, and so they shouted, "Hurrah for Pippi!" too. The ringmaster sat on the railing and wrung his hands. He was angry. But Mighty Adolf was angrier still. Never in his life had anything so terrible happened to him. But now he would show this little red-haired girl what kind of a man Mighty Adolf was! He rushed forward and took a strong grip on her, but Pippi stood as fast as a rock.

"You can do better than that," she said to encourage him. Then she prised herself free from his grip and, in a second, Mighty Adolf was lying on the mat again. Pippi stood beside him and waited. She didn't have to wait long. With a bellow he raised himself and stormed at her again.

"Tiddlelipom and poddeliday," said Pippi.

All the people at the circus stamped their feet and threw their caps up in the air, and shouted, "Hurrah for Pippi!"

The third time Mighty Adolf rushed at her, Pippi lifted him high into the air and carried him on her upstretched arms around the ring. After that, she laid him on the mat and held him there.

"Now, my boy, I think we've had enough of this sort of game," she said. "It won't get any more fun than this, anyway."

"Pippi is the winner! Pippi is the winner!" shouted all the

people at the circus. Mighty Adolf slunk out as fast as he could. And the ringmaster had to go forward and present Pippi the hundred-crown note, though he looked as if he would rather have eaten her up.

"Here you are, my young lady, here is your hundred crowns."

"That?" said Pippi scornfully. "What should I do with that piece of paper? You can have it to wrap fish in, if you want!"

Then she went back to her place.

"This is a long-lasting circus, this one," she said to Tommy and Annika. "Forty winks might not do any harm. But wake me if there's anything else I need to help with."

So she lay back in her chair and went to sleep immediately. There she lay snoring while clowns and sword-swallowers and snake-people showed their tricks to Tommy and Annika and all the other people at the circus.

"Somehow, I think Pippi was best of all," whispered Tommy to Annika.

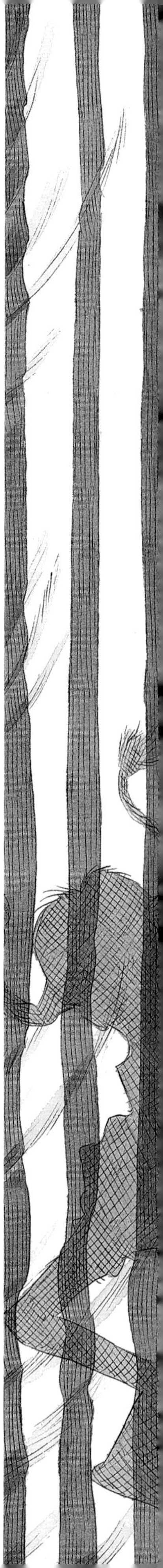

Introduction

I don't know how many books have been written about King Arthur. Hundreds probably – I've done one myself. But this must be the best of them all and it's certainly the funniest.

Two boys, the Wart (nickname for Art, which is short for Arthur) and Kay, grow up in a castle "in an enormous clearing in a still more enormous forest" with their father, Sir Ector. Kay is his real son, the Wart his adopted son. One day Sir Ector decides he must start a quest to find a tutor for the two boys. Then, quite by chance, after he has been hawking and is alone and lost in the forest, the Wart meets an old man with a long white beard and a long white moustache. It is the wizard Merlyn, who is to become his tutor and change his whole life.

M. M.

The Sword in the Stone

T. H. White

Merlyn took off his pointed hat when he came into this extraordinary chamber, because it was too high for the roof, and immediately there was a little scamper in one of the dark corners and a flap of soft wings, and a young tawny owl was sitting on the black skull-cap which protected the top of his head.

"Oh, what a lovely owl!" cried the Wart.

But when he went up to it and held out his hand, the owl grew half as tall again, stood up as stiff as a poker, closed its eyes so that there was only the smallest slit to peep through, as one is in the habit of doing when told to shut one's eyes at hide-and-seek, and said in a doubtful voice:

"There is no owl."

Then it shut its eyes entirely and looked the other way.

"It's only a boy," said Merlyn.

"There is no boy," said the owl hopefully, without turning round.

The Wart was so startled by finding that the owl could talk that he forgot his manners and came closer still. At this the owl became so nervous that it made a mess on Merlyn's head – the whole room was quite white with droppings – and flew off to perch on the farthest tip of the corkindrill's tail, out of reach.

"We see so little company," explained Merlyn, wiping his head with half a worn-out pair of pyjama tops which he kept for that purpose, "that Archimedes is a little shy of strangers. Come, Archimedes, I want you to meet a friend of mine called Wart."

Here he held out his hand to the owl, who came waddling like a goose along the corkindrill's back – he waddled with this rolling gait so as to keep his tail from being damaged – and hopped down on to Merlyn's finger with every sign of reluctance.

"Hold out your finger," said Merlyn, "and put it behind his legs. No, lift it up under his train."

When the Wart had done this Merlyn moved the owl gently backwards, so that the Wart's finger pressed against its legs from behind, and it either had to step back on the finger or get pushed off its balance altogether. It stepped back. The Wart stood there delighted, while the furry little feet held tight on to his finger and the sharp claws prickled his skin.

"Say how d'you do properly," said Merlyn.

"I won't," said Archimedes, looking the other way and holding very tight.

"Oh, he *is* lovely," said the Wart again. "Have you had him very long?"

"Archimedes has stayed with me since he was quite small, indeed since he had a tiny head like a chicken's."

"I wish he would talk to me," said the Wart.

"Perhaps if you were to give him this mouse here, politely, he might learn to know you better."

Merlyn took the dead mouse out of his skull-cap – "I always keep them there," he explained, "and worms too, for fishing. I find it most convenient" – and handed it to the Wart, who held it out rather gingerly towards Archimedes. The nutty little curved beak looked as if it were capable of doing damage, but Archimedes looked closely at the mouse, blinked at the Wart, moved nearer on the finger, closed his eyes and leant forward. He stood there with closed eyes and an expression of rapture on his face, as if he were saying grace, and then, with the absurdest little sideways nibble, took the morsel so gently that he would not have broken a soap bubble. He remained leaning forward with closed eyes, with the mouse suspended from his beak, as if he were not sure what to do with it. Then he lifted his right foot – he was right-handed – and took hold of the mouse. He held it up like a boy holding a stick of rock or a constable with his truncheon, looked at it, nibbled its tail. He turned it round so that it was head first, for the Wart had offered it the wrong way round, and gave one gulp. He looked round at the company with the tail hanging out of the corner of his mouth – as much as to say, "I wish you would not all stare at me so" – turned his head away, politely swallowed the tail, scratched his sailor's beard with his left toe, and began to ruffle out his feathers.

"Let him alone," said Merlyn, "now. For perhaps he does not want to be friends with you until he knows what you are like. With owls, it is never easy-come and easy-go."

"Perhaps he will sit on my shoulder," said the Wart, and with that he instinctively lowered his hand, so that the owl, who liked to be as high as possible, ran up the slope and stood shyly beside his ear.

"Now breakfast," said Merlyn.

The Wart saw that the most perfect breakfast was laid out neatly for two, on the table before the window. There were peaches. There were also melons, strawberries and cream, rusks, brown trout piping hot, grilled perch which were much nicer, chicken devilled enough to burn one's mouth out, kidneys and mushrooms on toast, fricassee, curry, and a choice of boiling coffee or best chocolate made with cream in large cups.

"Have some mustard," said Merlyn, when they had got to the kidneys.

The mustard-pot got up and walked over to his plate on thin silver legs that waddled like the owl's. Then it uncurled its handles and one handle lifted its lid with exaggerated courtesy while the other helped him to a generous spoonful.

"Oh, I love the mustard-pot!" cried the Wart. "Where ever did you get it?"

At this the pot beamed all over its face and began to strut a bit; but Merlyn rapped it on the head with a teaspoon, so that it sat down and shut up at once.

"It's not a bad pot," he said grudgingly. "Only it is inclined to give itself airs."

The Wart was so much impressed by the kindness of the old magician, and particularly by all the lovely things which he possessed, that he hardly liked to ask him personal questions. It seemed politer to sit still and speak when he was spoken to. But Merlyn did not speak very much, and when he did speak it was never in questions, so that the Wart had little opportunity for conversation. At last his curiosity got the better of him, and he asked something which had been puzzling him for some time.

"Would you mind if I ask you a question?"

"It is what I am for," said Merlyn sadly.

"How did you know to set the breakfast for two?"

The old gentleman leaned back in his chair and lit an enormous meerschaum pipe – Good gracious, he breathes fire, thought the Wart, who had never heard of tobacco – before he was ready to reply. Then he looked puzzled, took off his skull-cap – three mice fell out – and scratched in the middle of his bald head.

"Have you ever tried to draw in a looking-glass?" asked Merlyn.

"I don't think I have," said the Wart.

"Looking-glass," said the old gentleman, holding out his hand. Immediately there was a tiny lady's vanity-glass in his hand.

"Not that kind, you fool," said Merlyn angrily. "I want one big enough to shave in."

The vanity-glass vanished, and in its place there was a shaving mirror about a foot square. Merlyn then demanded pencil and paper in quick succession; got an unsharpened pencil and the *Morning Post*; sent them back; got a fountain-pen with no ink in it and six reams of brown-paper suitable for parcels; sent them back; flew into a passion in which he said by-our-lady quite often, and ended up with a carbon pencil and some cigarette papers which he said would have to do.

He put one of the papers in front of the glass and made five dots on it like this:

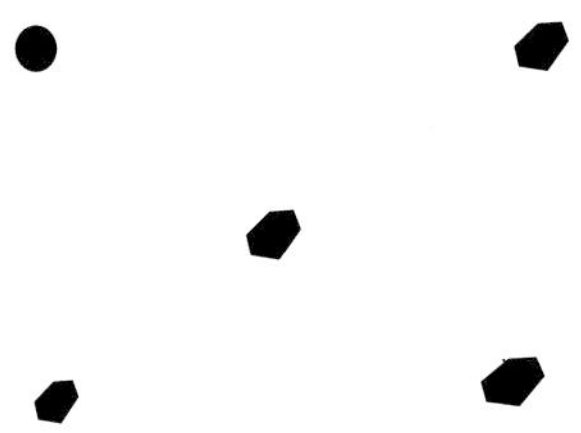

"Now," he said, "I want you to join those five dots up to make a W, looking only in the glass."

The Wart took the pen and tried to do as he was bid, but after a lot of false starts the letter which he produced was this:

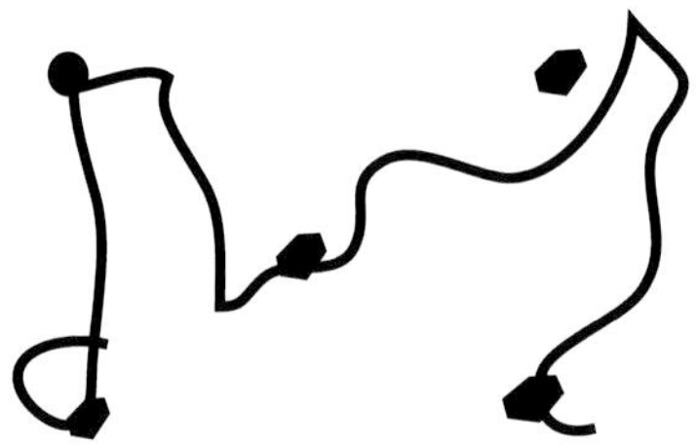

"Well, it isn't bad," said Merlyn doubtfully, "and in a way it does look a bit like an M."

Then he fell into a reverie, stroking his beard, breathing fire, and staring at the paper.

"About the breakfast?" asked the Wart timidly, after he had waited five minutes.

"Ah, yes," said Merlyn. "How did I know to set breakfast for two? That was why I showed you the looking-glass. Now ordinary people are born *forwards* in Time, if you understand what I mean, and nearly everything in the world goes forward too. This makes it quite easy for the ordinary people to live, just as it would be easy to join those five dots into a W if you were allowed to look at them forwards instead of backwards and inside out. But I unfortunately was born at the wrong end of time, and I have to live *backwards* from in front, while surrounded by a lot of people living forwards from behind. Some people call it having second sight."

Merlyn stopped talking and looked at the Wart in an anxious way.

"Have I told you this before?" he inquired suspiciously.

"No," said the Wart. "We only met about half an hour ago."

"So little time to pass as that?" said Merlyn, and a big tear ran down to the end of his nose. He wiped it off with his pyjama tops and added anxiously, "Am I going to tell it you again?"

"I don't know," said the Wart, "unless you haven't finished telling me yet."

"You see," said Merlyn, "one gets confused with Time, when it is like that. All one's tenses get muddled up, for one thing. If you know what's *going* to happen to people, and not what *has* happened to them, it makes it so difficult to prevent it happening, if you don't want it to have happened, if you see what I mean? Like drawing in a mirror."

The Wart did not quite see, but was just going to say that he was sorry for Merlyn if these things made him unhappy, when he felt a curious sensation at his ear. "Don't jump," said Merlyn, just as he was going to do so, and the Wart sat still. Archimedes, who had been standing forgotten on his shoulder all this time, was gently touching himself against him. His beak was right against the lobe of his ear, which its bristles made to tickle, and suddenly, a soft hoarse little voice whispered, "How d'you do," so that it sounded right inside his head.

"Oh, owl!" cried the Wart, forgetting about Merlyn's troubles instantly. "Look, he has decided to talk to me!"

The Wart gently leant his head against the soft feathers, and the brown owl, taking the rim of his ear in its beak, quickly nibbled right round it with the smallest nibbles.

"I shall call him Archie!" exclaimed the Wart.

"I trust you will do nothing of the sort," cried Merlyn instantly, in a stern and angry voice, and the owl withdrew to the farthest corner of his shoulder.

"Is it wrong?"

"You might as well call me Wol, or Olly," said the owl sourly, "and have done with it.

"Or Bubbles," added the owl in a bitter voice.

Merlyn took the Wart's hand and said kindly, "You are only young, and do not understand these things. But you will learn that owls are the politest and the most courteous, single-hearted and faithful creatures living. You must never be familiar, rude or vulgar with them, or make them to look ridiculous. Their mother is Athene, the goddess of wisdom, and, though they are often ready to play the buffoon for your amusement, such conduct is the prerogative of the truly wise. No owl can possibly be called Archie."

"I am sorry, owl," said the Wart.

"And I am sorry, boy," said the owl. "I can see that you spoke in ignorance, and I bitterly regret that I should have been so petty as to take offence where none was intended."

The owl really did regret it, and looked so remorseful and upset that Merlyn had to put on a very cheerful manner and change the conversation.

"Well," said he, "now that we have finished breakfast, I think it is high time that we should all three find our way back to Sir Ector."

"Excuse me a moment," he added as an afterthought, and, turning round to the breakfast things, he pointed a knobbly finger at them and said in a stern voice, "Wash up."

At this all the china and cutlery scrambled down off the table, the cloth emptied the crumbs out of the window, and the napkins folded themselves up. All ran off down the ladder, to where Merlyn had left the bucket, and there was such a noise and yelling as if a lot of children had been let out of school. Merlyn went to the door and shouted, "Mind, nobody is to get broken." But his voice was entirely drowned in shrill squeals, splashes, and cries of "My, it is cold," "I shan't stay in long," "Look out, you'll break me," or "Come on, let's duck the teapot."

"Are you really coming all the way home with me?" asked the Wart, who could hardly believe the good news.

"Why not?" said Merlyn. "How else can I be your tutor?"

At this the Wart's eyes grew rounder and rounder, until they were about as big as the owl's who was sitting on his shoulder, and his face got redder and redder, and a big breath seemed to gather itself beneath his heart.

"My!" exclaimed the Wart, while his eyes sparkled with excitement at the discovery. "I must have been on a Quest."

Introduction

Peter, Susan, Edmund and Lucy have all been sent down to the country to escape the air raids in the Second World War. They are living in a huge house with lots of corridors and spare rooms. In one of these rooms Lucy finds a wardrobe, climbs into it and finds herself in the magical land of Narnia. Soon all of them are there, and caught up in a titanic struggle between the White Witch and the noble Aslan. A struggle between good and evil in which Peter must now play his part. The White Witch has captured Edmund. With Aslan, Peter must save him and defeat the White Witch.

M. M.

THE LION, THE WITCH AND THE WARDROBE

C. S. LEWIS

Peter's First Battle

Aslan stood in the centre of a crowd of creatures who had grouped themselves round him in the shape of a half-moon. There were Tree-Women there and Well-Women (Dryads and Naiads as they used to be called in our world) who had stringed instruments; it was they who had made the music. There were four great centaurs. The horse part of them was like huge English farm horses, and the man part was like stern but beautiful giants. There was also a unicorn, and a bull with the head of a man, and a pelican, and an eagle, and a great Dog. And next to Aslan stood two leopards of whom one carried his crown and the other his standard.

But as for Aslan himself, the Beavers and the children didn't know what to do or say when they saw him. People who have not been in Narnia sometimes think that a thing cannot be good

and terrible at the same time. If the children had ever thought so, they were cured of it now. For when they tried to look at Aslan's face they just caught a glimpse of the golden mane and the great, royal, solemn, overwhelming eyes; and then they found they couldn't look at him and went all trembly.

"Go on," whispered Mr Beaver.

"No," whispered Peter, "you first."

"No, Sons of Adam before animals," whispered Mr Beaver back again.

"Susan," whispered Peter, "what about you? Ladies first."

"No, you're the eldest," whispered Susan. And of course the longer they went on doing this the more awkward they felt. Then at last Peter realized that it was up to him. He drew his sword and raised it to the salute and hastily saying to the others "Come on. Pull yourselves together," he advanced to the Lion and said:

"We have come – Aslan."

"Welcome, Peter, Son of Adam," said Aslan. "Welcome, Susan and Lucy, Daughters of Eve. Welcome He-Beaver and She-Beaver."

His voice was deep and rich and somehow took the fidgets out of them. They now felt glad and quiet and it didn't seem awkward to them to stand and say nothing.

"But where is the fourth?" asked Aslan.

"He has tried to betray them and joined the White Witch, O Aslan," said Mr Beaver. And then something made Peter say,

"That was partly my fault, Aslan. I was angry with him and I think that helped him to go wrong."

And Aslan said nothing either to excuse Peter or to blame him but merely stood looking at him with his great unchanging eyes. And it seemed to all of them that there was nothing to be said.

"Please – Aslan," said Lucy, "can anything be done to save Edmund?"

"All shall be done," said Aslan. "But it may be harder than you think." And then he was silent again for some time. Up to that moment Lucy had been thinking how royal and strong and peaceful his face looked; now it suddenly came into her head that he looked sad as well. But next minute that expression was quite gone.

The Lion shook his mane and clapped his paws together ("Terrible paws," thought Lucy, "if he didn't know how to velvet them!") and said,

"Meanwhile, let the feast be prepared. Ladies, take these Daughters of Eve to the pavilion and minister to them."

When the girls had gone Aslan laid his paw – and though it was velveted it was very heavy – on Peter's shoulder and said, "Come, Son of Adam, and I will show you a far-off sight of the castle where you are to be King."

And Peter with his sword still drawn in his hand went with the Lion to the eastern edge of the hilltop. There a beautiful sight met their eyes. The sun was setting behind their backs. That meant that the whole country below them lay in the evening light – forest and hills and valleys and, winding away like a silver snake, the lower part of the great river. And beyond all this, miles away, was the sea, and beyond the sea the sky, full of clouds which were just turning rose colour with the reflection of the sunset. But just where the land of Narnia met the sea – in fact, at the mouth of the great river – there was something on a little hill, shining. It was shining because it was a castle and of course the sunlight was reflected from all the windows which looked towards Peter and the sunset; but to Peter it looked like a great star resting on the seashore.

"That, O Man," said Aslan, "is Cair Paravel of the four thrones, in one of which you must sit as King. I show it to you because you are the first-born and you will be High King over all the rest."

And once more Peter said nothing, for at that moment a strange noise woke the silence suddenly. It was like a bugle, but richer.

"It is your sister's horn," said Aslan to Peter in a low voice; so low as to be almost a purr, if it is not disrespectful to think of a Lion purring.

For a moment Peter did not understand. Then, when he saw all the other creatures start forward and heard Aslan say with a wave of his paw, "Back! Let the Prince win his spurs," he did understand, and set off running as hard as he could to the pavilion. And there he saw a dreadful sight.

The Naiads and Dryads were scattering in every direction. Lucy was running towards him as fast as her short legs would carry her and her face was as white as paper. Then he saw Susan make a dash for a tree, and swing herself up, followed by a huge grey beast. At first Peter thought it was a bear. Then he saw it looked like an Alsatian, though it was far too big to be a dog. Then he realized that it was a wolf – a wolf standing on its hind legs, with its front paws against the tree-trunk, snapping and snarling. All the hair on its back stood up on end. Susan had not been able to get higher than the second big branch. One of her legs hung down so that her foot was only an inch or two above the snapping teeth. Peter wondered why she did not get higher or at least take a better grip; then he realized that she was just going to faint and that if she fainted she would fall off.

Peter did not feel very brave; indeed, he felt he was going to be sick. But that made no difference to what he had to do. He rushed straight up to the monster and aimed a slash of his sword at its side. That stroke never reached the Wolf. Quick as lightning it turned round, its eyes flaming, and its mouth wide open in a howl of anger. If it had not been so angry that it simply had to howl it would have got him by the throat at once. As it was – though all this happened too quickly for Peter to think at all – he had just time to duck down and plunge his sword, as hard as he could, between the brute's forelegs into its heart.

Then came a horrible, confused moment like something in a nightmare. He was tugging and pulling and the Wolf seemed neither alive nor dead, and its bared teeth knocked against his forehead, and everything was blood and heat and hair. A moment later he found that the monster lay dead and he had drawn his sword out of it and was straightening his back and rubbing the sweat off his face and out of his eyes. He felt tired all over.

Then, after a bit, Susan came down the tree. She and Peter felt pretty shaky when they met and I won't say there wasn't kissing and crying on both sides. But in Narnia no one thinks any the worse of you for that.

"Quick! Quick!" shouted the voice of Aslan. "Centaurs! Eagles! I see another wolf in the thickets. There – behind you. He has just darted away. After him, all of you. He will be going to his mistress. Now is your chance to find the Witch and rescue the fourth Son of Adam." And instantly with a thunder of hoofs and beating of wings a dozen or so of the swiftest creatures disappeared into the gathering darkness.

Peter, still out of breath, turned and saw Aslan close at hand.

"You have forgotten to clean your sword," said Aslan.

It was true. Peter blushed when he looked at the bright blade and saw it all smeared with the Wolf's hair and blood. He stooped down and wiped it quite clean on the grass, and then wiped it quite dry on his coat.

"Hand it to me and kneel, Son of Adam," said Aslan. And when Peter had done so he struck him with the flat of the blade and said, "Rise up, Sir Peter Wolf's-Bane. And, whatever happens, never forget to wipe your sword."

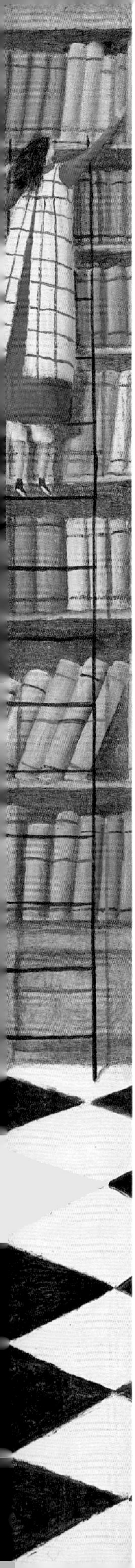

Introduction

Katy Carr has five younger brothers and sisters, and since the death of their mother she has helped their well-meaning yet perplexed aunt to take care of them. But they all run circles round poor Aunt Izzie: playing rough games, exploring – never still for a moment. Katy longs to set the others a good example, but her head is so full of plans and schemes and building castles in the air that all her good resolutions are quickly forgotten. When she gets into a fight at school and her rowdy game runs out of control, she vows never to get into a scrape again. But what does poor, thoughtless Katy do the following Monday? Well, having been cooped up inside all day because of the rain doesn't help her good intentions . . .

R. S.

WHAT KATY DID

SUSAN COOLIDGE

Kikeri

Katy was naturally fond of reading. Papa encouraged it. He kept a few books locked up, and then turned her loose in the library. She read all sorts of things: travels, and sermons, and old magazines. Nothing was so dull that she couldn't get through with it. Anything really interesting absorbed her so that she never knew what was going on about her. The little girls to whose houses she went visiting had found this out, and always hid away their storybooks, when she was expected to tea. If they didn't do this, she was sure to pick one up and plunge in, and then it was no use to call her or tug at her dress, for she neither saw nor heard anything more till it was time to go home.

This afternoon she read the *Jerusalem* till it was too dark to see any more. On her way upstairs she met Aunt Izzie, with bonnet and shawl on.

"Where *have* you been?" she said. "I have been calling you for the last half-hour."

"I didn't hear you, ma'am."

"But where were you?" persisted Miss Izzie.

"In the library, reading," replied Katy.

Her aunt gave a sort of sniff, but she knew Katy's ways, and said no more.

"I'm going out to drink tea with Mrs Hall and attend the evening lecture," she went on. "Be sure that Clover gets her lesson, and if Cecy comes over as usual, you must send her home early. All of you must be in bed by nine."

"Yes'm," said Katy; but I fear she was not attending much, but thinking in her secret soul, how jolly it was to have Aunt Izzie go out for once. Miss Carr was very faithful to her duties, and seldom left the children, even for an evening; so whenever she did, they felt a certain sense of novelty and freedom, which was dangerous as well as pleasant.

Still, I am sure that on this occasion Katy meant no mischief. Like all excitable people, she seldom did *mean* to do wrong; she just did it when it came into her head. Supper passed off successfully, and all might have gone well had it not been that after the lessons were learned and Cecy had come in, they fell to talking about "Kikeri".

Kikeri was a game which had been very popular with them a year before. They had invented it themselves, and chosen for it this queer name out of an old fairy story. It was a sort of mixture of blindman's-buff and tag – only, instead of anyone's eyes being bandaged, they all played in the dark. One of the children would

stay out in the hall, which was dimly lighted from the stairs, while the others hid themselves in the nursery. When they were all hidden they would call out "Kikeri!" as a signal for the one in the hall to come in and find them. Of course, coming from the light he could see nothing, while the others could see only dimly. It was very exciting to stand crouching up in a corner and watch the dark figure stumbling about and feeling to right and left, while every now and then somebody, just escaping his clutches, would slip past and gain the hall – which was "Freedom Castle" – with a joyful shout of "Kikeri, Kikeri, Kikeri, Ki!" Whoever was caught had to take the place of the catcher. For a long time this game was the delight of the Carr children; but so many scratches and black-and-blue spots came of it, and so many of the nursery things were thrown down and broken, that at last Aunt Izzie issued an order that it should not be played any more. This was almost a year since; but talking of it now put it into their heads to want to try it again.

"After all, we didn't promise," said Cecy.

"No, and *Papa* never said a word about our not playing it," added Katy, to whom "Papa" was authority, and must always be minded, while Aunt Izzie might now and then be defied.

So they all went upstairs. Dorry and John, though half undressed, were allowed to join the game. Philly was fast asleep in another room.

It was certainly splendid fun. Once Clover climbed up on the mantelpiece and sat there, and when Katy, who was finder, groped about a little more wildly than usual, she caught hold of Clover's foot, and couldn't imagine where it came from. Dorry got a hard knock, and cried, and at another time Katy's dress caught on the bureau handle and was frightfully torn; but these were too much affairs of every day to interfere in the least with the pleasures of Kikeri. The fun and frolic seemed to grow greater the longer they

played. In the excitement time went on so much faster than any of them dreamed. Suddenly, in the midst of the noise, came a sound – the sharp distinct slam of the carry-all door at the side entrance. Aunt Izzie had returned from her lecture!

The dismay and confusion of that moment! Cecy slipped downstairs like an eel, and fled on the wings of fear along the path which led to her home. Mrs Hall, as she bade Aunt Izzie goodnight, and shut Dr Carr's front door behind her with a bang, might have been struck with the singular fact that a distant bang came from her own front door like a sort of echo. But she was not a suspicious woman; and when she went upstairs there were Cecy's clothes neatly folded on a chair, and Cecy herself in bed, fast asleep, only with a little more colour than usual in her cheeks.

Meantime, Aunt Izzie was on *her* way upstairs and such a panic as prevailed in the nursery! Katy felt it, and basely scuttled off to her own room, where she went to bed with all possible speed. But the others found it much harder to go to bed; there were so many of them, all getting into each other's way, and with no lamp to see by. Dorry and John popped under the clothes half undressed, Elsie disappeared, and Clover, too late for either, and hearing Aunt Izzie's step in the hall, did this horrible thing – fell on her knees with her face buried in a chair, and began to say her prayers very hard indeed.

Aunt Izzie, coming in with a candle in her hand, stood in the doorway, astonished at the spectacle. She sat down and waited for Clover to get through, while Clover, on her part, didn't dare to get through, but went on repeating "Now I lay me" over and over again, in a sort of despair. At last Aunt Izzie said very grimly: "That will do, Clover, you can get up!" and Clover rose, feeling like a culprit, which she was, for it was much naughtier to pretend to be praying than to disobey Aunt Izzie and be out of bed after

ten o'clock, though I think Clover hardly understood this then.

Aunt Izzie began at once to undress her, and while doing so asked so many questions, and before long she had got at the truth of the whole matter. She gave Clover a sharp scolding; and, leaving her to wash her tearful face, she went to the bed where John and Dorry lay fast asleep and snoring as conspicuously as they knew how. Something strange in the appearance of the bed made her look more closely; she lifted the clothes, and there, sure enough, they were – half dressed, and with their school boots on.

Such a shake as Aunt Izzie gave the little scamps at this discovery would have roused a couple of dormice. Much against their will, John and Dorry were forced to wake up and be slapped and scolded, and made ready for bed, Aunt Izzie standing over them all the while, like a dragon. She had just tucked them warmly in, when for the first time she missed Elsie.

"Where is my poor Elsie?" she exclaimed.

"In bed," said Clover, meekly.

"In bed!" repeated Aunt Izzie, much amazed. Then stooping down she gave a vigorous pull. The trundle-bed came into view, and, sure enough, there was Elsie, in full dress, shoes and all, but so fast asleep that not all Aunt Izzie's shakes and pinches and calls were able to rouse her. Her clothes were taken off, her boots unlaced, her nightgown put on; but through it all Elsie slept, and she was the only one of the children who did not get the scolding she deserved that dreadful night.

Katy did not even pretend to be asleep when Aunt Izzie went to her room. Her tardy conscience had waked up, and she was lying in bed, very miserable at having drawn the others into a scrape as well as herself, and at the failure of her last set of resolutions about "setting an example to the younger ones". So unhappy was she, that Aunt Izzie's severe words were almost a relief; and though she cried herself to sleep, it was rather from the burden of her own thoughts than because she had been scolded.

She cried even harder the next day, for Dr Carr talked to her more seriously than he had ever done before. He reminded her of the time when her Mamma died, and of how she said, "Katy must be a Mamma to the little ones, when she grows up." And he asked her if she didn't think the time was come for beginning to take this dear place towards the children. Poor Katy! She sobbed as if her heart would break at this, and though she made no promises, I think she was never so thoughtless again after that day.

As for the rest, Papa called them together and made them distinctly understand that "Kikeri" was never to be played any more. It was so seldom that Papa forbade any games, however boisterous, that this order really made an impression on the unruly brood, and they never have played Kikeri again from that day to this.

Introduction

It all begins on a hot summer's afternoon when the White Rabbit runs past Alice as she lies dozing in a meadow, takes a watch out of his waistcoat pocket, and hurries down a large rabbit hole. Not once considering how she will get out, Alice follows him – down, down into a topsy-turvy world where anything can happen. She shrinks to only ten inches tall one minute, the next she has grown to a massive nine feet. Remarkable characters appear at every turn, and Alice has the strangest adventures. She swims with a mouse, takes advice from a caterpillar smoking a hookah pipe, chats to the grinning Cheshire Cat, cradles a baby who turns into a pig, and argues with two fishy liveried footmen. Nothing is what it seems in this Wonderland, and when Alice reaches the March Hare's house, there is something even more curious in store for her.

R. S.

ALICE'S ADVENTURES IN WONDERLAND

LEWIS CARROLL

A Mad Tea-Party

There was a table set out under a tree in front of the house, and the March Hare and the Hatter were having tea at it: a Dormouse was sitting between them, fast asleep, and the other two were using it as a cushion, resting their elbows on it, and talking over its head. "Very uncomfortable for the Dormouse," thought Alice; "only, as it's asleep, I suppose it doesn't mind."

The table was a large one, but the three were all crowded together at one corner of it. "No room! No room!" they cried out when they saw Alice coming. "There's *plenty* of room!" said Alice indignantly, and she sat down in a large armchair at one end of the table.

"Have some wine," the March Hare said in an encouraging tone.

Alice looked all round the table, but there was nothing on it but tea. "I don't see any wine," she remarked.

"There isn't any," said the March Hare.

"Then it wasn't very civil of you to offer it," said Alice angrily.

"It wasn't very civil of you to sit down without being invited," said the March Hare.

"I didn't know it was *your* table," said Alice; "it's laid for a great many more than three."

"Your hair wants cutting," said the Hatter. He had been looking at Alice for some time with great curiosity, and this was his first speech.

"You should learn not to make personal remarks," Alice said with some severity; "it's very rude."

The Hatter opened his eyes very wide on hearing this; but all he *said* was, "Why is a raven like a writing-desk?"

"Come, we shall have some fun now!" thought Alice. "I'm glad they've begun asking riddles. – I believe I can guess that," she added aloud.

"Do you mean that you think you can find out the answer to it?" said the March Hare.

"Exactly so," said Alice.

"Then you should say what you mean," the March Hare went on.

"I do," Alice hastily replied; "at least – at least I mean what I say – that's the same thing, you know."

"Not the same thing a bit!" said the Hatter. "You might just as well say that 'I see what I eat' is the same thing as 'I eat what I see'!"

"You might just as well say," added the March Hare, "that 'I like what I get' is the same thing as 'I get what I like'!"

"You might just as well say," added the Dormouse, who seemed to be talking in his sleep, "that 'I breathe when I sleep' is the same thing as 'I sleep when I breathe'!"

"It *is* the same thing with you," said the Hatter, and here the conversation dropped, and the party sat silent for a minute, while Alice thought over all she could remember about ravens and writing-desks, which wasn't much.

The Hatter was the first to break the silence.

"What day of the month is it?" he said, turning to Alice: he had taken his watch out of his pocket, and was looking at it uneasily, shaking it every now and then, and holding it to his ear.

Alice considered a little, and then said, "The fourth."

"Two days wrong!" sighed the Hatter. "I told you butter wouldn't suit the works!" he added, looking angrily at the March Hare.

"It was the *best* butter," the March Hare meekly replied.

"Yes, but some crumbs must have got in as well," the Hatter grumbled: "you shouldn't have put it in with the bread-knife."

The March Hare took the watch and looked at it gloomily: then he dipped it into his cup of tea, and looked at it again: but he could think of nothing better to say than his first remark, "It was the *best* butter, you know."

Alice had been looking over his shoulder with some curiosity. "What a funny watch!" she remarked. "It tells the day of the month, and doesn't tell what o'clock it is!"

"Why should it?" muttered the Hatter. "Does *your* watch tell you what year it is?"

"Of course not," Alice replied very readily: "but that's because it stays the same year for such a long time together."

"Which is just the case with *mine*," said the Hatter.

Alice felt dreadfully puzzled. The Hatter's remark seemed to have no sort of meaning in it, and yet it was certainly English. "I don't quite understand you," she said, as politely as she could.

"The Dormouse is asleep again," said the Hatter, and he poured a little hot tea upon its nose.

The Dormouse shook its head impatiently, and said, without opening its eyes, "Of course, of course; just what I was going to remark myself."

"Have you guessed the riddle yet?" the Hatter said, turning to Alice again.

"No, I give it up," Alice replied: "what's the answer?"

"I haven't the slightest idea," said the Hatter.

"Nor I," said the March Hare.

Alice sighed wearily. "I think you might do something better with the time," she said, "than waste it in asking riddles that have no answers."

"If you knew Time as well as I do," said the Hatter, "you wouldn't talk about wasting *it*. It's *him*."

"I don't know what you mean," said Alice.

"Of course you don't!" the Hatter said, tossing his head contemptuously. "I dare say you never even spoke to Time!"

"Perhaps not," Alice cautiously replied: "but I know I have to beat time when I learn music."

"Ah! that accounts for it," said the Hatter. "He won't stand beating. Now, if you only kept on good terms with him, he'd do almost anything you liked with the clock. For instance, suppose it were nine o'clock in the morning, just time to begin lessons: you'd only have to whisper a hint to Time, and round goes the clock in a twinkling! Half past one, time for dinner!"

("I only wish it was," the March Hare said to itself in a whisper.)

"That would be grand, certainly," said Alice thoughtfully: "but then – I shouldn't be hungry for it, you know."

"Not at first, perhaps," said the Hatter: "but you could keep it to half past one as long as you liked."

"Is that the way *you* manage?" Alice asked.

The Hatter shook his head mournfully. "Not I!" he replied. "We quarrelled last March – just before *he* went mad, you know –" (pointing with his teaspoon at the March Hare) "– it was at the great concert given by the Queen of Hearts, and I had to sing:

'Twinkle, twinkle, little bat!
How I wonder what you're at!'

You know the song, perhaps?"

"I've heard something like it," said Alice.

"It goes on, you know," the Hatter continued, "in this way:

'Up above the world you fly,
Like a tea-tray in the sky.
Twinkle, twinkle –'"

Here the Dormouse shook itself, and began singing in its sleep

"Twinkle, twinkle, twinkle, twinkle –" and went on so long that they had to pinch it to make it stop.

"Well, I'd hardly finished the first verse," said the Hatter, "when the Queen jumped up and bawled out, 'He's murdering the time! Off with his head!'"

"How dreadfully savage!" exclaimed Alice.

"And ever since that," the Hatter went on in a mournful tone, "he won't do a thing I ask! It's always six o'clock now."

A bright idea came into Alice's head. "Is that the reason so many tea-things are put out here?" she asked.

"Yes, that's it," said the Hatter with a sigh: "it's always tea-time, and we've no time to wash the things between whiles."

"Then you keep moving round, I suppose?" said Alice.

"Exactly so," said the Hatter: "as the things get used up."

"But what happens when you come to the beginning again?" Alice ventured to ask.

"Suppose we change the subject," the March Hare interrupted, yawning. "I'm getting tired of this. I vote the young lady tells us a story."

"I'm afraid I don't know one," said Alice, rather alarmed at the proposal.

"Then the Dormouse shall!" they both cried. "Wake up, Dormouse!" And they pinched it on both sides at once.

The Dormouse slowly opened his eyes. "I wasn't asleep," he said in a hoarse, feeble voice: "I heard every word you fellows were saying."

"Tell us a story!" said the March Hare.

"Yes, please do!" pleaded Alice.

"And be quick about it," added the Hatter, "or you'll be asleep again before it's done."

"Once upon a time there were three little sisters," the

Dormouse began in a great hurry; "and their names were Elsie, Lacie, and Tillie; and they lived at the bottom of a well –"

"What did they live on?" said Alice, who always took a great interest in questions of eating and drinking.

"They lived on treacle," said the Dormouse, after thinking a minute or two.

"They couldn't have done that, you know," Alice gently remarked; "they'd have been ill."

"So they were," said the Dormouse; "*very* ill."

Alice tried to fancy to herself what such an extraordinary way of living would be like, but it puzzled her too much, so she went on: "But why did they live at the bottom of a well?"

"Take some more tea," the March Hare said to Alice, very earnestly.

"I've had nothing yet," Alice replied in an offended tone, "so I can't take more."

"You mean you can't take *less*," said the Hatter: "it's very easy to take *more* than nothing."

"Nobody asked *your* opinion," said Alice.

"Who's making personal remarks now?" the Hatter asked triumphantly.

Alice did not quite know what to say to this: so she helped herself to some tea and bread-and-butter, and then turned to the Dormouse, and repeated her question. "Why did they live at the bottom of a well?"

The Dormouse again took a minute or two to think about it, and then said, "It was a treacle-well."

"There's no such thing!" Alice was beginning very angrily, but the Hatter and the March Hare went "Sh! Sh!" and the Dormouse sulkily remarked, "If you can't be civil, you'd better finish the story for yourself."

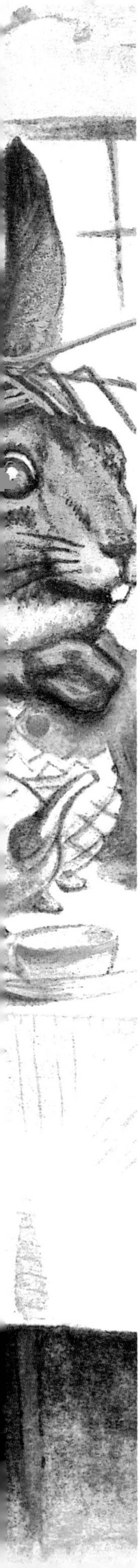

"No, please go on!" Alice said very humbly; "I won't interrupt again. I dare say there may be *one*."

"One, indeed!" said the Dormouse indignantly. However, he consented to go on. "And so these three little sisters – they were learning to draw, you know –"

"What did they draw?" said Alice, quite forgetting her promise.

"Treacle," said the Dormouse, without considering at all this time.

"I want a clean cup," interrupted the Hatter: "let's all move one place on."

He moved on as he spoke, and the Dormouse followed him: the March Hare moved into the Dormouse's place, and Alice rather unwillingly took the place of the March Hare. The Hatter was the only one who got any advantage from the change: and Alice was a good deal worse off than before, as the March Hare had just upset the milk-jug into his plate.

Alice did not wish to offend the Dormouse again, so she began very cautiously: "But I don't understand. Where did they draw the treacle from?"

"You can draw water out of a water-well," said the Hatter; "so I should think you could draw treacle out of a treacle-well – eh, stupid?"

"But they were *in* the well," Alice said to the Dormouse, not choosing to notice this last remark.

"Of course they were," said the Dormouse; "– well in."

This answer so confused poor Alice, that she let the Dormouse go on for some time without interrupting it.

"They were learning to draw," the Dormouse went on, yawning and rubbing its eyes, for it was getting very sleepy; "and they drew all manner of things – everything that begins with an M –"

"Why with an M?" said Alice.

"Why not?" said the March Hare.

Alice was silent.

The Dormouse had closed its eyes by this time, and was going off into a doze; but, on being pinched by the Hatter, it woke up again with a little shriek, and went on: "– that begins with an M, such as mouse-traps, and the moon, and memory, and muchness – you know you say things are 'much of a muchness' – did you ever see such a thing as a drawing of a muchness?"

"Really, now you ask me," said Alice, very much confused, "I don't think –"

"Then you shouldn't talk," said the Hatter.

This piece of rudeness was more than Alice could bear: she got up in great disgust, and walked off; the Dormouse fell asleep instantly, and neither of the others took the least notice of her going, though she looked back once or twice, half hoping that they would call after her: the last time she saw them, they were trying to put the Dormouse into the teapot.

"At any rate I'll never go *there* again!" said Alice as she picked her way through the wood. "It's the stupidest tea-party I ever was at in all my life!"

Introduction

Exiled from his home – because his parents do not want him to catch measles from his brother, Peter – Tom has to go and stay with his Uncle Alan and Aunt Gwen. It's a bleak house, a big old place, now divided up into flats. Strangely, there's a grandfather clock on the stairs that never chimes the right hours, that even chimes thirteen sometimes. There is no garden, nowhere to play. Tom's bored. He's not sleeping well, either. One night, hearing the clock strike thirteen again, he gets up. He finds the house changed – carpets where there were none, different furniture and a maid scurrying past who does not seem to know he's there. There's a back door, which opens easily, and Tom steps into a huge garden with hyacinths growing, a sundial, a greenhouse. It's no dream. It's real.

M. M.

Tom's Midnight Garden

Philippa Pearce

Through a Door

Every night now Tom slipped downstairs to the garden. At first he used to be afraid that it might not be there. Once, with his hand already upon the garden door to open it, he had turned back, sick with grief at the very thought of absence. He had not dared, then, to look; but, later the same night, he had forced himself to go again and open that door: there the garden was. It had not failed him.

He saw the garden at many times of its day, and at different seasons – its favourite season was summer, with perfect weather. In earliest summer hyacinths were still out in the crescent beds on the lawn, and wallflowers in the round ones. Then the hyacinths bowed and died; and the wallflowers were uprooted, and stocks and asters bloomed in their stead. There was a clipped box bush by the greenhouse, with a cavity like a great mouth cut into the side of it: this was stacked full of pots of geraniums in flower. Along the sundial path, heavy red poppies came out, and roses;

and, in summer dusk, the evening primroses glimmered like little moons. In the latest summer the pears on the wall were muffled in muslin bags for safe ripening.

Tom was not a gardener, however; his first interest in a garden, as Peter's would have been, was tree-climbing. He always remembered his first tree in this garden – one of the yews round the lawn. He had never climbed a yew before, and was inclined to think ever afterwards that yews were best.

The first branches grew conveniently low, and the main trunk had bosses and crevices. With the toes of his left foot fitted into one of these last, Tom curved his hands round the branch over his head. Then he gave a push, a spring and a strong haul on the arms: his legs and feet were dangling free, and the branch was under his chest, and then under his middle. He drew himself still farther forward, at the same time twisting himself expertly: now he was sitting on the bough, a man's height above ground.

The rest of the ascent was easy but interesting: sometimes among the spreading, outermost branches; sometimes working close to the main trunk. Tom loved the dry feel of the bark on the main trunk. In places the bark had peeled away, and then a deep pink showed beneath, as though the tree were skin and flesh beneath its brown.

Up he went – up and up, and burst at last from the dim interior into an openness of blue and fiery gold. The sun was the gold, in a blue sky. All round him was a spreading, tufted surface of evergreen. He was on a level with all the yew-tree tops round the lawn; nearly on a level with the top of the tall south wall.

Tom was on a level, too, with the upper windows of the house, just across the lawn from him. His attention was caught by a movement inside one of the rooms: it came, he saw, from the same maid he had once seen in the hall. She was dusting

a bedroom, and came now to the window to raise the sash and shake her duster outside. She looked casually across to the yew-trees as she did so, and Tom tried waving to her. It was like waving to the He in blindman's-buff.

The maid went back into the depths of the room, to her dusting. She left the window open behind her, and Tom could now see more. There was someone else in the room besides the maid – someone who stood against the far wall, facing the window. The maid evidently spoke to her companion occasionally as she worked, for Tom could hear the faint coming and going of voices. He could not see the other figure at all clearly, except that it was motionless, and there was the whiteness and shape of a face that was always turned in his direction. That steadfastness of direction embarrassed Tom. Very gradually he began to draw his head downwards, and then suddenly ducked it below tree-level altogether.

Tom saw more people later, in the garden itself. He stalked

them warily, and yet – remembering his invisibility to the house-maid – with a certain confidence too.

He was pretty sure that the garden was used more often than he knew. He often had the feeling of people having just gone – and an uncomfortable feeling, out of which he tried to reason himself, again and again, of someone who had *not* gone: someone who, unobserved, observed him. It was a relief really to see people, even when they ignored his presence: the maid, the gardener, and a severe-looking woman in a long dress of rustling purple silk, face to face with whom Tom once came unexpectedly, on a corner. She cut him dead.

Visibility . . . invisibility . . . If he were invisible to the people of the garden, he was not completely so at least to some of the other creatures. How truly they saw him he could not say; but birds cocked their heads at him, and flew away when he approached.

And had he any bodily weight in this garden, or had he not? At first, Tom thought not. When he climbed the yew-tree he had been startled to feel that no bough swung beneath him, and not a twig broke. Later – and this was a great disappointment to him – he found that he could not, by the ordinary grasping and pushing of his hand, open any of the doors in the garden, to go through them. He could not push open the door of the greenhouse or of the little heating-house behind it, or the door in the south wall by the sundial.

The doors shut against Tom were a check upon his curiosity, until he saw a simple way out: he would get through the doorways that interested him by following at the heels of the gardener. He regularly visited the greenhouse, the heating-house, and used the south wall door.

Tom concentrated upon getting through the south wall door.

That entry promised to be the easiest, because the gardener went through so often, with his tools. There must be a tool-shed somewhere through there.

The gardener usually went through so quickly and shut the door so smartly behind him, that there was not time for anyone else to slip through as well. However, he would be slower with a wheelbarrow, Tom judged; and he waited patiently for that opportunity. Yet even then the man somehow only made a long arm to open the door ahead of the wheelbarrow, wheeled it very swiftly through, caught the door-edge with the toe of his boot as he passed and slammed the door in Tom's face.

Tom glared at the door that once more was his barrier. Once more, without hope, he raised his hand to the latch and pressed it. As usual, he could not move it: his fingers seemed to have no substance. Then, in anger, he pressed with all imaginable might: he knitted his brows, and brought all his will to bear upon the latch, until he felt that something had to happen. It did: his fingers began to go through the latch, as though the latch, and not his fingers, now, were without substance. His fingers went through the ironwork of the latch altogether, and his hand fell back into place by his side.

Tom stared down at that ever-memorable right hand. He felt it tenderly with his left, to see if it were bruised or broken: it was quite unhurt – quite as before. Then he looked at the latch: it looked as real as any latch he had ever seen anywhere.

Then the idea came to Tom that the door might be no more solid than the latch, if he really tried it.

Deliberately he set his side against the door, shoulder, hip and heel, and pressed. At first, nothing gave, either of himself or the door. Yet he continued the pressure, with still greater force and greater determination; and gradually he became aware of a strange sensation, that at first he thought was a numbness all down his side – but no, it was not that.

"I'm going through," Tom gasped, and was seized with alarm and delight.

On the other side of the wall, the gardener had emptied his barrow-load of weeds and was sitting on the handle of his barrow, in front of a potting-shed, eating his midday dinner. If he had been able to see Tom at all he would have seen a most curious sight: a very thin slice of boy, from shoulder to foot, coming through a perfectly solid wooden door. At first the body came through evenly from top to bottom; then, the upper part seemed to stop, and the bottom part came through in its entirety, legs first. Then one arm came through, then another. Finally, everything was through except the head.

The truth was that Tom was now a little lacking courage. The passing through the door of so much of his body had not been without enormous effort and peculiar, if indescribable, sensations. "I'm just resting a minute," said Tom's head, on the garden side of the door; yet he knew that he was really delaying because he was nervous. His stomach, for instance, had felt most uncomfortable as it passed through the door; what would the experience be like for his head – his eyes, his ears?

On the other hand – and the new idea was even worse than the old – supposing that, like a locomotive-engine losing steam-pressure, he lost his present force of body and will-power in this delay? Then, he would be unable to move either forwards or backwards. He would be caught here by the neck, perhaps for ever. And just supposing someone came along, on the far side of the wall, who by some evil chance *could* see him – supposing a whole company came: they would see an entirely defenceless stern sticking out – an invitation to ridicule and attack.

With a convulsive effort, eyes closed, lips sealed, Tom dragged his head through the door, and stood, dizzy, dazed, but whole, on the far side of it.

When his vision cleared, he saw that he was standing directly in front of the potting-shed and the gardener. Tom had never been front to front with the gardener before: he was a large-framed young man, with a weather-reddened face, and eyes the colour of the sky itself – they now looked straight through Tom and far away. Into his mouth he was putting the last fragments of a thick bacon-and-bread sandwich. He finished the sandwich, closed his eyes and spoke aloud: "For all good things I thank the Lord; and may He keep me from all the works of the Devil that he hurt me not."

He spoke with a country voice, clipping short his t's and widening his vowels, so that Tom had to listen attentively to understand him.

The gardener opened his eyes again, and, reaching behind him, brought out another sandwich. Tom wondered, in some surprise, whether he said grace after every sandwich. Perhaps he never knew how many he was going to eat.

The gardener went on eating, and Tom turned away to look around him. He was in an orchard, that also served for the keeping of hens, the pegging out of washing and the kindling of a bonfire. Beyond the orchard were meadows and trees, from among which rose the roofs of what must be a village.

While he looked, Tom was also keeping a sharp eye upon the gardener. When the man had really finished his meal he grasped the handles of his wheelbarrow, to return to his work in the garden. In a moment, Tom was beside him. He had not at all enjoyed the experience of going through a shut door, and he did not now intend to have to repeat it. This time there was an easy way through: he got nimbly up into the empty barrow and was wheeled back into the garden in comfort.

It was a long time before Tom literally forced his way through a door again. Anyway, he had seen the orchard, and that was enough in that direction; other doors could wait. Meanwhile, he climbed the low wall at the bottom of the garden and explored the wood beyond. On the third side of the garden he wormed his way through the hedge again and crossed the meadow. The only surprise there was the boundary: a river, clear, gentle-flowing, shallow, and green with reeds and water-plants.

The garden and its surroundings, then, were not, in themselves, outside the natural order of things; nor was Tom alarmed by his own unnatural abilities. Yet to some things his mind came back again and again, troubled: the constant fine weather, the rapid coming and going of the seasons and the times of day, the feeling of being watched.

One night all his uneasiness came to a head. He had gone from his bed in the flat upstairs and crept down to the hall at about midnight, as usual; he had opened the garden door. He had found for the first time that it was night, too, in the garden. The moon was up, but clouds fled continuously across its face. Although there was this movement in the upper air, down below there was none: a great stillness lay within the garden, and a heavier heat than at any noon. Tom felt it: he unbuttoned his pyjama jacket and let it flap open as he walked.

One could smell the storm coming. Before Tom had reached the bottom of the garden, the moon had disappeared, obscured altogether by cloud. In its place came another light that seemed instantaneously to split the sky from top to bottom, and a few seconds later came the thunder.

Tom turned back to the house. As he reached the porch, the winds broke out into the lower air, with heavy rain and a deathly chilling of the temperature. Demons of the air seemed let loose in that garden; and, with the increasing frequency of the lightning, Tom could watch the foliage of the trees ferociously tossed and torn at by the wind, and, at the corner of the lawn, the tall, tapering fir-tree swinging to and fro, its ivy-wreathed arms struggling wildly in the tempest like the arms of a swaddling-child.

To Tom it seemed that the fir-tree swung more widely each time. "It can't be blown over," thought Tom. "Strong trees are not often blown over."

As if in answer to this, and while the winds still tore, there came the loudest thunder, with a flash of lightning that was not to one side nor even above, but seemed to come down into the garden itself, to the tree. The glare was blinding, and Tom's eyes closed against it, although only for a part of a second. When he opened them again, he saw the tree like one flame, and falling. In the long instant while it fell, there seemed to be a horrified silence of all the winds; and, in that quiet, Tom heard something – a human cry – an "Oh!" of the terror he himself felt. It came from above him – from the window of one of the upper rooms.

Then the fir-tree fell, stretching its length – although Tom did not know this until much later – along the grave-beds of the asparagus in the kitchen-garden. It fell in darkness and the resumed rushing of wind and rain.

Tom was shaken by what he had seen and heard. He went back into the house and shut the garden door behind him. Inside, the grandfather clock ticked peacefully; the hall was still. He wondered if perhaps he had only imagined what he had seen outside. He opened the door again, and looked out. The summer storm was still raging. The flashes of lightning were distant now:

they lit up the ugly gap in the trees round the lawn, where the fir-tree had stood.

The tree had fallen, that had been a sight terrible enough; but the cry from above troubled Tom more. On the next night came the greatest shock of all. He opened the garden door as usual, and surveyed the garden. At first, he did not understand what was odd in its appearance; then, he realized that its usual appearance was in itself an oddity. In the trees round the lawn there was no gap: the ivy-grown fir-tree still towered above them.

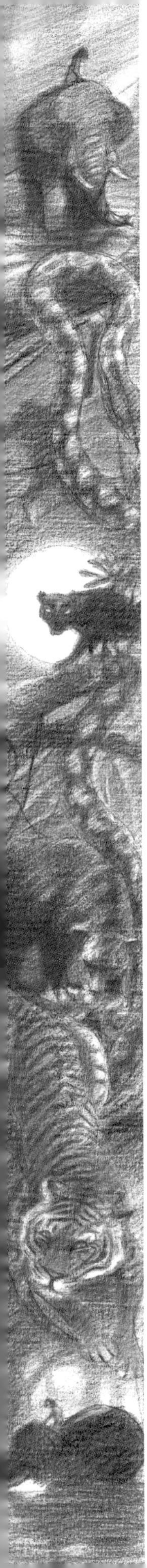

Introduction

Abandoned in the jungle, the helpless infant Mowgli has been taken in by a pack of wolves, saved by them from the evil tiger, Shere Khan. As he grows up he learns the laws of the jungle from the wolves, from Bagheera the black panther and from Baloo the bear. Now eleven years old, this boy cub needs to learn more – for Akela the lone wolf, pack leader and Mowgli's protector, is weaker now in his old age. Bagheera knows that Mowgli will soon have to fend for himself. Mowgli must get the Red Flower, fire – for every beast, even Shere Khan, lives in deadly fear of it.

M. M.

THE JUNGLE BOOK

RUDYARD KIPLING

Mowgli was far and far through the forest, running hard, and his heart was hot in him. He came to the cave as the evening mist rose, and drew breath, and looked down the valley. The cubs were out, but Mother Wolf, at the back of the cave, knew by his breathing that something was troubling her frog.

"What is it, Son?" she said.

"Some bat's chatter of Shere Khan," he called back. "I hunt among the ploughed fields tonight," and he plunged downward through the bushes, to the stream at the bottom of the valley. There he checked, for he heard the yell of the Pack hunting, heard the bellow of a hunted sambhur, and the snort as the buck turned at bay. Then there were wicked, bitter howls from the young wolves: "Akela! Akela! Let the Lone Wolf show his strength. Room for the leader of the Pack! Spring, Akela!"

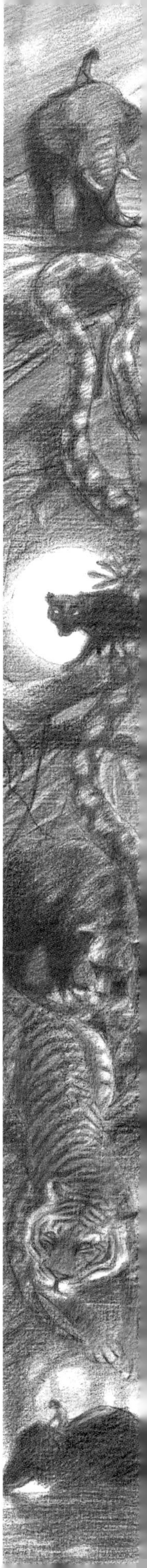

The Lone Wolf must have sprung and missed his hold, for Mowgli heard the snap of his teeth and then a yelp as the sambhur knocked him over with his forefoot.

He did not wait for anything more, but dashed on; and the yells grew fainter behind him as he ran into the croplands where the villagers lived.

"Bagheera spoke truth," he panted, as he nestled down in some cattle-fodder by the window of a hut. "Tomorrow is one day both for Akela and for me."

Then he pressed his face close to the window and watched the fire on the hearth. He saw the husband-man's wife get up and feed it in the night with black lumps; and when the morning came and the mists were all white and cold, he saw the man's child pick up a wicker pot plastered inside with earth, fill it with lumps of red-hot charcoal, put it under his blanket, and go out to tend the cows in the byre.

"Is that all?" said Mowgli. "If a cub can do it, there is nothing to fear"; so he strode round the corner and met the boy, took the pot from his hand, and disappeared into the mist while the boy howled with fear.

"They are very like me," said Mowgli, blowing into the pot, as he had seen the woman do. "This thing will die if I do not give it things to eat"; and he dropped twigs and dried bark on the red stuff. Half-way up the hill he met Bagheera with the morning dew shining like moonstones on his coat.

"Akela has missed," said the Panther. "They would have killed him last night, but they needed thee also. They were looking for thee on the hill."

"I was among the ploughed lands. I am ready. See!" Mowgli held up the fire-pot.

"Good! Now, I have seen men thrust a dry branch into that

stuff, and presently the Red Flower blossomed at the end of it. Art thou not afraid?"

"No. Why should I fear? I remember now – if it is not a dream – how, before I was a Wolf, I lay beside the Red Flower, and it was warm and pleasant."

All that day Mowgli sat in the cave tending his fire-pot and dipping dry branches into it to see how they looked. He found a branch that satisfied him, and in the evening when Tabaqui came to the cave and told him rudely enough that he was wanted at the Council Rock, he laughed till Tabaqui ran away. Then Mowgli went to the Council, still laughing.

Akela the Lone Wolf lay by the side of his rock as a sign that the leadership of the Pack was open, and Shere Khan with his following of scrapfed wolves walked to and fro openly, being flattered. Bagheera lay close to Mowgli, and the fire-pot was between Mowgli's knees. When they were all gathered together, Shere Khan began to speak – a thing he would never have dared to do when Akela was in his prime.

"He has no right," whispered Bagheera. "Say so. He is a dog's son. He will be frightened."

Mowgli sprang to his feet. "Free People," he cried, "does Shere Khan lead the Pack? What has a tiger to do with our leadership?"

"Seeing that the leadership is yet open, and being asked to speak –" Shere Khan began.

"By whom?" said Mowgli. "Are we *all* jackals, to fawn on this cattle-butcher? The leadership of the Pack is with the Pack alone."

There were yells of "Silence, thou man's cub!" "Let him speak. He has kept our Law"; and at last the seniors of the Pack thundered: "Let the Dead Wolf speak." When a leader of the Pack has missed his kill, he is called the Dead Wolf as long as he lives, which is not long, as a rule.

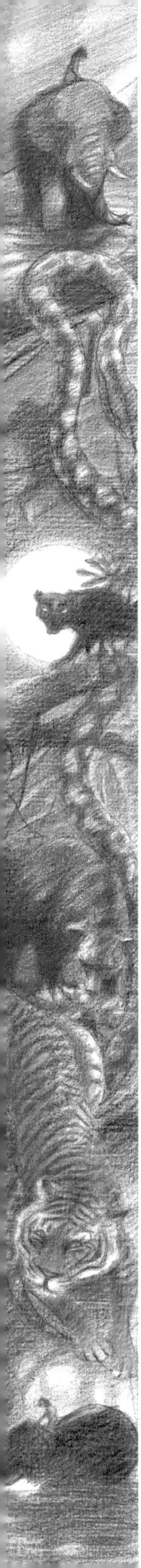

Akela raised his old head wearily:

"Free People, and ye too, jackals of Shere Khan, for many seasons I have led ye to and from the kill, and in all my time not one has been trapped or maimed. Now I have missed my kill. Ye know how that plot was made. Ye know how ye brought me up to an untried buck to make my weakness known. It was cleverly done. Your right is to kill me here on the Council Rock now. Therefore, I ask, who comes to make an end of the Lone Wolf? For it is my right, by the Law of the Jungle, that ye come one by one."

There was a long hush, for no single wolf cared to fight Akela to the death. Then Shere Khan roared: "Bah! what have we to do with this toothless fool? He is doomed to die! It is the man-cub who has lived too long. Free People, he was my meat from the first. Give him to me. I am weary of this man-wolf folly. He has troubled the Jungle for ten seasons. Give me the man-cub, or I will hunt here always, and not give you one bone. He is a man, a man's child, and from the marrow of my bones I hate him!"

Then more than half the Pack yelled: "A man! a man! What has a man to do with us? Let him go to his own place."

"And turn all the people of the villages against us?" clamoured Shere Khan. "No; give him to me. He is a man, and none of us can look him between the eyes."

Akela lifted his head again, and said: "He has eaten our food. He has slept with us. He has driven game for us. He has broken no word of the Law of the Jungle."

"Also, I paid for him with a bull when he was accepted. The worth of a bull is little, but Bagheera's honour is something that he will perhaps fight for," said Bagheera, in his gentlest voice.

"A bull paid ten years ago!" the Pack snarled. "What do we care for bones ten years old?"

"Or for a pledge?" said Bagheera, his white teeth bared under his lip. "Well are ye called the Free People!"

"No man's cub can run with the people of the Jungle," howled Shere Khan. "Give him to me!"

"He is our brother in all but blood," Akela went on; "and ye would kill him here! In truth, I have lived too long. Some of ye are eaters of cattle, and of others I have heard that, under Shere Khan's teaching, ye go by dark night and snatch children from the villager's doorstep. Therefore I know ye to be cowards, and it is to cowards I speak. It is certain that I must die, and my life is of no worth, or I would offer that in the Man-cub's place. But for the sake of the honour of the Pack – a little matter that by being without a leader ye have forgotten – I promise that if ye let the Man-cub go to his own place, I will not, when my time comes to die, bare one tooth against ye. I will die without fighting. That will at least save the Pack three lives. More I cannot do; but if ye will, I can save ye the shame that comes of killing a brother against whom there is no fault – a brother spoken for and bought into the Pack according to the Law of the Jungle."

"He is a man – a man – a man!" snarled the Pack; and most of the wolves began to gather round Shere Khan, whose tail was beginning to switch.

"Now the business is in thy hands," said Bagheera to Mowgli. "*We* can do no more except fight."

Mowgli stood upright – the fire-pot in his hands. Then he stretched out his arms, and yawned in the face of the Council; but he was furious with rage and sorrow, for, wolf-like, the wolves had never told him how they hated him. "Listen, you!" he cried. "There is no need for this dog's jabber. Ye have told me so often tonight that I am a man (and indeed I would have been a wolf with you to my life's end), that I feel your words are true.

So I do not call ye my brothers any more, but *sag* [dogs], as a man should. What ye will do, and what ye will not do, is not yours to say. That matter is with *me*; and that we may see the matter more plainly, I, the man, have brought here a little of the Red Flower which ye, dogs, fear."

He flung the fire-pot on the ground, and some of the red coals lit a tuft of dried moss that flared up, as all the Council drew back in terror before the leaping flames.

Mowgli thrust his dead branch into the fire till the twigs lit and crackled, and whirled it above his head among the cowering wolves.

"Thou art the master," said Bagheera, in an undertone. "Save Akela from the death. He was ever thy friend."

Akela, the grim old wolf who had never asked for mercy in his life, gave one piteous look at Mowgli as the boy stood all naked, his long black hair tossing over his shoulders in the light of the blazing branch that made the shadows jump and quiver.

"Good!" said Mowgli, staring round slowly. "I see that ye are dogs. I go from you to my own people – if they be my own people. The Jungle is shut to me, and I must forget your talk and your companionship; but I will be more merciful than ye are. Because I was all but your brother in blood, I promise that when I am a man among men I will not betray ye to men as ye have betrayed me." He kicked the fire with his foot, and the sparks flew up. "There shall be no war between any of us and the Pack. But here is a debt to pay before I go." He strode forward to where Shere Khan sat blinking stupidly at the flames, and caught him by the tuft on his chin. Bagheera followed in case of accidents. "Up, dog!" Mowgli cried. "Up, when a man speaks, or I will set that coat ablaze!"

Shere Khan's ears lay flat back on his head, and he shut his eyes, for the blazing branch was very near.

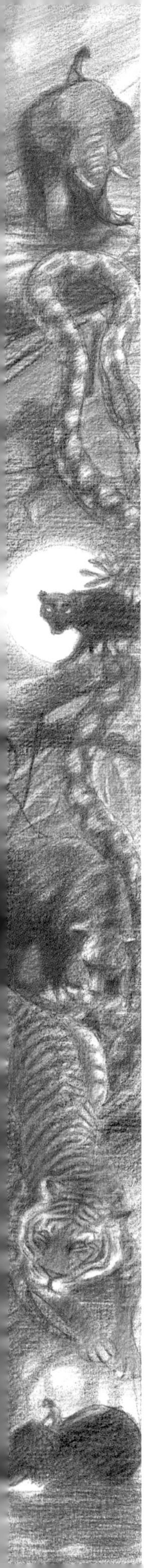

"This cattle-killer said he would kill me in the Council because he had not killed me when I was a cub. Thus and thus, then, do we beat dogs when we are men. Stir a whisker, Lungri, and I ram the Red Flower down thy gullet!" He beat Shere Khan over the head with the branch, and the tiger whimpered and whined in an agony of fear.

"Pah! Singed jungle-cat – go now! But remember when next I come to the Council Rock, as a man should come, it will be with Shere Khan's hide on my head. For the rest, Akela goes free to live as he pleases. Ye will *not* kill him, because that is not my will. Nor do I think that ye will sit here any longer, lolling out your tongues as though ye were somebodies, instead of dogs whom I drive out – thus! Go!" The fire was burning furiously at the end of the branch, and Mowgli struck right and left round the circle, and the wolves ran howling with the sparks burning their fur. At last there were only Akela, Bagheera, and perhaps ten wolves that had taken Mowgli's part. Then something began to hurt Mowgli inside him, as he had never been hurt in his life before, and he caught his breath and sobbed, and the tears ran down his face.

"What is it? What is it?" he said. "I do not wish to leave the Jungle, and I do not know what this is. Am I dying, Bagheera?"

"No, Little Brother. Those are only tears such as men use," said Bagheera. "Now I know thou art a man, and a man's cub no longer. The Jungle is shut indeed to thee henceforward. Let them fall, Mowgli. They are only tears." So Mowgli sat and cried as though his heart would break; and he had never cried in all his life before.

"Now," he said, "I will go to men. But first I must say farewell to my mother"; and he went to the cave where she lived with Father Wolf, and he cried on her coat, while the four cubs howled miserably.

"Ye will not forget me?" said Mowgli.

"Never while we can follow a trail," said the cubs. "Come to the foot of the hill when thou art a man, and we will talk to thee; and we will come into the croplands to play with thee by night."

"Come soon!" said Father Wolf. "Oh, wise little frog, come again soon; for we be old, thy mother and I."

"Come soon," said Mother Wolf, "little naked son of mine; for, listen, child of man, I loved thee more than ever I loved my cubs."

"I will surely come," said Mowgli, "and when I come it will be to lay out Shere Khan's hide upon the Council Rock. Do not forget me! Tell them in the Jungle never to forget me!"

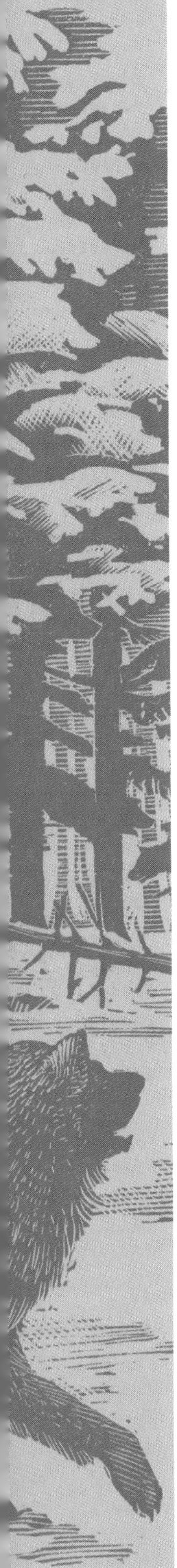

Introduction

Set in the late 1890s, The Call of the Wild *is the story of Buck, a St Bernard-collie cross-breed. As a young dog, he is captured by dog thieves who eventually sell him to be a sled-dog in Alaska during the Klondike gold rush. Only when he meets his new master, Thornton, does he begin to experience any kind of human affection. The bond between man and dog becomes one of absolute trust and respect.*

M. M.

THE CALL OF THE WILD

JACK LONDON

That winter, at Dawson, Buck performed another exploit, not so heroic, perhaps, but one that put his name many notches higher on the totem pole of Alaskan fame. This exploit was particularly gratifying to the three men; for they stood in need of the outfit which it furnished, and were enabled to make a long-desired trip into the virgin East, where miners had not yet appeared. It was brought about by a conversation in the Eldorado Saloon, in which men waxed boastful of their favourite dogs. Buck, because of his record, was the target for these men, and Thornton was driven stoutly to defend him. At the end of half an hour one man stated that his dog could start a sled with five hundred pounds and walk off with it; a second bragged six hundred for his dog; and a third, seven hundred.

"Pooh! Pooh!" said John Thornton; "Buck can start a thousand pounds."

"And break it out? And walk off with it for a hundred yards?" demanded Matthewson, a Bonanza King, he of the seven hundred vaunt.

"And break it out, and walk off with it for a hundred yards," John Thornton said coolly.

"Well," Matthewson said, slowly and deliberately, so that all could hear, "I've got a thousand dollars that says he can't. And there it is." So saying, he slammed a sack of gold dust of the size of a bologna sausage down upon the bar.

Nobody spoke. Thornton's bluff, if bluff it was, had been called. He could feel a flush of warm blood creeping up his face. His tongue had tricked him. He did not know whether Buck could start a thousand pounds. Half a ton! The enormousness of it appalled him. He had great faith in Buck's strength and had often thought him capable of starting such a load; but never, as now, had he faced the possibility of it, the eyes of a dozen men fixed upon him, silent and waiting. Further, he had no thousand dollars; nor had Hans or Pete.

"I've got a sled standing outside now, with twenty fifty-pound sacks of flour on it," Matthewson went on with brutal directness; "so don't let that hinder you."

Thornton did not reply. He did not know what to say. He glanced from face to face in the absent way of a man who has lost the power of thought and is seeking somewhere to find the thing that will start it going again. The face of Jim O'Brien, a Mastodon King and old-time comrade, caught his eyes. It was as a cue to him, seeming to rouse him to do what he would never have dreamed of doing.

"Can you lend me a thousand?" he asked, almost in a whisper.

"Sure," answered O'Brien, thumping down a plethoric sack by the side of Matthewson's. "Though it's little faith I'm having, John, that the beast can do the trick."

The Eldorado emptied its occupants into the street to see the test. The tables were deserted, and the dealers and gamekeepers came forth to see the outcome of the wager and to lay odds. Several hundred men, furred and mittened, banked around the sled within easy distance. Matthewson's sled, loaded with a thousand pounds of flour, had been standing for a couple of hours, and in the intense cold (it was sixty below zero) the runners had frozen fast to the hard-packed snow. Men offered odds of two to one that Buck could not budge the sled.

A quibble arose concerning the phrase "break out". O'Brien contended it was Thornton's privilege to knock the runners loose, leaving Buck to "break it out" from a dead standstill. Matthewson insisted that the phrase included breaking the runners from the frozen grip of the snow. A majority of the men who had witnessed the making of the bet decided in his favour, whereat the odds went up to three to one against Buck.

There were no takers. Not a man believed him capable of the feat. Thornton had been hurried into the wager, heavy with doubt; and now that he looked at the sled itself, the concrete fact, with the regular team of ten dogs curled up in the snow before it, the more impossible the task appeared. Matthewson waxed jubilant.

"Three to one!" he proclaimed. "I'll lay you another thousand at that figure, Thornton. What d'ye say?"

Thornton's doubt was strong in his face, but his fighting spirit was aroused – the fighting spirit that soars above odds, fails to recognize the impossible, and is deaf to all save the clamour for battle. He called Hans and Pete to him. Their sacks were slim, and with his own the three partners could rake together only two hundred dollars. In the ebb of their fortunes, this sum was their total capital; yet they laid it unhesitatingly against Matthewson's six hundred.

The team of ten dogs was unhitched, and Buck, with his own harness, was put into the sled. He had caught the contagion of the excitement, and he felt that in some way he must do a great thing for John Thornton. Murmurs of admiration at his splendid appearance went up. He was in perfect condition, without an ounce of superfluous flesh, and the one hundred and fifty pounds that he weighed were so many pounds of grit and virility. His furry coat shone with the sheen of silk. Down the neck and across the shoulders, his mane, in repose as it was, half bristled and seemed to lift with every movement, as though excess of vigour made each particular hair alive and active. The great breast and heavy forelegs were no more than in proportion with the rest of the body, where the muscles showed in tight rolls underneath the skin. Men felt these muscles and proclaimed them hard as iron, and the odds went down to two to one.

"Gad, sir! Gad, sir!" stuttered a member of the latest dynasty, a king of the Skookum Benches. "I offer you eight hundred for him, sir, before the test, sir; eight hundred just as he stands."

Thornton shook his head and stepped to Buck's side.

"You must stand off from him," Matthewson protested. "Free play and plenty of room."

The crowd fell silent; only could be heard the voices of the gamblers vainly offering two to one. Everybody acknowledged Buck a magnificent animal, but twenty fifty-pound sacks of flour bulked too large in their eyes for them to loosen their pouch-strings.

Thornton knelt down by Buck's side. He took his head in his two hands and rested cheek on cheek. He did not playfully shake him, as was his wont, or murmur soft love curses; but he whispered in his ear. "As you love me, Buck. As you love me," was what he whispered. Buck whined with suppressed eagerness.

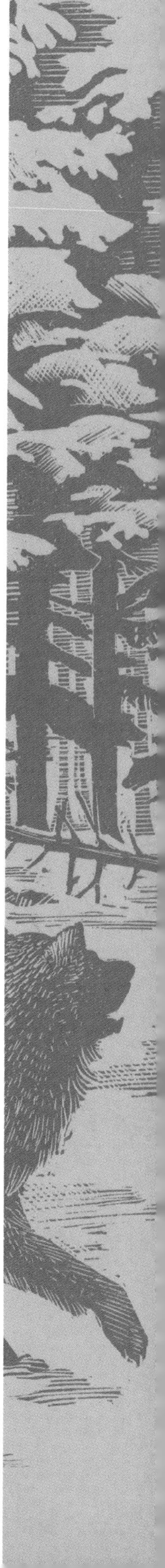

The crowd was watching curiously. The affair was growing mysterious. It seemed like a conjuration. As Thornton got to his feet, Buck seized his mittened hand between his jaws, pressing in with his teeth and releasing slowly, half-reluctantly. It was the answer, in terms, not of speech, but of love. Thornton stepped well back.

"Now, Buck," he said.

Buck tightened the traces, then slacked them for a matter of several inches. It was the way he had learned.

"Gee!" Thornton's voice rang out, sharp in the tense silence.

Buck swung to the right, ending the movement in a plunge that took up the slack and with a sudden jerk arrested his one hundred and fifty pounds. The load quivered, and from under the runners arose a crisp crackling.

"Haw!" Thornton commanded.

Buck duplicated the manoeuvre, this time to the left. The crackling turned into a snapping, the sled pivoting and the runners slipping and grating several inches to the side. The sled was broken out. Men were holding their breaths, intensely unconscious of the fact.

"Now, MUSH!"

Thornton's command cracked out like a pistol shot. Buck threw himself forward, tightening the traces with a jarring lunge. His whole body was gathered compactly together in the tremendous effort, the muscles writhing and knotting like live things under the silky fur. His great chest was low to the ground, his head forward and down, while his feet were flying like mad, the claws scarring the hard-packed snow in parallel grooves. The sled swayed and trembled, half-started forward. One of his feet slipped, and one man groaned aloud. Then the sled lurched ahead in what appeared a rapid succession of jerks, though it never really came to a dead stop again . . . half an inch . . . an inch . . .

two inches . . . The jerks perceptibly diminished; as the sled gained momentum, he caught them up, till it was moving steadily along.

Men gasped and began to breathe again, unaware that for a moment they had ceased to breathe. Thornton was running behind, encouraging Buck with short, cheery words. The distance had been measured off, and as he neared the pile of firewood which marked the end of the hundred yards, a cheer began to grow and grow, which burst into a roar as he passed the firewood and halted at command. Every man was tearing himself loose, even Matthewson. Hats and mittens were flying in the air. Men were shaking hands, it did not matter with whom, and bubbling over in a general incoherent babel.

But Thornton fell on his knees beside Buck. Head was against head, and he was shaking him back and forth. Those who hurried up heard him cursing Buck, and he cursed him long and fervently, and softly and lovingly.

"Gad, sir! Gad, sir!" spluttered the Skookum Bench king. "I'll give you a thousand for him, sir, a thousand, sir – twelve hundred, sir."

Thornton rose to his feet. His eyes were wet. The tears were streaming frankly down his cheeks. "Sir," he said to the Skookum Bench king, "no, sir. You can go to hell, sir. It's the best I can do for you, sir."

Buck seized Thornton's hand in his teeth. Thornton shook him back and forth. As though animated by a common impulse, the onlookers drew back to a respectful distance; nor were they again indiscreet enough to interrupt.

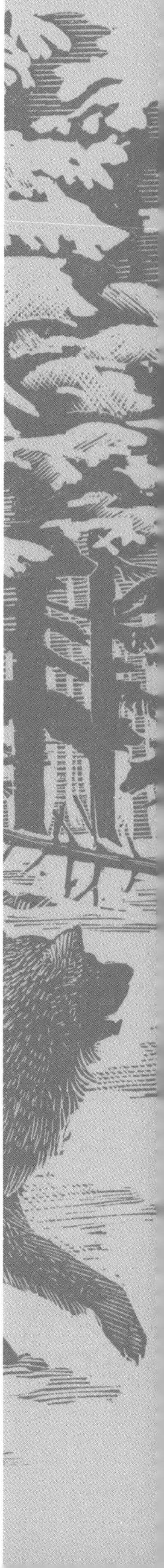

Introduction

"Without doubt Judy was the worst of the seven, probably because she was the cleverest." So Ethel Turner describes the most highly spirited member of Captain Woolcot's large family, who all run wild in their rambling riverside home in Sydney. He calls them "a disgraceful tribe" and after a particularly naughty episode, forbids them to go to the pantomime they are so looking forward to. The next day, Pat, the stable lad, is taking the dogcart into town for repairs. Pip, the eldest boy, goes with him, to deliver a coat to his father ("the governor") at the army barracks. Judy (christened Helen and sometimes called Fizz) goes along for the ride, taking with her the youngest member of the family, the baby they call "the General".

R. S.

Seven Little Australians

Ethel Turner

The General Sees Active Service

On the way to Paddington a gentleman on horseback slackened pace a little. Pip took off his hat with a flourish, and Judy gave a frank, pleased smile, for it was a certain old Colonel they had known for years, and had cause to remember his good humour and liberality.

"Well, my little maid – well, Philip, lad," he said smiling genially, while his horse danced round the dogcart, "And the General too – where are you all off too?"

"The Barracks. I'm taking something up for the governor," Pip answered. Judy was watching the plunging horse with admiring eyes. "And then we're going back home."

The old gentleman managed, in spite of the horse's tricks, to slip his hand in his pocket. "Here's something to make yourself ill with on the way," he said, handing them two half-crowns, "but don't send me the doctor's bill."

He flicked the General's cheek with his whip, gave Judy a nod, and cantered off.

The children looked at each other with sparkling eyes.

"Coconuts," Pip said, "and tarts and toffee, and save the rest for a football?" Judy shook her head.

"Where do *I* come in?" she said. "You'd keep the football at school. I vote pink jujubes, and ice creams, and a wax doll."

"A wax grandmother!" Pip retorted. "You wouldn't be such a girl, I hope." Then he added, with almost pious fervour, "Thank goodness you've always hated dolls, Fizz."

Judy gave a sudden leap in her seat, almost upsetting the General, and bringing down upon her head a storm of reproaches from the coachman. "*I* know!" she said. "And we're almost halfway there now. Oh-h-h! it *will* be lovely."

Pip urged her to explain herself.

"Bondi Aquarium – skating, boats, merry-go-round, switchback threepence a go!" she returned succinctly.

"Good iron," Pip whistled softly, while he revolved the thing in his mind. "There'd be something over, too, to get some tucker with, and perhaps something for the football, too." Then his brow clouded.

"There's the kid – whatever did you go bringing him for? Just like a girl, to spoil everything!"

Judy looked nonplussed. "I quite forgot him," she said, vexedly. "Couldn't we leave him somewhere? Couldn't we ask someone to take care of him while we go? Oh, it would be *too* bad to have to give it up just because of him. It's beginning to rain, too. We couldn't take him with us."

They were at the foot of Barrack Hill now, and Pat told them they must get out and walk the rest of the way up, or he would never get the dogcart finished to take back that evening.

Pip tumbled out and took the General, all in a bunched-up heap, and Judy alighted carefully after him, the precious coat parcel in her arms. And they walked up the asphalt hill to the gate leading to the officers' quarters in utter silence.

"Well?" Pip said querulously, as they reached the top. "Be quick – haven't you thought of anything?"

That levelling of brows, and pursing of lips, always meant deep and intricate calculation on his sister's part, as he knew full well.

"Yes," Judy said quietly. "I've got a plan that will do, I think." Then a sudden fire entered her manner.

"Who is the General's father? Tell me that," she said, in a rapid, eager way. "And isn't it right and proper fathers should look after their sons? And doesn't he deserve we should get even with him for doing us out of the pantomime? And isn't the Aquarium too lovely to miss?"

"Well?" Pip said. His slower brain did not follow such rapid reasoning.

"Only I'm going to leave the General here at the Barracks for a couple of hours till we come back, his father being the proper person to watch over him." Judy grasped the General's small fat hand in a determined way, and opened the gate.

"Oh, I say," remarked Pip, "we'll get into an awful row, you know, Fizz. I don't think we'd better – I don't really know, old girl."

"Not a bit," said Judy stoutly, "at least, only a bit, and the Aquarium's worth that. Look how it's raining – the child will get croup, or rheumatism, or something if we take him. There's Father standing over on the green near the tennis court talking to a man. I'll slip quietly along the verandah and into his own room, and put the coat and the General on the bed; then I'll tell a soldier to go and tell Father his parcels have come, and while he's gone I'll fly back to you, and we'll catch the tram and go to the Aquarium."

Pip whistled again, softly. He was used to bold proposals from this sister of his, but this was beyond everything. "B-b-but," he said uneasily, "but, Judy, whatever would he do with that kid for two mortal hours?"

"Mind him," Judy returned promptly. "It's a pretty thing if a father can't mind his own child for two hours. Afterwards, you see, when we've been to the Aquarium, we will come back and fetch him, and we can explain to Father how it was raining and that we thought we'd better not take him with us for fear of rheumatism, and that we were in a hurry to catch the tram, and as he wasn't in his room we just put him on the bed till he came. Why, Pip, it's beautifully simple!"

Pip still looked uncomfortable. "I don't like it, Fizz," he said again. "He'll be in a fearful wax."

Judy gave him one exasperated look. "Go and see if that's the Bondi tram coming," she said, and, glad of a moment's respite, he went down the path again to the pavement and looked down the hill. When he turned round again she had gone.

He stuck his hands in his pockets and walked up and down the path a few times. "Fizz'll get us hanged yet," he muttered, looking darkly at the door in the wall through which she had disappeared.

He pushed his hat to the back of his head and stared gloomily at his boots, wondering what would be the consequences of this new mischief. There was a light footfall behind him.

"Come on," said Judy, pulling his sleeve, "it's done now, come on, let's go and have our fun. Have you got the money safe?"

It was two o'clock as they passed out of the gate and turned their faces up the hill to the tram stopping-place. And it was half past four when they jumped out of a town-bound tram and entered the gates again to pick up their charge.

Such an afternoon as they had had! Once inside the Aquarium, even Pip had put his conscience qualms on one side, and bent all his energies to enjoying himself thoroughly. And Judy was like a

little mad thing. She spent a shilling of her money on the switchback railway, pronouncing the swift, bewildering motion "heavenly". The first journey made Pip feel sick, so he eschewed a repetition of it, and watched Judy go off from time to time, waving gaily from the perilous little car, almost with his heart in his mouth. Then they hired a pair of rollerskates each, and bruised themselves black and blue with heavy falls on the asphalt. After that they had a ride on the merry-go-round, but Judy found it tame after the switchback, and refused to squander a second threepence on it, contenting herself with watching Pip fly round, and madly running by his side to keep up as long as she could. They finished the afternoon with a prolonged inspection of the fish tanks, a light repast of jam tarts of questionable freshness, and twopenny-worth of peanuts. And, as I said, it was half past four as they hastened up the path again to the top gate of the Barracks.

"I *hope* he's been good," Judy said, as she turned the handle. "Yes, you come, too, Pip," – for that young gentleman hung back one agonized second – "twenty kicks or blows divided by two only make ten, you see."

They went up the long stone verandah and stopped at one door. There was a little knot of young officers laughing and talking close by.

"Take my word, 'twas as good as a play to see Wooly grabbing his youngster, and stuffing it into a cab, and getting in himself, all with a look of ponderous injured dignity," one said, and laughed at the recollection.

Another blew away a cloud of cigar smoke. "It was a jolly little beggar," he said. "It doubled its fists and landed His High Mightiness one in the eye – and then its shoe dropped off, and we all rushed to pick it up, and it was muddy and generally dilapidated, and old Wooly went red slowly up to his ear-tips as he tried to put it on."

A little figure stepped into the middle of the group – a little figure with an impossibly short and shabby ulster, thin, black-stockinged legs, and a big hat crushed over a tangle of curls.

"It is my father you are speaking of," she said, her head very high, her tone haughty, "and I cannot tell where your amusement is. Is my father here, or did I hear you say he had gone away?"

Two of the men looked foolish, the third took off his cap.

"I am sorry you should have overheard us, Miss Woolcot," he said pleasantly. "Still, there is no irreparable harm done, is there? Yes, your father has gone away in a cab. He couldn't imagine how the little boy came on his bed, and, as he couldn't keep him here very well, I suppose he has taken him home."

Something like a look of shame came into Judy's bright eyes.

"I am afraid I must have put my father to some inconvenience," she said quietly. "It was I who left the Gen – my brother here, because I didn't know what to do with him for an hour or two. But I quite meant to take him home myself. Has he been gone long?"

"About half an hour," the officer said, and tried not to look amused at the little girl's old-fashioned manner.

"Ah, thank you. Perhaps we can catch him up. Come on, Pip," and, nodding in a grave, distant manner, she turned away, and went down the verandah and through the gate with her brother.

"A nice hole we're in," he said.

Judy nodded.

"It's about the very awfullest thing we've ever done in our lives. Fancy the governor carting that child all the way from here! Oh, lor'!"

Judy nodded again.

"Can't you speak?" he said irritably. "You've got us into this – I didn't want to do it – but I'll stand by you, of course. Only you'll have to think of something quick."

Judy bit three finger-tips off her right-hand glove, and looked melancholy.

"There's absolutely nothing to do, Pip," she said slowly. "I didn't think it would turn out like this. I suppose we'd better just go straight back and hand ourselves over for punishment. He'll be too angry to hear any sort of an excuse, so we'd better just grin and bear whatever he does to us. I'm really sorry, too, that I made a laughing-stock of him up there."

Pip was explosive. He called her a little ass and a gowk and a stupid idiot for doing such a thing, and she did not reproach him or answer back once.

They caught a tram and went into Sydney, and afterwards to the boat. They ensconced themselves in a corner at the far end, and discussed the state of affairs with much seriousness. Then Pip got up and strolled about a little to relieve his feelings, coming back in a second with a white, scared face.

"He's on the boat," he said, in a horrified whisper.

"Where – where – where? What – what – what?" Judy cried, unintentionally mimicking a long-buried monarch.

"In the cabin, looking as glum as a boiled wallaby, and hanging on to the poor little General as if he thinks he'll fly away."

Judy looked a little frightened for the first time.

"Can't we hide? Don't let him see us. It wouldn't be any good offering to take the General now. We're in for it now, Pip – there'll be no quarter."

Pip groaned, then Judy stood up.

"Let's creep down as far as the engine," she said, "and see if he does look very bad."

They made their way cautiously along the deck, and took up a position where they could see without being seen. The dear little General was sitting on the seat next to his stern father, who had a firm hold of the back of his woolly pelisse. He was sucking his little dirty hand, and casting occasional longing glances at his tan shoe, which he knew was delicious to bite. Once or twice he had pulled it off and conveyed it to his mouth, but his father intercepted it, and angrily buttoned it on again in its rightful place. He wanted, too, to slither off that horrid seat, and crawl all over the deck, and explore the ground under the seats, and see where the puffing noise came from, but there was that iron grasp on his coat that no amount of wriggling would move. No wonder the poor child looked unhappy.

At last the boat stopped at a wharf not far from Misrule, and the Captain alighted, carrying his small dirty son gingerly in his arms. He walked slowly up the red road along which the dogcart had sped so blithesomely some six or seven hours ago, and Judy and Pip followed at a respectful – a very respectful – distance. At the gate he saw them, and gave a large, angry beckon for them to come up. Judy went very white, but obeyed instantly, and Pip, pulling himself together, brought up the rear.

Afterwards Judy only had a very indistinct remembrance of what happened during the next half hour. She knew there was a stormy scene, in which Esther and the whole family came in for an immense amount of vituperation.

Then Pip received a thrashing, in spite of Judy's persistent avowal that it was all her fault, and Pip hadn't done anything. She remembered wondering whether she would be treated as summarily as Pip, so angry was her father's face as he pushed the boy aside and stood looking at her, riding whip in hand.

But he flung it down and laid a heavy hand on her shrinking shoulder.

"Next Monday," he said slowly – "next Monday morning you will be going to boarding school. Esther, kindly see Helen's clothes are ready for boarding school – next Monday morning."

Introduction

Sam Gribley lives in an apartment in New York with his mum and dad and four sisters and four brothers. None of them likes it and Sam's dad hates it worse than all of them. It is from his dad that Sam discovers where his great-grandfather came from – the Catskill Mountains. He'd had a farm there. "Somewhere in the Catskills is an old beech with the name Gribley carved on it." That sets Sam thinking, dreaming. In the New York Public Library he reads up about how to survive on the land. But Sam doesn't just dream his dream of escape. He lives his dream. He runs away.

M. M.

My Side of the Mountain

Jean Craighead George

I left New York in May. I had a penknife, a ball of cord, an axe, and $40, which I had saved from selling magazine subscriptions. I also had some flint and steel which I had bought at a Chinese store in the city. The man in the store had showed me how to use it. He had also given me a little purse to put it in, and some tinder to catch the sparks. He had told me that if I ran out of tinder, I should burn cloth, and use the charred ashes.

I thanked him and said, "This is the kind of thing I am not going to forget."

On the train north to the Catskills I unwrapped my flint and steel and practised hitting them together to make sparks. On the wrapping paper I made these notes.

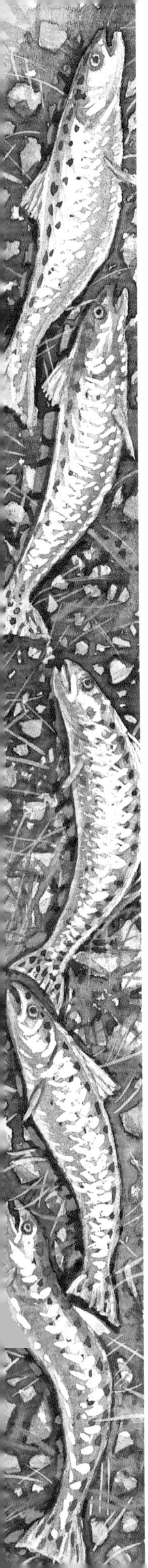

A hard brisk strike is best. Remember to hold the steel in the left hand and the flint in the right, and hit the steel with the flint. The trouble is the sparks go every which way.

And that *was* the trouble. I did not get a fire going that night, and as I mentioned, this was a scary experience.

I hitched rides into the Catskill Mountains. At about four o'clock a truck driver and I passed through a beautiful dark hemlock forest, and I said to him, "This is as far as I am going."

He looked all around and said, "You live here?"

"No," I said, "but I am running away from home, and this is just the kind of forest I have always dreamed I would run to. I think I'll camp here tonight." I hopped out of the cab.

"Hey, boy," the driver shouted. "Are you serious?"

"Sure," I said.

"Well, now, ain't that sumpin'? You know, when I was your age, I did the same thing. Only thing was, I was a farm boy and ran to the city, and you're a city boy running to the woods. I was scared of the city – do you think you'll be scared of the woods?"

"Heck, no!" I shouted loudly.

As I marched into the cool shadowy woods, I heard the driver call to me, "I'll be back in the morning, if you want to ride home."

He laughed. Everybody laughed at me. Even Dad. I told Dad that I was going to run away to Great-grandfather Gribley's land. He had roared with laughter and told me about the time he had run away from home. He got on a boat headed for Singapore, but when the whistle blew for departure, he was down the gangplank and home in bed before anybody knew he was gone. Then he told me, "Sure, go try it. Every boy should try it."

I must have walked a mile into the woods until I found a stream.

It was a clear athletic stream that rushed and ran and jumped and splashed. Ferns grew along its bank, and its rocks were upholstered with moss.

I sat down, smelled the piney air, and took out my penknife. I cut off a green twig and began to whittle. I have always been good at whittling. I carved a ship once that my teacher exhibited for parents' night at school.

First I whittled an angle on one end of the twig. Then I cut a smaller twig and sharpened it to a point. I whittled an angle on that twig, and bound the two angles face to face with a strip of green bark. It was supposed to be a fishhook.

According to a book on how to survive on the land that I read in the New York Public Library, this was the way to make your own hooks. I then dug for worms. I had hardly chopped the moss away with my axe before I hit frost. It had not occurred to me that there would be frost in the ground in May, but then, I had not been on a mountain before.

This did worry me, because I was depending on fish to keep me alive until I got to my great-grandfather's mountain, where I was going to make traps and catch game.

I looked into the stream to see what else I could eat, and as I did, my hand knocked a rotten log apart. I remembered about old logs and all the sleeping stages of insects that are in it. I chopped away until I found a cold white grub.

I swiftly tied a string to my hook, put the grub on, and walked up the stream looking for a good place to fish. All the manuals I had read were very emphatic about where fish lived, and so I had memorized this: "In streams, fish usually congregate in pools and deep calm water. The heads of riffles, small rapids, the tail of a pool, eddies below rocks or logs, deep undercut banks, in the shade of overhanging bushes – all are very likely places to fish."

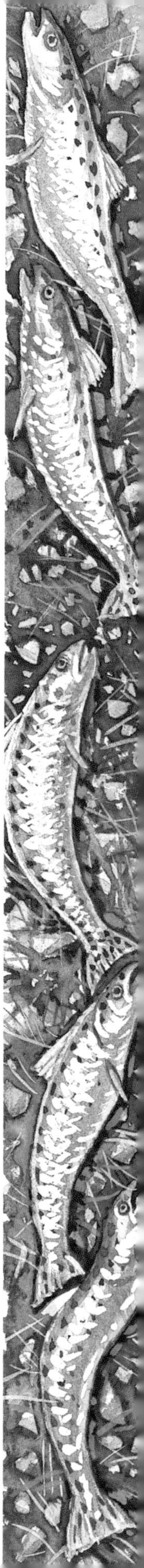

This stream did not seem to have any calm water, and I must have walked a thousand miles before I found a pool by a deep undercut bank in the shade of overhanging bushes. Actually, it wasn't that far, it just seemed that way because as I went looking and finding nothing, I was sure I was going to starve to death.

I squatted on this bank and dropped in my line. I did so want to catch a fish. One fish would set me upon my way, because I had read how much you can learn from one fish. By examining the contents of its stomach you can find what the other fish are eating or you can use the internal organs as bait.

The grub went down to the bottom of the stream. It swirled around and hung still. Suddenly the string came to life, and rode back and forth and around in a circle. I pulled with a powerful jerk. The hook came apart, and whatever I had went circling back to its bed.

Well, that almost made me cry. My bait was gone, my hook was broken, and I was getting cold, frightened, and mad. I whittled another hook, but this time I cheated and used string to wind it together instead of bark. I walked back to the log and luckily found another grub. I hurried to the pool, and I flipped a trout out of the water before I knew I had a bite.

The fish flopped, and I threw my whole body over it. I could not bear to think of it flopping itself back into the stream.

I cleaned it like I had seen the man at the fish market do, examined its stomach, and found it empty. This horrified me. What I didn't know was that an empty stomach means the fish are hungry and will eat about anything. However, I thought at the time that I was a goner. Sadly, I put some of the internal organs on my hook, and before I could get my line to the bottom I had another bite. I lost that one, but got the next one. I stopped when I had five nice little trout and looked around for a place to build a camp and make a fire.

It wasn't hard to find a pretty spot along that stream. I selected a place beside a mossy rock in a circle of hemlocks.

I decided to make a bed before I cooked. I cut off some boughs for a mattress, then I leaned some dead limbs against the boulder and covered them with hemlock limbs. This made a kind of tent. I crawled in, lay down, and felt alone and secret and very excited.

But, ah, the rest of this story! I was on the northeast side of the mountain. It grew dark and cold early. Seeing the shadows slide down on me, I frantically ran around gathering firewood. This is about the only thing I did right from that moment until dawn, because I remembered that the driest wood in a forest is the dead limbs that are still on the trees, and I gathered an enormous pile of them. That pile must still be there, for I never got a fire going.

I got sparks, sparks, sparks. I even hit the tinder with the sparks. The tinder burned all right, but that was as far as I got. I blew on it, I breathed on it, I cupped it in my hands, but no sooner did I add twigs than the whole thing went black.

Then it got too dark to see. I clicked steel and flint together, even though I couldn't see the tinder. Finally, I gave up and crawled into my hemlock tent, hungry, cold, and miserable.

I can talk about that first night now, although it is still embarrassing to me because I was so stupid, and scared, that I hate to admit it.

I had made my hemlock bed right in the stream valley where the wind drained down from the cold mountaintop. It might have been all right if I had made it on the other side of the boulder, but I didn't. I was right on the main highway of the cold winds as they tore down upon the valley below. I didn't have enough hemlock boughs under me, and before I had my head down, my stomach was cold and damp. I took some boughs off the roof and stuffed them under me, and then my shoulders were cold. I curled up in a ball and was almost asleep when a whippoorwill called. If you have ever been within forty feet of a whippoorwill, you will understand why I couldn't even shut my eyes. They are deafening!

Well, anyway, the whole night went like that. I don't think I slept fifteen minutes, and I was so scared and tired that my throat was dry. I wanted a drink but didn't dare go near the stream for fear of making a misstep and falling in and getting wet. So I sat tight, and shivered and shook – and now I am able to say – I cried a little tiny bit.

Fortunately, the sun has a wonderfully glorious habit of rising every morning. When the sky lightened, when the birds

awoke, I knew I would never again see anything so splendid as the round red sun coming up over the earth.

I was immediately cheered, and set out directly for the highway. Somehow, I thought that if I was a little nearer the road, everything would be all right.

I climbed a hill and stopped. There was a house. A house warm and cosy, with smoke coming out the chimney and lights in the windows, and only a hundred feet from my torture camp.

Without considering my pride, I ran down the hill and banged on the door. A nice old man answered. I told him everything in one long sentence, and then said, "And so, can I cook my fish here, because I haven't eaten in years."

He chuckled, stroked his whiskery face, and took the fish. He had them cooking in a pan before I knew what his name was.

When I asked him, he said Bill something, but I never heard his last name because I fell asleep in his rocking chair that was pulled up beside his big hot glorious wood stove in the kitchen.

I ate the fish some hours later, also some bread, jelly, oatmeal, and cream. Then he said to me, "Sam Gribley, if you are going to run off and live in the woods, you better learn how to make a fire. Come with me."

We spent the afternoon practising. I pencilled these notes on the back of a scrap of paper, so I wouldn't forget.

When the tinder glows, keep blowing and add fine dry needles one by one – and keep blowing, steadily, lightly, and evenly. Add one inch dry twigs to the needles and then give her a good big handful of small dry stuff. Keep blowing.

The next day I told Bill goodbye, and as I strode, warm and fed, on to the road, he called to me, "I'll see you tonight. The back door will be open if you want a roof over your head."

I said, "Okay," but I knew I wouldn't see Bill again. I knew how to make fire, and that was my weapon. With fire I could conquer the Catskills. I also knew how to fish. To fish and to make a fire. That was all I needed to know, I thought.

Introduction

he young Geat, Beowulf, hears from a sea captain the story of how Grendel the Night-Stalker, Grendel the Man-Wolf, the Death-Shadow, is terrorizing the Danish King Hrothgar's court, how thirty of his thanes have been slaughtered in one night. Beowulf knows at once he must go to Hrothgar's aid, for Hrothgar had given shelter and help to his father and mother in their time of need. Hrothgar, with the wisdom of age, knows only too well how terrible this Grendel is, and how impossible is Beowulf's task. But Beowulf has the strength and courage of youth . . .

M. M.

Beowulf: Dragonslayer

Rosemary Sutcliff

But now the shadows were gathering in the corners of the hall, and as the daylight faded, a shadow seemed to gather on the hearts of all men there, a shadow that was all too long familiar to the Danes. Then Hrothgar rose in his High Seat, and called Beowulf to him again.

"Soon it will be dusk," he said, when the young Geat stood before him. "And yet again the time of dread comes upon Heorot. You are still determined upon this desperate venture?"

"I am not one to change my purpose without cause," Beowulf said, "and those with me are of a like mind, or they would not have taken ship with me from Geatland in the first place."

"So. Keep watch, then. If you prevail in the combat before you, you shall have such reward from me as never yet heroes had from a King. I pray to the All-Father that when the light grows again out of tonight's dark, you may stand here to claim it. Heorot is yours until morning." And he turned and walked out through the postern door, a tall old man stooping under the burden of his own height, to his sleeping quarters, where Wealhtheow the Queen had gone before him.

All up and down the hall men were taking leave of each other, dwindling away to their own sleeping places for the night. The thralls set back the benches and stacked the trestle boards against the gable-walls, and spread out straw-filled bolsters and warm wolfskin rugs for the fifteen warriors. Then they too were gone, and Heorot was left to the band of Geats, and the dreadful thing whose shadow was already creeping towards them through the dark.

"Bar the doors," Beowulf said, when the last footsteps of the last thrall had died away. "Bars will not keep him out, but at least they may give us some warning of his coming."

And when two of them had done his bidding, and the seldom-used bars were in their sockets, there was nothing more that could be done.

For a little, as the last fire sank lower, they stood about it, sometimes looking at each other, sometimes into the glowing embers, seldom speaking. Not one of them had much hope that he would see the daylight again, yet none repented of having followed their leader upon the venture. One by one, the fourteen lay down in their harness, with their swords beside them. But Beowulf stripped off his battle-sark and gave it with his sword and boar-crested helmet to Waegmund his kinsman and the dearest to him of all his companions, for he knew that mortal weapons were of no use against the Troll-kind; such creatures must be mastered, if they could be mastered at all, by a man's naked strength, and the red courage of his heart.

Then he too lay down, as though to sleep.

In the darkest hour of the spring night Grendel came to Heorot as he had come so many times before, up from his lair and over the high moors, through the mists that seemed to travel with him under the pale moon; Grendel, the Night-Stalker, the Death-Shadow. He came to the foreporch and snuffed about it, and smelled the man-smell, and found that the door which had stood unlatched for him so long was barred and bolted. Snarling in rage that any man should dare attempt to keep him out, he set the flat of his talon-tipped hands against the timbers and burst them in.

Dark as it was, the hall seemed to fill with a monstrous shadow at his coming; a shadow in which Beowulf, half springing up, then holding himself in frozen stillness, could make out no shape nor clear outline save two eyes filled with a wavering greenish flame.

The ghastly corpse-light of his own eyes showed Grendel the shapes of men as it seemed sleeping, and he did not notice among them one who leaned up on his elbow. Laughing in his throat, he reached out and grabbed young Hondscio who lay nearest to him, and almost before his victim had time to cry out, tore him limb from limb and drank the warm blood. Then, while the young warrior's dying shriek still hung upon the air, he reached for another. But this time his hand was met and seized in a grasp such as he had never felt before; a grasp that had in it the strength of thirty men. And for the first time he who had brought fear to so many caught the taste of it himself, knowing that at last he had met his match and maybe his master.

Beowulf leapt from the sleeping bench and grappled him in the darkness; and terror broke over Grendel in full force, the terror of a wild animal trapped; so that he thought no more of his hunting but only of breaking the terrible hold upon his arm and flying back into the night and the wilderness, and he howled and bellowed as he struggled for his freedom. Beowulf set his teeth and summoned all his strength and tightened his grip until the sinews cracked; and locked together they reeled and staggered up and down the great hall. Trestles and sleeping benches went over with crash on crash as they strained this way and that, trampling even through the last red embers of the dying fire; and the very walls seemed to groan and shudder as though the stout timbers would burst apart. And all the while Grendel snarled and shrieked and Beowulf fought in silence save for his gasping breaths.

Outside, the Danes listened in horror to the turmoil that seemed as though it must split Heorot asunder; and within, the Geats had sprung from their sleeping benches sword in hand, forgetful of their powerlessness against the Troll-kind, but in the dark, lit only by stray gleams of bale-fire from the monster's eyes, they dared not strike for fear of slaying their leader, and when one or other of them did contrive to get in a blow, the sword blade glanced off Grendel's charmed hide as though he were sheathed in dragon scales.

At last, when the hall was wrecked to the walls, the Night-Stalker gathered himself for one last despairing effort to break free. Beowulf's hold was as fierce as ever; yet none the less the two figures burst apart – and Grendel with a frightful shriek staggered to the doorway and through it, and fled wailing into the night, leaving his arm and shoulder torn from the roots in the hero's still unbroken grasp.

Beowulf sank down sobbing for breath on a shattered bench, and his fellows came crowding round him with torches rekindled at the scattered embers of the fire; and together they looked at the thing he held across his knees. "Not even the Troll-kind could live half a day with a wound such as that upon them," one of them said; and Waegmund agreed. "He is surely dead as though he lay here among the benches."

"Hondscio is avenged, at all events," said Beowulf. "Let us hang up this thing for a trophy, and a proof that we do not boast idly as the wind blows over."

So in triumph they nailed up the huge scaly arm on one of the roof beams above the High Seat of Hrothgar.

The first thin light of day was already washing over the moors, and almost before the grizzly thing was securely in place the Danes returned to Heorot. They came thronging in to beat

Beowulf in joyful acclaim upon his bruised and claw-marked shoulders, and gaze up in awe at the huge arm whose taloned fingers seemed even now to be striving to claw down the roof beam. Many of them called for their horses and followed the blood trail that Grendel had left in his flight up through the tilled land and over the moors until they came to the deep sea-inlet where the monster had his lair, and saw the churning waves between the rocks all fouled and boiling with blood. Meanwhile others set all things on foot for a day of rejoicing, and the young men wrestled together and raced their horses against each other, filling the day with their merrymaking, while the King's harper walked to and fro by himself under the apple trees, making a song in praise of Beowulf ready for the evening's feasting which this night would not end when darkness fell.

Introduction

When Matthew Cuthbert goes to the station to collect a boy from the orphanage to help on the farm, imagine his surprise to find that the "boy" is an eleven-year-old red-headed girl called Anne. He takes her back to the house with green gables, where his sister Marilla is most displeased to be offered this odd girl as a helper. But her feistiness and impulsive nature intrigue Marilla, who soon invites Anne to make Green Gables her home. Life is full of things to do and places to explore. Best of all will be the Sunday school picnic beside the Lake of Shining Waters (as Anne has romantically renamed the local pond). Anne's imagination is filled with thoughts of boating on the Lake with her new friend, Diana – and of tasting ice cream for the first time. But will her dreams come true?

R. S.

ANNE OF GREEN GABLES

L. M. MONTGOMERY

Anne's Confession

On the Monday evening before the picnic Marilla came down from her room with a troubled face.

"Anne," she said to that small personage, who was shelling peas by the spotless table and singing "Nelly of the Hazel Dell" with a vigour and expression that did credit to Diana's teaching, "did you see anything of my amethyst brooch? I thought I stuck it in my pincushion when I came home from church yesterday evening but I can't find it anywhere."

"I – I saw it this afternoon when you were away at the Aid Society," said Anne, a little slowly. "I was passing your door when I saw it on the cushion, so I went in to look at it."

"Did you touch it?" said Marilla sternly.

"Y-e-e-s," admitted Anne. "I took it up and I pinned it on my breast just to see how it would look."

"You had no business to do anything of the sort. It's very wrong in a little girl to meddle. You shouldn't have gone into my room in the first place and you shouldn't have touched a brooch that didn't belong to you in the second. Where did you put it?"

"Oh, I put it back on the bureau. I hadn't it on a minute. Truly, I didn't mean to meddle, Marilla. I didn't think about its being wrong to go in and try on the brooch; but I see now that it was, and I'll never do it again. That's one good thing about me. I never do the same naughty thing twice."

"You didn't put it back," said Marilla. "That brooch isn't anywhere on the bureau. You've taken it out or something, Anne."

"I *did* put it back," said Anne quickly – pertly, Marilla thought. "I don't just remember whether I stuck it on the pincushion or laid it in the china tray. But I'm perfectly certain I put it back."

"I'll go and have another look," said Marilla, determining to be just. "If you put that brooch back it's there still. If it isn't I'll know you didn't, that's all!"

Marilla went to her room and made a thorough search, not only over the bureau but in every other place she thought the brooch might possibly be. It was not to be found and she returned to the kitchen.

"Anne, the brooch is gone. By your own admission you were the last person to handle it. Now, what have you done with it? Tell me the truth at once. Did you take it out and lose it?"

"No, I didn't," said Anne solemnly, meeting Marilla's angry gaze squarely. "I never took the brooch out of your room and that is the truth, if I was to be led to the block for it – although I'm not very certain what a block is. So there, Marilla."

Anne's "so there" was only intended to emphasize her

assertion, but Marilla took it as a display of defiance.

"I believe you are telling me a falsehood, Anne," she said sharply. "I know you are. There, now, don't say anything more unless you are prepared to tell the whole truth. Go to your room and stay there until you are ready to confess."

"Will I take the peas with me?" said Anne meekly.

"No, I'll finish shelling them myself. Do as I bid you."

When Anne was gone, Marilla went about her evening tasks in a very disturbed state of mind. She was worried about her valuable brooch. What if Anne had lost it? And how wicked of the child to deny having taken it, when anybody could see she must have! With such an innocent face, too!

"I don't know what I wouldn't sooner have had happen," thought Marilla, as she nervously shelled the peas. "Of course I don't suppose she meant to steal it or anything like that. She's just taken it to play with or help along that imagination of hers. She must have taken it, that's clear, for there hasn't been a soul in that room since she was in it, by her own story, until I went up tonight. And the brooch is gone, there's nothing surer. I suppose she has lost it and is afraid to own up for fear she'll be punished. It's a dreadful thing to think she tells falsehoods. It's a far worse thing than her fit of temper. It's a fearful responsibility to have a child in your house you can't trust. Slyness and untruthfulness – that's what she has displayed. I declare I feel worse about that than about the brooch. If she'd only have told the truth about it I wouldn't mind so much."

Marilla went to her room at intervals all through the evening and searched for the brooch, without finding it. A bedtime visit to the east gable produced no result. Anne persisted in denying that she knew anything about the brooch but Marilla was only the more firmly convinced that she did.

She told Matthew the story the next morning. Matthew was confounded and puzzled; he could not so quickly lose faith in Anne but he had to admit that circumstances were against her.

"You're sure it hasn't fell down behind the bureau?" was the only suggestion he could offer.

"I've moved the bureau and I've taken out the drawers and I've looked in every crack and cranny," was Marilla's positive answer. "The brooch is gone and that child has taken it and lied about it. That's the plain, ugly truth, Matthew Cuthbert, and we might as well look it in the face."

"Well, now, what are you going to do about it?" Matthew asked forlornly, feeling secretly thankful that Marilla and not he had to deal with the situation. He felt no desire to put his oar in this time.

"She'll stay in her room until she confesses," said Marilla grimly, remembering the success of this method in the former case. "Then we'll see. Perhaps we'll be able to find the brooch if she'll only tell where she took it; but in any case she'll have to be severely punished, Matthew."

"Well, now, you'll have to punish her," said Matthew, reaching for his hat. "I've nothing to do with it, remember. You warned me off yourself."

Marilla felt deserted by everyone. She could not even go to Mrs Lynde for advice. She went up to the east gable with a very serious face and left it with a face more serious still. Anne steadfastly refused to confess. She persisted in asserting that she had not taken the brooch. The child had evidently been crying and Marilla felt a pang of pity which she sternly repressed. By night she was, as she expressed it, "beat out".

"You'll stay in this room until you confess, Anne. You can make up your mind to that," she said firmly.

"But the picnic is tomorrow, Marilla," cried Anne. "You won't keep me from going to that, will you? You'll just let me out for the afternoon, won't you? Then I'll stay here as long as you like afterwards *cheerfully*. But I *must* go to the picnic."

"You'll not go to picnics nor anywhere else until you've confessed, Anne."

"Oh, Marilla," gasped Anne.

But Marilla had gone out and shut the door.

Wednesday morning dawned as bright and fair as if expressly made to order for the picnic. Birds sang around Green Gables; the Madonna lilies in the garden sent out whiffs of perfume that entered in on viewless winds at every door and window, and wandered through halls and rooms like spirits of benediction. The birches in the hollow waved joyful hands as if watching for Anne's usual morning greeting from the east gable. But Anne was not at her window. When Marilla took her breakfast up to her she found the child sitting primly on her bed, pale and resolute, with tight-shut lips and gleaming eyes.

"Marilla, I'm ready to confess."

"Ah!" Marilla laid down her tray. Once again her method had succeeded; but her success was very bitter to her. "Let me hear what you have to say then, Anne."

"I took the amethyst brooch," said Anne, as if repeating a lesson she had learned. "I took it just as you said. I didn't mean to take it when I went in. But it did look so beautiful, Marilla, when I pinned it on my breast that I was overcome by an irresistible temptation. I imagined how perfectly thrilling it would be to take it to Idlewild and play I was the Lady Cordelia Fitzgerald. It would be so much easier to imagine I was the Lady Cordelia if I had a real amethyst brooch on. Diana and I made necklaces of roseberries, but what are roseberries compared to amethysts? So I took the brooch. I thought I could put it back before you came home. I went all the

way around by the road to lengthen out the time. When I was going over the bridge across the Lake of Shining Waters I took the brooch off to have another look at it. Oh, how it did shine in the sunlight! And then, when I was leaning over the bridge, it just slipped through my fingers – so – and went down – down – down, all purply-sparkling and sank for evermore beneath the Lake of Shining Waters. And that's the best I can do at confessing, Marilla."

Marilla felt hot anger surge up into her heart again. This child had taken and lost her treasured amethyst brooch and now sat there calmly reciting the details thereof without the least apparent compunction or repentance.

"Anne, this is terrible," she said, trying to speak calmly. "You are the very wickedest girl I ever heard of."

"Yes, I suppose I am," agreed Anne tranquilly. "And I know I'll have to be punished. It'll be your duty to punish me, Marilla. Won't you please get it over right off because I'd like to go to the picnic with nothing on my mind."

"Picnic, indeed! You'll go to no picnic today, Anne Shirley! That shall be your punishment. And it isn't half severe enough either for what you've done!"

"Not go to the picnic!" Anne sprang to her feet and clutched Marilla's hand. "But you *promised* me I might! Oh, Marilla, I must go to the picnic. That was why I confessed. Punish me any way you like but that. Oh, Marilla, please, please, let me go to the picnic. Think of the ice cream! For anything you know I may never have a chance to taste ice cream again."

Marilla disengaged Anne's clinging hands stonily.

"You needn't plead, Anne. You are not going to the picnic and that's final. No, not a word."

Anne realized that Marilla was not to be moved. She clasped her hands together, gave a piercing shriek, and then flung herself

face downwards on the bed, crying and writhing in an utter abandonment of disappointment and despair.

"For the land's sake!" gasped Marilla, hastening from the room. "I believe the child is crazy. No child in her senses would behave as she does. If she isn't she's utterly bad. Oh, dear, I'm afraid Rachel was right from the first. But I've put my hand to the plough, and I won't look back."

That was a dismal morning. Marilla worked fiercely and scrubbed the porch floor and the dairy shelves when she could find nothing else to do. Neither the shelves nor the porch needed it but Marilla did. Then she went out and raked the yard.

When dinner was ready she went to the stairs and called Anne. A tear-stained face appeared, looking tragically over the banisters.

"Come down to your dinner, Anne."

"I don't want my dinner, Marilla," said Anne sobbingly. "I couldn't eat anything. My heart is broken. You'll feel remorse of conscience some day, I expect, for breaking it, Marilla, but I forgive you. Remember when the time comes that I forgive you. But please don't ask me to eat anything, especially boiled pork and greens. Boiled pork and greens are so unromantic when one is in affliction."

Exasperated, Marilla returned to the kitchen and poured out her tale of woe to Matthew, who, between his sense of justice and his unlawful sympathy with Anne, was a miserable man.

"Well now, she shouldn't have taken the brooch, Marilla, or told stories about it," he admitted, mournfully surveying his plateful of unromantic pork and greens as if he, like Anne, thought it a food unsuited to crises of feeling, "but she's such a little thing – such an interesting little thing. Don't you think it's pretty rough not to let her go to the picnic when she's so set on it?"

"Matthew Cuthbert, I'm amazed at you. I think I've let her off entirely too easy. And she doesn't appear to realize how wicked she's been at all – that's what worries me most. If she'd really felt sorry it wouldn't be so bad. And you don't seem to realize it neither; you're making excuses for her all the time to yourself – I can see that."

"Well now, she's such a little thing," feebly reiterated Matthew. "And there should be allowances made, Marilla. You know she's never had any bringing up."

"Well, she's having it now," retorted Marilla.

The retort silenced Matthew if it did not convince him. That dinner was a very dismal meal. The only cheerful thing about it was Jerry Buote, the hired boy, and Marilla resented his cheerfulness as a personal insult.

When her dishes were washed and her bread sponge set and her hens fed Marilla remembered that she had noticed a small rent in her best black lace shawl when she had taken it off on Monday afternoon on returning from the Ladies' Aid. She would go and mend it.

The shawl was in a box in her trunk. As Marilla lifted it out, the sunlight, falling through the vines that clustered thickly about the window, struck upon something caught in the shawl – something that glittered and sparkled in facets of violet light. Marilla snatched at it with a gasp. It was the amethyst brooch, hanging to a thread of the lace by its catch!

"Dear life and heart," said Marilla blankly, "what does this mean? Here's my brooch safe and sound that I thought was at the bottom of Barry's pond. Whatever did that girl mean by saying she took it and lost it? I declare I believe Green Gables is bewitched. I remember now that when I took off my shawl Monday afternoon I laid it on the bureau for a minute. I suppose the brooch got caught in it somehow. Well!"

Marilla betook herself to the east gable, brooch in hand. Anne had cried herself out and was sitting dejectedly by the window.

"Anne Shirley," said Marilla solemnly, "I've just found my brooch hanging to my black lace shawl. Now I want to know what that rigmarole you told me this morning meant."

"Why, you said you'd keep me here until I confessed," returned Anne wearily, "and so I decided to confess because I was bound to get to the picnic. I thought out a confession last night after I went to bed and made it as interesting as I could. And I said it over and over so that I wouldn't forget it. But you wouldn't let me go to the picnic after all, so all my trouble was wasted."

Marilla had to laugh in spite of herself. But her conscience pricked her.

"Anne, you do beat all! But I was wrong – I see that now. I shouldn't have doubted your word when I'd never known you to tell a story. Of course, it wasn't right for you to confess to a thing you hadn't done – it was very wrong to do so. But I drove you to it so if you'll forgive me, Anne, I'll forgive you and we'll start square again. And now get yourself ready for the picnic."

Anne flew up like a rocket.

"Oh, Marilla, isn't it too late?"

"No, it's only two o'clock. They won't be more than well gathered yet and it'll be an hour before they have tea. Wash your face and comb your hair and put on your gingham. I'll fill a basket for you. There's plenty of stuff baked in the house. And I'll get Jerry to hitch up the sorrel and drive you down to the picnic ground."

"Oh, Marilla," exclaimed Anne, flying to the washstand. "Five minutes ago I was so miserable I was wishing I'd never been born and now I wouldn't change places with an angel!"

That night a thoroughly happy, completely tired-out Anne

returned to Green Gables in a state of beatification impossible to describe.

"Oh, Marilla, I've had a perfectly scrumptious time. Scrumptious is a new word I learned today. I heard Mary Alice Bell use it. Isn't it very expressive? Everything was lovely. We had a splendid tea and then Mr Harmon Andrews took us all for a row on the Lake of Shining Waters – six of us at a time. And Jane Andrews nearly fell overboard. She was leaning out to pick water lilies and if Mr Andrews hadn't caught her by her sash just in the nick of time she'd have fallen in and prob'ly been drowned. I wish it had been me. It would have been such a romantic experience to have nearly drowned. It would be such a thrilling tale to tell. And we had the ice cream. Words fail me to describe that ice cream. Marilla, I assure you it was sublime."

That evening Marilla told the whole story to Matthew over her stocking basket.

"I'm willing to own up that I made a mistake," she concluded candidly, "but I've learned a lesson. I have to laugh when I think of Anne's 'confession', although I suppose I shouldn't, for it really was a falsehood. But it doesn't seem as bad as the other would have been, somehow, and anyhow I'm responsible for it. That child is hard to understand in some respects. But I believe she'll turn out all right yet. And there's one thing certain, no house will ever be dull that she's in."

Introduction

It wasn't all that long ago when "foundlings" (orphans with no family or home) were picked up like stray dogs and taken to the workhouse. Here life was hard and often short, and it is in the workhouse that young Oliver finds himself at the beginning of Oliver Twist. *How he copes with it, you will see. And when you read the whole book you will discover how Oliver manages to survive despite all the sadness and cruelty and wickedness of the world around him. He's a real hero of our time, for although we no longer have workhouses, Oliver is a reminder that many children today suffer great unhappiness, great unkindness – and survive.*

M. M.

Oliver Twist

Charles Dickens

Oliver had not been within the walls of the workhouse a quarter of an hour, and had scarcely completed the demolition of a second slice of bread, when Mr Bumble, who had handed him over to the care of an old woman, returned; and, telling him it was a board night, informed him that the board had said he was to appear before it forthwith.

Not having a very clearly defined notion of what a live board was, Oliver was rather astounded by this intelligence, and was not quite certain whether he ought to laugh or cry. He had no time to think about the matter, however; for Mr Bumble gave him a tap on the head, with his cane, to wake him up: and another on the back to make him lively: and bidding him follow, conducted him into a large white-washed room, where eight or ten fat gentlemen were sitting round a table. At the top of the table, seated in an armchair rather higher than the rest, was a particularly fat gentleman with a very round, red face.

"Bow to the board," said Bumble. Oliver brushed away two or three tears that were lingering in his eyes; and seeing no board but the table, fortunately bowed to that.

"What's your name, boy?" said the gentleman in the high chair.

Oliver was frightened at the sight of so many gentlemen, which made him tremble: and the beadle gave him another tap behind, which made him cry. These two causes made him answer in a very low and hesitating voice; whereupon a gentleman in a white waistcoat said he was a fool. Which was a capital way of raising his spirits, and putting him quite at his ease.

"Boy," said the gentleman in the high chair, "listen to me. You know you're an orphan, I suppose?"

"What's that, sir?" inquired poor Oliver.

"The boy *is* a fool – I thought he was," said the gentleman in the white waistcoat.

"Hush!" said the gentleman who had spoken first. "You know you've got no father or mother, and that you were brought up by the parish, don't you?"

"Yes, sir," replied Oliver, weeping bitterly.

"What are you crying for?" inquired the gentleman in the white waistcoat. And to be sure it was very extraordinary. What *could* the boy be crying for?

"I hope you say your prayers every night," said another gentleman in a gruff voice; "and pray for the people who feed you, and take care of you – like a Christian."

"Yes, sir," stammered the boy. The gentleman who spoke last

was unconsciously right. It would have been *very* like a Christian, and a marvellously good Christian, too, if Oliver had prayed for the people who fed and took care of *him*. But he hadn't, because nobody had taught him.

"Well! You have come here to be educated, and taught a useful trade," said the red-faced gentleman in the high chair.

"So you'll begin to pick oakum tomorrow morning at six o'clock," added the surly one in the white waistcoat.

For the combination of both these blessings in the one simple process of picking oakum, Oliver bowed low by the direction of the beadle, and was then hurried away to a large ward: where, on a rough, hard bed, he sobbed himself to sleep. What a noble illustration of the tender laws of England! They let the paupers go to sleep!

Poor Oliver! He little thought, as he lay sleeping in happy unconsciousness of all around him, that the board had that very day arrived at a decision which would exercise the most material influence over all his future fortunes. But they had. And this was it:

The members of this board were very sage, deep philosophical men; and when they came to turn their attention to the workhouse they found out at once what ordinary folks would never have discovered – the poor people liked it! It was a regular place of public entertainment for the poorer classes; a tavern where there was nothing to pay; a public breakfast, dinner, tea, and supper all the year round; a brick and mortar elysium, where it was all play and no work. "Oho!" said the board, looking very knowing; "we are the fellows to set this to rights; we'll stop it all, in no time." So, they established the rule, that all poor people should have the alternative (for they would compel nobody, not they), of being starved by a gradual process in the house, or by a quick one out of it. With this view, they contracted with the water-works to lay on an unlimited supply of water; and with a corn-factor to supply periodically small quantities of oatmeal; and issued three meals of thin gruel a day, with an onion twice a week, and half a roll on Sundays. They made a great many other wise and humane regulations, having reference to the ladies, which it is not necessary to repeat; kindly undertook to divorce poor married people, in consequence of the great expense of a suit in Doctors' Commons; and, instead of compelling a man to support his family, as they had theretofore done, took his family away from him, and made him a bachelor! There is no saying how many applicants for relief, under these last two heads, might have started up in all classes of society, if it had not been coupled with the workhouse; but the board were long-headed men, and had provided for this difficulty. The relief was inseparable from the workhouse and the gruel; and that frightened people.

For the first six months after Oliver Twist was removed, the system was in full operation. It was rather expensive at first, in consequence of the increase in the undertaker's bill, and the necessity of taking in the clothes of all the paupers, which fluttered loosely on their wasted, shrunken forms, after a week or two's gruel. But the number of workhouse inmates got thin as well as the paupers; and the board were in ecstasies.

The room in which the boys were fed was a large stone hall, with a copper at one end: out of which the master, dressed in an apron for the purpose, and assisted by one or two women, ladled the gruel at meal-times. Of this festive composition each boy had one porringer, and no more – except on occasions of great public rejoicing, when he had two ounces and a quarter of bread besides. The bowls never wanted washing. The boys polished them with their spoons till they shone again; and when they had performed this operation (which never took very long, the spoons being nearly as large as the bowls), they would sit staring at the copper, with such eager eyes, as if they could have devoured the very bricks of which it was composed; employing themselves, meanwhile, in sucking their fingers most assiduously, with the view of catching up any stray splashes of gruel that might have been cast thereon. Boys have generally excellent appetites. Oliver Twist and his companions suffered the tortures of slow starvation for three months: at last they got so voracious and wild with hunger, that one boy, who was tall for his age, and hadn't been used to that sort of thing (for his father had kept a small cook-shop), hinted darkly to his companions, that unless he had another basin of gruel *per diem*, he was afraid he might some night happen to eat the boy who slept next him, who happened to be a weakly youth of tender age. He had a wild, hungry eye; and they implicitly believed him. A council was held; lots were cast who should walk up to the master after supper that evening, and ask for more; and it fell to Oliver Twist.

The evening arrived; the boys took their places. The master, in his cook's uniform, stationed himself at the copper; his pauper assistants ranged themselves behind him; the gruel was served out; and a long grace was said over the short commons. The gruel disappeared; the boys whispered to each other, and winked at Oliver; while his next neighbours nudged him. Child as he was, he was desperate with hunger, and reckless with misery. He rose from the table; and advancing to the master, basin and spoon in hand, said: somewhat alarmed at his own temerity:

"Please, sir, I want some more."

The master was a fat, healthy man; but he turned very pale. He gazed in stupefied astonishment on the small rebel for some seconds, and then clung for support to the copper. The assistants were paralysed with wonder; the boys with fear.

"What!" said the master at length, in a faint voice.

"Please, sir," replied Oliver, "I want some more."

The master aimed a blow at Oliver's head with the ladle; pinioned him in his arms; and shrieked aloud for the beadle.

The board were sitting in solemn conclave, when Mr Bumble rushed into the room in great excitement, and addressing the gentleman in the high chair, said,

"Mr Limbkins, I beg your pardon, sir! Oliver Twist has asked for more!"

There was a general start. Horror was depicted on every countenance.

"For *more*!" said Mr Limbkins. "Compose yourself, Bumble, and answer me distinctly. Do I understand that he asked for more, after he had eaten the supper allotted by the dietary?"

"He did, sir," replied Bumble.

"That boy will be hung," said the gentleman in the white waistcoat. "I know that boy will be hung."

Nobody controverted the prophetic gentleman's opinion. An animated discussion took place. Oliver was ordered into instant confinement; and a bill was next morning pasted on the outside of the gate, offering a reward of five pounds to anybody who would take Oliver Twist off the hands of the parish. In other words, five pounds and Oliver Twist were offered to any man or woman who wanted an apprentice to any trade, business, or calling.

"I never was more convinced of anything in my life," said the gentleman in the white waistcoat, as he knocked at the gate and read the bill next morning: "I never was more convinced of anything in my life, than I am that that boy will come to be hung."

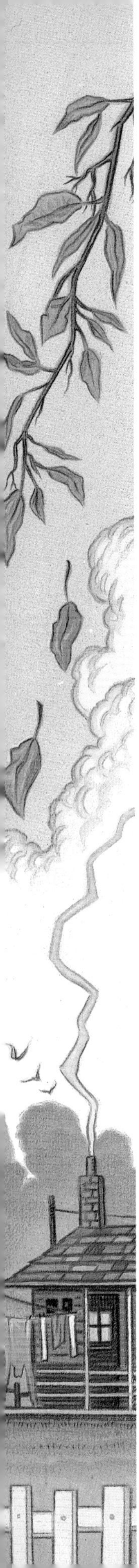

Introduction

Eleven-year-old Gilly is tough and resourceful. She has to be, to cope with the succession of foster families her social worker, Miss Ellis, places her with. Always at the back of Gilly's mind is the forlorn hope that her mother will come back for her. In the meantime, she uses her ingenuity and quick thinking as she moves from home to home: "I am too clever and too hard to manage. Gruesome Gilly, they call me." Will things be any different in the Trotter household, with Maime and her foster son William Ernest? It is only when Miss Ellis arrives to take her away after a particularly hairy incident, that Gilly realizes perhaps Maime Trotter is on her side after all.

R. S.

THE GREAT GILLY HOPKINS

KATHERINE PATERSON

Pow

There was a fight between Trotter and Miss Ellis. Gilly heard the sounds of battle in the living-room when she came in from school the next afternoon. "Never, never, never!" Trotter was bellowing, like an old cow deprived of its calf.

Gilly stopped still in the hallway, closing the door without a sound.

"Mrs Trotter, nobody at the agency looks at it as any indication of failure on your part –"

"You think I care what the agency thinks?"

"You're one of our most capable foster parents. You've been with us for more than twenty years. This won't affect your record with us. You're too valuable –"

"I don't give a spit about no record. You ain't taking Gilly."

"We're trying to think of you –"

"No, you ain't. If you was thinking of me, you'd never come to me with such a fool notion."

"This is a troubled child, Maime. She needs special –"

"No! I ain't giving her up. Never!"

"If you won't think of yourself, think of William Ernest. He's come too far in the last year to let – I've seen myself how she upsets him."

"It was William Ernest got her to come home last night." Trotter's voice was square and stubborn.

"Because he saw how upset you were. That doesn't mean she can't damage him."

"William Ernest has lived with me for over two years. He's gonna make it. I know he is. Sometimes, Miz Ellis, you gotta walk on your heel and favour your toe even if it makes your heel a little sore."

"I don't understand what you're driving at."

"Somebody's got to favour Gilly for a little while. She's long overdue."

"That's exactly it, Mrs Trotter. I'm quite aware of Gilly's needs. I've been her caseworker for nearly five years, and whether you believe it or not, I really care about her. But I don't think it's her needs we're talking about right now, is it?"

"What do you mean?"

"It's *your* needs." Said very quietly.

A silence and then, "Yes, Lord knows, I need her." A funny broken sound like a sob came from Trotter. "I like to die when I found her gone."

"You can't do that, Mrs Trotter. You can't let them tear you to pieces."

"Don't try to tell a mother how to feel."

"You're a foster mother, Mrs Trotter." Miss Ellis's voice was firm. "You can't afford to forget that."

Gilly's whole body was engulfed in a great aching. She opened and slammed the front door, pretending to have just come in. This time they heard her.

"That you, Gilly, honey?"

She went to the doorway of the living-room. Both women were on their feet, flushed as though they'd been running a race.

"Well, Gilly," Miss Ellis began, voice glittering like a fake Christmas tree.

"Miz Ellis," Trotter broke in loudly, "was just saying how it's up to you." There was a flash of alarm from the social worker which Trotter pretended not to see. "You want to stay on here with William Ernest and me – that's fine. You want her to find you someplace else – that's fine, too. You got to be the one to decide." Her eyes shifted uneasily towards Miss Ellis.

"What about," Gilly asked, her mouth going dry as a stale soda cracker, "what about my real mother?"

Miss Ellis's eyebrows jumped. "I wrote her, Gilly, several months ago, when we decided to move you from the Nevinses. She never answered."

"She wrote me. She wants me to come out there."

Miss Ellis looked at Trotter. "Yes. I know about the postcard," the caseworker said.

Those damned cops reading people's mail and blabbing, passing it around, snickering over it probably.

"Gilly. If – if she had really wanted you with her –"

"She does want me. She said so!"

"Then why hasn't she come to get you?" A hard edge had come into Miss Ellis's voice, and her eyebrows were twitching madly.

"It's been over eight years, Gilly. Even when she lived close by, she never came to see you."

"It's different now!" – wasn't it? – "She's gonna come! She really wants me!" – didn't she?

Trotter came over to her and laid her arm heavily on Gilly's shoulder. "If she knowed you – if she just knowed what a girl she has – she'd be here in a minute."

Oh, Trotter, don't be a fool. If she knew what I was like, she'd never come. It takes someone stupid like you – Gilly removed herself gently from under the weighty embrace and addressed herself to Miss Ellis, eye to eyebrow.

"Till she comes . . . till she comes for me, I guess I'll just stay here."

Trotter wiped her face with her big hand and snuffled. "Well, I'm sure we'll be seeing you sometime, Miz Ellis."

The social worker wasn't going to be swept out quite so easily. She set her feet apart as though fearing Trotter might try to remove her bodily and said, "Officer Rhine told me when he called that you had well over a hundred dollars with you last night."

"Yeah?"

It came out sassy, but Miss Ellis just squinted her eyes and went on: "It's hard to believe that it was all your money."

"So?"

"So I call taking other people's money *stealing*, Miss Hopkins."

"Yeah?"

Trotter patted Gilly's arm as if to shush her. "So do we, Miz Ellis. Surely you don't think this is the first time something like this has happened to me over the last twenty years?"

"No, I know it's not."

"Then how 'bout trusting me to handle it?"

Miss Ellis shook her head and smoothed her trouser suit down over her rump before she put on her coat. "I'll be in close touch," she said.

Trotter nearly shoved her out the front door. "We're going to do just fine. Don't worry your pretty little head about us, hear?"

"I get paid to worry, Mrs Trotter."

Trotter smiled impatiently and closed the door quickly. When she turned back towards Gilly, her face was like Mount Rushmore stone.

Gilly blinked in surprise at the sudden and absolute change.

"I don't take lightly to stealing, you know."

Gilly nodded. No use pretending sassiness.

"I figure that money ain't all mine, right?"

"No."

"Well, where'd you get it?"

"I found it," said Gilly softly.

Trotter came over and with two hands lifted Gilly's face to look into her own. "Where did you get it, Gilly?"

"I found it behind some books next door."

Trotter dropped her hands in disbelief. "You stole from Mr Randolph?"

"It was just lying there behind the books. He probably didn't even –"

"Gilly, you stole it. Don't put no fancy name on it. It was his, and you took it, right?"

"I guess so."

"How much?"

"Uh, for– thir–"

"Don't fool with me. How much?"

"Forty-four dollars," Gilly said miserably.

"Well, you gotta take it back."

"I can't." Trotter stood there, hand on hip, staring at her until

Gilly continued, "I gave five dollars to Agnes Stokes."

"You did, huh?"

Gilly nodded.

"Well" – a great sigh – "I'll lend you the five to pay Mr Randolph back, and you can work it off."

Giving back Mr Randolph's money was not as bad as it might have been. The old man apparently had no idea that there had been any money behind his books. Either he'd forgotten, or it had been put there by his wife, dead long before Trotter's Melvin. At any rate, when Gilly gave the forty-four dollars to him, Trotter looming behind her like a mighty army, he accepted her mumbled explanation without showing shock or undue curiosity, but with a strange little dignity.

"Thank you," he said, for once not doubling the phrase. He put the money in his pocket, rubbed his hands together briefly, and then put out his hand to be led to supper.

Gilly hesitated for a moment, waiting for the sermon that was bound to pour forth, if not from him, surely from Trotter. But neither spoke, so she took Mr Randolph's hand, instead of his elbow as she usually did, as a kind of thank you.

Trotter had obviously never heard of either the minimum wage or the child labour laws. She posted the following sign in the kitchen:

Washing dishes and cleaning kitchen 10¢
Vacuuming downstairs 10¢
Cleaning both bathrooms including floors 10¢
Dusting 10¢
Helping William Ernest with schoolwork, one hour 25¢

Gilly began to spend a lot of time with W. E. She discovered several things. One was that the boy was not as dumb as he looked. If you held back and didn't press him, he could often figure out things for himself, but when you crowded him, he would choke right up, and if you laughed at him, he'd throw his hands up as if to protect his head from a blow. It finally occurred to Gilly that he really thought she would smack him every time he made a mistake.

Which was why, of course, Trotter tiptoed around the boy as though he would shatter at the least commotion, and why she was death on anyone she caught fooling around with him.

But it wasn't going to work. W. E. wasn't a fluted antique cup in Mrs Nevins's china cupboard. He was a kid – a foster kid. And if he didn't toughen up, what would happen to him when there was no Trotter to look after him?

So Gilly asked him, "What do you do when somebody socks you?"

His squinty little eyes went wild behind the glasses.

"I'm not going to hit you. I was just wondering what you do."

He stuck his right index finger into his mouth and began to tug at the nail.

She took out the finger and studied his stubby-nailed hand for a minute. "Nothing wrong with this, I can see. Ever think of smacking them back?"

He shook his head, wide-eyed.

"You going to go through life letting people pick on you?"

He hung his head. The finger went back in.

"Look, William Ernest" – she bent over close to his ear and whispered hoarsely into it – "I'm going to teach you how to fight. No charge or anything. Then when some big punk comes up to you and tries to start something, you can just let them have it."

His finger dropped from his mouth as he stared at her, unbelieving.

"You hear how I fought six boys one day – all by myself?"

He nodded solemnly.

"Before I get through with you, you're going to do the same thing. *Pow! Pow! Pow! Pow! Pow! Pow!*" She landed six imaginary punches sending six imaginary bullies flying.

"*Pow*," he echoed softly, tentatively doubling up his fist and giving a feeble swing.

"First thing, when somebody yells at you, don't throw your hands up" – she imitated him – "and act like you think they're going to kill you."

"*Pow?*" He swung his little fist in a kind of question mark.

"Naw, not *first* thing. See, they may not be even meaning to hit you. First thing is, you take a deep breath –" She filled her diaphragm and waited while he tried to imitate her, his ribs poking through his shirt. "Then you yell like this: *Get the hell outa my way!*"

Before the sentence was out, Trotter was filling the doorway like the wrath of God Almighty.

"OK, OK," Gilly said. "Leave out the hell part. The main thing –"

"What are you kids doing? I thought I was paying you to help William Ernest with his reading?"

"Naw. This is on my own time. No charge."

Trotter looked dubiously at W. E. He was standing on tiptoe, fists clenched, eyes squeezed shut in his red face, sucking in a huge breath.

"*Get the hell out my way!*" He turned to Gilly, smiling. "Was that good, Gilly?"

"Better leave the hell part out in front of Trotter. But that was pretty good for a start. Really not bad."

"Gilly," said Trotter.

"Look, Trotter. He's got to learn to take care of himself, and I'm the best damn – the best teacher around."

Trotter just went on standing in the doorway as though she couldn't think what to do next, when the little guy marched over to her, put his fists up in front of her huge bosom, took in a breath, and said squeakily, "Get out my way."

Tears started in the woman's eyes. She threw her arms around W. E. and bear-hugged him.

"I was just practising, Trotter. I didn't mean you."

"I know, William Ernest, honey," she said. "I know."

"He's got to learn to take care of himself in the world, Trotter."

The big woman wiped her face with her apron and sniffed.

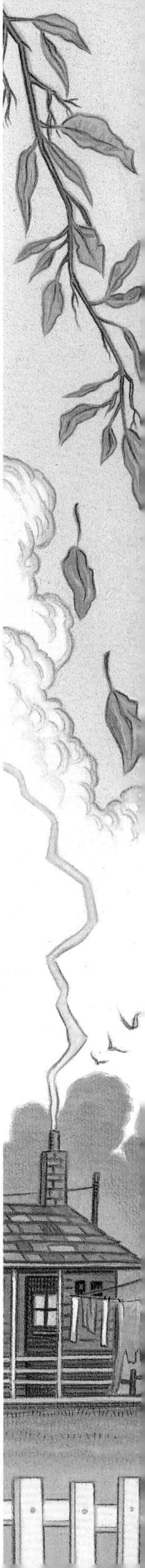

"Don't I know that, baby?" She patted the boy and straightened up. "How 'bout you finishing this lesson outside? I don't b'lieve it's something I want to listen to."

"C'mon, Gilly." William Ernest slid around Trotter and started for the back door. "*Pow! Pow!*" they could hear him exploding softly down the hall.

"I'm not going to teach him to pick on people," Gilly said, "just how to take care of himself. He can't come hiding behind your skirt every time someone looks at him cross-eyed."

"I s'pose not."

"Even real mothers can't watch out for kids the rest of their lives, and you're just his foster mother."

"So they keep telling me."

Gilly hadn't meant to be cruel, but she needed to make Trotter understand. "If he knows how to read and how to stick up for himself, he'll be OK."

"You got it all figured out, ain't you, Gilly, honey?" She relaxed into a smile. "Well, I ain't stopping your boxing lessons. I just don't care to watch."

Boxing lessons? The woman was a throwback to another century. Gilly started to pass her at the door, but as she brushed by the big body, Trotter grabbed her and planted a wet kiss on her forehead. One hand went up automatically to wipe the spot, but a look at Trotter's face, and Gilly stopped her arm midway.

"Don't know what got into me," Trotter mumbled, trying to turn it into a joke. "I know you don't allow no kissing. Sometimes I just haul off and go crazy."

"At Sunday school Miss Applegate calls it demon possession."

"Does she now? Demon possession, is it?" She began to laugh so hard, Gilly could feel the boards vibrating under her feet. "Demon possession – Mercy, girl, I'd have to catch me a jet to keep one step ahead of you. Well – you better get going before the devil grabs me one more time."

She waved her hand to land a mock spank on Gilly's bottom, but by the time it swept the air, Gilly's bottom, along with the rest of her, was well down the hall.

Introduction

All on board the Hispaniola *are bound for Treasure Island, but there's treachery afoot. Young Jim Hawkins, until now a great admirer of Long John Silver, climbs into a barrel to help himself to an apple. There he hears how Silver has nothing but mutiny and murder in his black heart, how he plans to kill Captain Smollett and all Jim's friends once they have found the treasure they seek. Trapped in the barrel, the worst is about to happen. It's Silver's voice, telling one of his cronies, ". . . you just jump up, like a sweet lad, and get me an apple . . .". But Jim is saved in the nick of time by the look-out's shout of "Land ho!" Now he must alert Captain Smollett to the danger ahead . . .*

M. M.

TREASURE ISLAND

ROBERT LOUIS STEVENSON

Council of War

There was a great rush of feet across the deck. I could hear people tumbling up from the cabin and the foc's'le; and, slipping in an instant outside my barrel, I dived behind the foresail, made a double towards the stern, and came out upon the open deck in time to join Hunter and Dr Livesey in the rush for the weather bow.

There all hands were already congregated. A belt of fog lifted almost simultaneously with the appearance of the moon. Away to the south-west of us we saw two low hills, about a couple of miles apart, and rising behind one of them a third and higher hill, whose peak was still buried in the fog. All three seemed sharp and conical in figure.

So much I saw, almost in a dream, for I had not yet recovered from my horrid fear of a minute or two before. And then I heard the voice of Captain Smollett issuing orders. The *Hispaniola* was laid a couple of points nearer the wind, and now sailed a course

that would just clear the island on the east.

"And now, men," said the captain, when all was sheeted home, "has any one of you ever seen that land ahead?"

"I have, sir," said Silver. "I've watered there with a trader I was cook in."

"The anchorage is on the south, behind an islet, I fancy?" asked the captain.

"Yes, sir; Skeleton Island they calls it. It were a main place for pirates once, and a hand we had on board knowed all their names for it. That hill to the nor'ard they calls the Fore-mast Hill; there are three hills in a row running south'ard – fore, main, and mizzen, sir. But the main – that's the big 'un, with the cloud on it – they usually calls the Spy-glass, by reason of a look-out they kept when they was in the anchorage cleaning; for it's there they cleaned their ships, sir, asking your pardon."

"I have a chart here," says Captain Smollett. "See if that's the place."

Long John's eyes burned in his head as he took the chart; but, by the fresh look of the paper, I knew he was doomed to disappointment. This was not the map we found in Billy Bones's chest, but an accurate copy, complete in all things – names and heights and soundings – with the single exception of the red crosses and the written notes. Sharp as must have been his annoyance, Silver had the strength of mind to hide it.

"Yes, sir," said he, "this is the spot to be sure; and very prettily drawed out. Who might have done that, I wonder? The pirates were too ignorant, I reckon. Ay, here it is: 'Capt. Kidd's Anchorage' – just the name my shipmate called it. There's a strong current runs along the south, and then away nor'ard up the west coast. Right you was, sir," says he, "to haul your wind and keep the weather of the island. Leastways, if such was your intention as to enter and careen, and there ain't no better place for that in these waters."

"Thank you, my man," says Captain Smollett. "I'll ask you, later on, to give us a help. You may go."

I was surprised at the coolness with which John avowed his knowledge of the island; and I own I was half-frightened when I saw him drawing nearer to myself. He did not know, to be sure, that I had overheard his council from the apple barrel, and yet I had, by this time, taken such a horror of his cruelty, duplicity, and power, that I could scarce conceal a shudder when he laid his hand upon my arm.

"Ah," says he, "this here is a sweet spot, this island – a sweet spot for a lad to get ashore on. You'll bathe, and you'll climb trees, and you'll hunt goats, you will; and you'll get aloft on them hills like a goat yourself. Why, it makes me young again. I was going to forget my timber leg, I was. It's a pleasant thing to be young, and have ten toes, and you may lay to that. When you want to go a bit of exploring, you just ask old John, and he'll put up a snack for you to take along."

And clapping me in the friendliest way upon the shoulder, he hobbled off forward and went below.

Captain Smollett, the squire, and Dr Livesey were talking together on the quarterdeck, and, anxious as I was to tell them my story, I durst not interrupt them openly. While I was still casting about in my thoughts to find some probable excuse, Dr Livesey called me to his side. He had left his pipe below, and being a slave to tobacco, had meant that I should fetch it; but as soon as I was near enough to speak and not to be overheard, I broke out immediately: "Doctor, let me speak. Get the captain and squire down to the cabin, and then make some pretence to send for me. I have terrible news."

The doctor changed countenance a little, but next moment he was master of himself.

"Thank you, Jim," said he, quite loudly, "that was all I wanted to know," as if he had asked me a question.

And with that he turned on his heel and rejoined the other two. They spoke together for a little, and though none of them started, or raised his voice, or so much as whistled, it was plain enough that Dr Livesey had communicated my request; for the next thing that I heard was the captain giving an order to Job Anderson, and all hands were piped on deck.

"My lads," said Captain Smollett, "I've a word to say to you. This land that we have sighted is the place we have been sailing for. Mr Trelawney, being a very open-handed gentleman, as we all know, has just asked me a word or two, and as I was able to tell him that every man on board had done his duty, alow and aloft, as I never ask to see it done better, why, he and I and the doctor are going below to the cabin to drink *your* health and luck, and you'll have grog served out for you to drink *our* health and luck. I'll tell you what I think of this: I think it handsome.

And if you think as I do, you'll give a good sea cheer for the gentleman that does it."

The cheer followed – that was a matter of course; but it rang out so full and hearty, that I confess I could hardly believe these same men were plotting for our blood.

"One more cheer for Cap'n Smollett," cried Long John, when the first had subsided.

And this also was given with a will.

On the top of that the three gentlemen went below, and not long after, word was sent forward that Jim Hawkins was wanted in the cabin.

I found them all three seated round the table, a bottle of Spanish wine and some raisins before them, and the doctor smoking away, with his wig on his lap, and that, I knew, was a sign that he was agitated. The stern window was open, for it was a warm night, and you could see the moon shining behind on the ship's wake.

"Now, Hawkins," said the squire, "you have something to say. Speak up."

I did as I was bid, and as short as I could make it, told the whole details of Silver's conversation. Nobody interrupted me till I was done, nor did any one of the three of them make so much as a movement, but they kept their eyes upon my face from first to last.

"Jim," said Dr Livesey, "take a seat."

And they made me sit down at table beside them, poured me out a glass of wine, filled my hands with raisins, and all three, one after the other, and each with a bow, drank my good health, and their service to me, for my luck and courage.

"Now, captain," said the squire, "you were right, and I was wrong. I own myself an ass, and I await your orders."

"No more an ass than I, sir," returned the captain. "I never heard of a crew that meant to mutiny but what showed signs before, for any man that had an eye in his head to see the mischief and take steps according. But this crew," he added, "beats me."

"Captain," said the doctor, "with your permission, that's Silver. A very remarkable man."

"He'd look remarkably well from a yard-arm, sir," returned the captain. "But this is talk; this don't lead to anything. I see three or four points, and with Mr Trelawney's permission, I'll name them."

"You, sir, are the captain. It is for you to speak," says Mr Trelawney, grandly.

"First point," began Mr Smollett. "We must go on, because we can't turn back. If I gave the word to go about, they would rise at once. Second point, we have time before us – at least, until this treasure's found. Third point, there are faithful hands. Now, sir, it's got to come to blows sooner or later; and what I propose is, to take time by the forelock, as the saying is, and come to blows

some fine day when they least expect it. We can count, I take it, on your own home servants, Mr Trelawney?"

"As upon myself," declared the squire.

"Three," reckoned the captain, "ourselves make seven, counting Hawkins, here. Now, about the honest hands?"

"Most likely Trelawney's own men," said the doctor; "those he had picked up for himself, before he lit on Silver."

"Nay," replied the squire, "Hands was one of mine."

"I did think I could have trusted Hands," added the captain.

"And to think that they're all Englishmen!" broke out the squire. "Sir, I could find it in my heart to blow the ship up."

"Well, gentlemen," said the captain, "the best that I can say is not much. We must lay to, if you please, and keep a bright look-out. It's trying on a man, I know. It would be pleasanter to come to blows. But there's no help for it till we know our men. Lay to, and whistle for a wind, that's my view."

"Jim here," said the doctor, "can help us more than anyone. The men are not shy with him, and Jim is a noticing lad."

"Hawkins, I put prodigious faith in you," added the squire.

I began to feel pretty desperate at this, for I felt altogether helpless; and yet, by an odd train of circumstances, it was indeed through me that safety came. In the meantime, talk as we pleased, there were only seven out of the twenty-six on whom we knew we could rely; and out of these seven one was a boy, so that the grown men on our side were six to their nineteen.

Introduction

No animal book has captivated readers and changed attitudes as much as Black Beauty, *published in 1877. Anna Sewell deliberately set out to show how badly horses were often treated, how they were used and abused, whether as carriage horses, cab horses or work horses. In* Black Beauty *we experience the story through Beauty's own eyes. We live with him, feel his pain and his joy. No one can doubt after reading this novel that horses have feelings, and that they should be treated with respect and kindness, as we should treat each other.*

M. M.

Black Beauty

Anna Sewell

A Stormy Day

One day late in the autumn, my master had a long journey to go on business. I was put into the dog-cart, and John went with his master. I always liked to go in the dog-cart, it was so light, and the high wheels ran along so pleasantly. There had been a great deal of rain, and now the wind was very high, and blew the dry leaves across the road in a shower. We went along merrily till we came to the toll-bar, and the low wooden bridge. The river banks were rather high, and the bridge, instead of rising, went across just level, so that in the middle, if the river was full, the water would be nearly up to the woodwork and planks; but as there were good substantial rails on each side, people did not mind it.

The man at the gate said the river was rising fast, and he feared it would be a bad night. Many of the meadows were under water, and in one low part of the road the water was halfway up to my

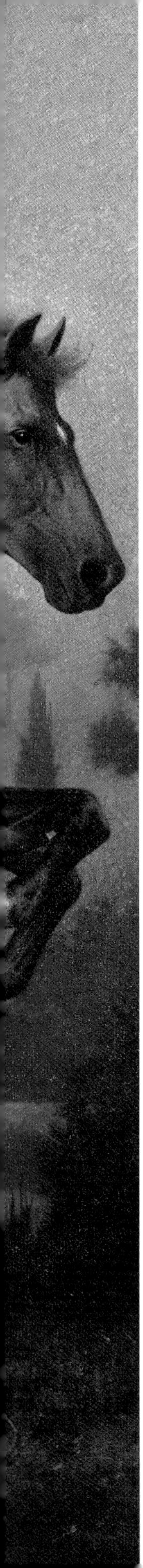

knees; the bottom was good, and the master drove gently, so it was no matter.

When we got to the town, of course, I had a good wait, but as the master's business engaged him a long time, we did not start for home till rather late in the afternoon. The wind was then much higher, and I heard the master say to John, he had never been out in such a storm; and so I thought, as we went along the skirts of a wood, where the great branches were swaying about like twigs, and the rushing sound was terrible.

"I wish we were well out of this wood," said my master.

"Yes, sir," said John, "it would be rather awkward if one of these branches came down upon us."

The words were scarcely out of his mouth, when there was a groan, and a crack, and a splitting sound, and tearing, crashing down amongst the other trees came an oak, torn up by the roots, and it fell right across the road just before us. I will never say I was not frightened, for I was. I stopped still, and I believe I trembled; of course, I did not turn round or run away; I was not brought up to that. John jumped out and was in a moment at my head.

"That was a very near touch," said my master. "What's to be done now?"

"Well, sir, we can't drive over that tree nor yet get round it; there will be nothing for it but to go back to the four crossways, and that will be a good six miles before we get round to the wooden bridge again; it will make us late, but the horse is fresh."

So back we went, and round by the crossroads; but by the time we got to the bridge it was very nearly dark, we could just see that the water was over the middle of it; but as that happened sometimes when the floods were out, master did not stop. We were going along at a good pace, but the moment my feet touched the first part of the bridge, I felt sure there was something wrong.

I dare not go forward, and I made a dead stop. "Go on, Beauty," said my master, and he gave me a touch with the whip, but I dare not stir; he gave me a sharp cut, I jumped, but I dare not go forward.

"There's something wrong, sir," said John, and he sprang out of the dog-cart and came to my head and looked all about. He tried to lead me forward, "Come on, Beauty, what's the matter?" Of course I could not tell him, but I knew very well that the bridge was not safe.

Just then, the man at the tollgate on the other side ran out of the house, tossing a torch about like one mad.

"Hoy, hoy, hoy, halloo, stop!" he cried.

"What's the matter?" shouted my master.

"The bridge is broken in the middle, and part of it is carried away; if you come on you'll be into the river."

"Thank God!" said my master. "You Beauty!" said John, and took the bridle and gently turned me round to the right-hand road by the river side. The sun had set some time, the wind seemed to have lulled off after that furious blast which tore up the tree. It grew darker and darker, stiller and stiller. I trotted quietly along, the wheels hardly making a sound on the soft road. For a good while neither master nor John spoke, and then master began in a serious voice. I could not understand much of what they said, but I found they thought, if I had gone on as the master wanted me, most likely the bridge would have given way under us, and horse, chaise, master and man would have fallen into the river; and as the current was flowing very strongly, and there was no light and no help at hand, it was more than likely we should all have been drowned. Master said God had given men reason by which they could find out things for themselves, but He had given animals knowledge which did not depend on reason, and which was

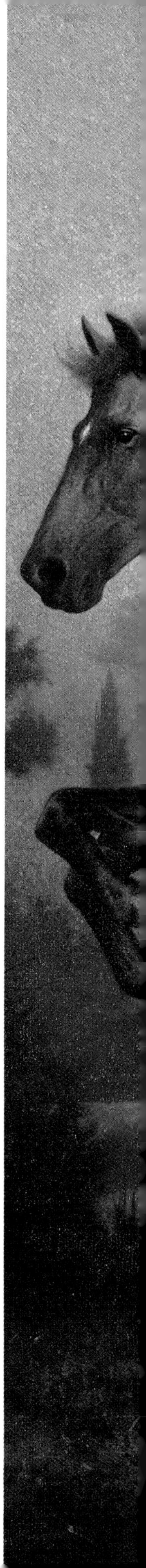

much more prompt and perfect in its way, and by which they had often saved the lives of men. John had many stories to tell of dogs and horses, and the wonderful things they had done; he thought people did not value their animals half enough, nor make friends of them as they ought to do. I am sure he makes friends of them if ever a man did.

At last we came to the Park gates, and found the gardener looking out for us. He said that mistress had been in a dreadful way ever since dark, fearing some accident had happened, and that she had sent James off on Justice, the roan cob, towards the wooden bridge to make enquiry after us.

We saw a light at the Hall door and at the upper windows, and as we came up mistress ran out, saying, "Are you really safe, my dear? Oh! I have been so anxious, fancying all sorts of things. Have you had no accident?"

"No, my dear; but if your Black Beauty had not been wiser than we were, we should all have been carried down the river at the wooden bridge." I heard no more, as they went into the house, and John took me to the stable. Oh, what a good supper he gave me that night, a good bran mash and some crushed beans with my oats, and such a thick bed of straw, and I was glad of it, for I was tired.

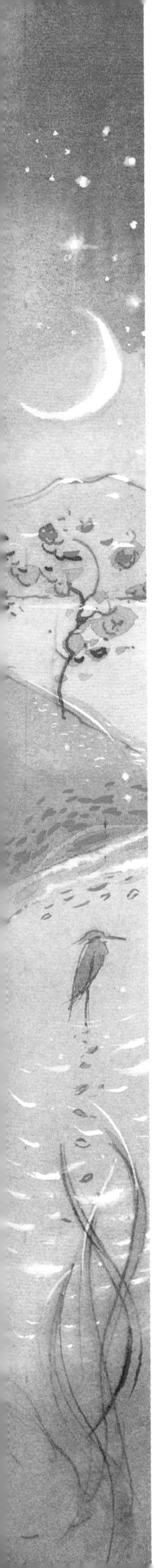

Introduction

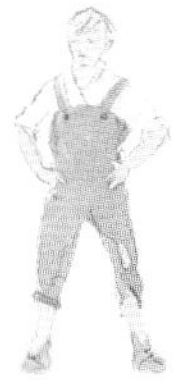

Tom Sawyer grows up in a small town on the Mississippi River. Whether with his Aunt Polly at home, or at school, Tom's always getting himself into a pickle of some sort. Here he's all crushed and crestfallen and feeling sorry for himself because his girlfriend, Becky Thatcher, who he's done his very best to impress, won't pay him any attention. So Tom decides he will leave home forever and roam abroad in the great world with his friends, Huckleberry Finn and Joe Harper. This is one of their marvellous capers – my favourite one, too.

M. M.

The Adventures of Tom Sawyer

Mark Twain

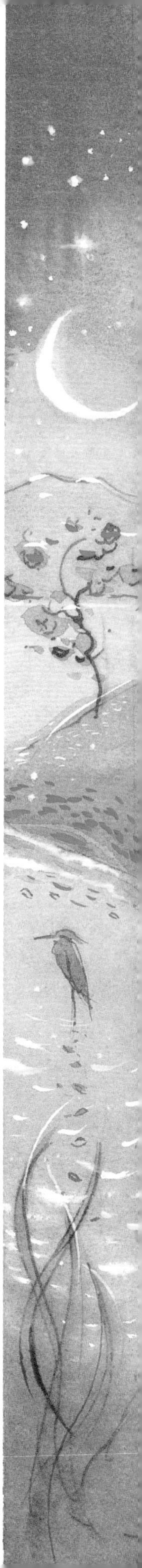

Tom's mind was made up now. He was gloomy and desperate. He was a forsaken, friendless boy, he said; nobody loved him; when they found out what they had driven him to, perhaps they would be sorry; he had tried to do right and get along, but they would not let him; since nothing would do them but to be rid of him, let it be so; and let them blame him for the consequences – why shouldn't they? What right had the friendless to complain? Yes, they had forced him to it at last: he would lead a life of crime. There was no choice.

By this time he was far down Meadow Lane, and the bell for school to "take up" tinkled faintly upon his ear. He sobbed, now, to think he should never, never hear that old familiar sound any more – it was very hard, but it was forced on him; since he was driven out into the cold world, he must submit – but he forgave them. Then the sobs came thick and fast.

Just at this point he met his soul's sworn comrade, Joe Harper – hard-eyed, and with evidently a great and dismal purpose in his heart. Plainly here were "two souls with but a single thought". Tom, wiping his eyes with his sleeve, began to blubber out something about a resolution to escape from hard usage and lack of sympathy at home by roaming abroad into the great world, never to return; and ended by hoping that Joe would not forget him.

But it transpired that this was a request which Joe had just been going to make of Tom, and had come to hunt him up for that purpose. His mother had whipped him for drinking some cream which he had never tasted and knew nothing about; it was plain that she was tired of him and wished him to go; if she felt that way, there was nothing for him to do but to succumb; he hoped she would be happy, and never regret having driven her poor boy out into the unfeeling world to suffer and die.

As the two boys walked sorrowing along, they made a new compact to stand by each other and be brothers, and never separate till death relieved them of their troubles. Then they began to lay their plans. Joe was for being a hermit, and living on crusts in a remote cave, and dying, sometime, of cold, and want, and grief; but, after listening to Tom, he conceded that there were some conspicuous advantages about a life of crime, and so he consented to be a pirate.

Three miles below St Petersburg, at a point where the Mississippi river was a trifle over a mile wide, there was a long, narrow, wooded island, with a shallow bar at the head of it, and this offered well as a rendezvous. It was not inhabited; it lay far over towards the farther shore, abreast a dense and almost wholly unpeopled forest. So Jackson's Island was chosen.

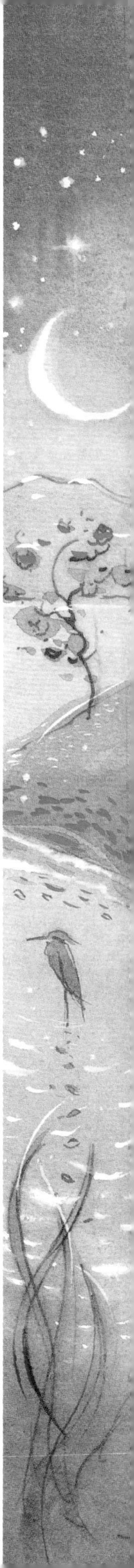

Who were to be the subjects of their piracies was a matter that did not occur to them. Then they hunted up Huckleberry Finn, and he joined them promptly, for all careers were one to him; he was indifferent. They presently separated, to meet at a lonely spot on the river bank two miles above the village, at the favourite hour, which was midnight. There was a small log raft there which they meant to capture. Each would bring hooks and lines, and such provisions as he could steal in the most dark and mysterious way – as became outlaws; and before the afternoon was done, they had all managed to enjoy the sweet glory of spreading the fact that pretty soon the town would "hear something". All who got this vague hint were cautioned to "be mum and wait".

About midnight Tom arrived with a boiled ham and a few trifles, and stopped in a dense undergrowth on a small bluff overlooking the meeting-place. It was starlight, and very still. The mighty river lay like an ocean at rest. Tom listened a moment, but no sound disturbed the quiet. Then he gave a low, distinct whistle. It was answered from under the bluff. Tom whistled twice more; these signals were answered in the same way. Then a guarded voice said:

"Who goes there?"

"Tom Sawyer, the Black Avenger of the Spanish Main. Name your names."

"Huck Finn the Red-handed, and Joe Harper the Terror of the Seas." Tom had furnished these titles from his favourite literature.

"'Tis well. Give the countersign."

Two hoarse whispers delivered the same awful word simultaneously to the brooding night:

"BLOOD!"

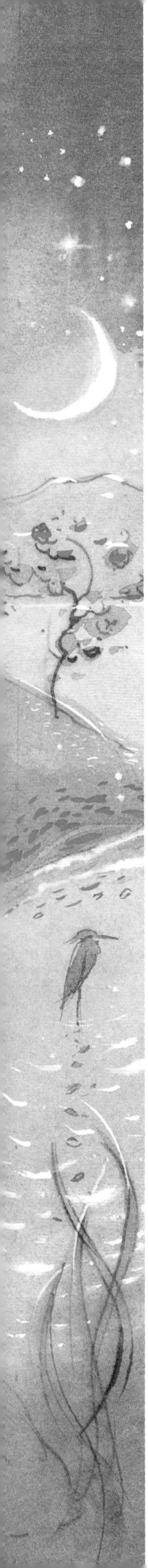

Then Tom tumbled his ham over the bluff and let himself down after it, tearing both skin and clothes to some extent in the effort. There was an easy, comfortable path along the shore under the bluff, but it lacked the advantages of difficulty and danger so valued by a pirate.

The Terror of the Seas had brought a side of bacon, and had about worn himself out with getting it there. Finn the Red-handed had stolen a skillet, and a quantity of half-cured leaf-tobacco, and had also brought a few corn-cobs to make pipes with. But none of the pirates smoked or "chewed" but himself. The Black Avenger of the Spanish Main said it would never do to start without some fire. That was a wise thought; matches were hardly known there in that day. They saw a fire smouldering upon a great raft a hundred yards above, and they went stealthily thither and helped themselves to a chunk. They made an imposing adventure of it, saying "hist" every now and then and suddenly halting with finger on lip; moving with hands on imaginary dagger-hilts; and giving orders in dismal whispers that if "the foe" stirred to "let him have it to the hilt", because "dead men tell no tales". They knew well enough that the raftmen were all down at the village laying in stores or having a spree, but still that was no excuse for their conducting this thing in an unpiratical way.

They shoved off presently, Tom in command, Huck at the left oar and Joe at the forward. Tom stood amidships, gloomy-browed and with folded arms, and gave his orders in a low, stern whisper.

"Luff, and bring her to the wind!"

"Aye, aye, sir!"

"Steady, steady-y-y-y!"

"Steady it is, sir!"

"Let her go off a point!"

"Point it is, sir!"

As the boys steadily and monotonously drove the raft towards mid-stream, it was no doubt understood that these orders were given only for "style", and were not intended to mean anything in particular.

"What sail's she carrying?"

"Courses, tops'ls, and flying-jib, sir!"

"Send the r'yals up! Lay out aloft there, half a dozen of ye, foretomast-stuns'l! Lively, now!"

"Aye, aye, sir!"

"Shake out that mainto-galans'l! Sheets and braces! *Now*, my hearties!"

"Aye, aye, sir!"

"Hellum-a-lee – hard a-port! Stand by to meet her when she comes! Port, port! *Now*, men! With a will! Stead-y-y!"

"Steady it is, sir!"

The raft drew beyond the middle of the river; the boys pointed her head right and then lay on their oars. The river was not high, so there was not more than a two or three mile current.

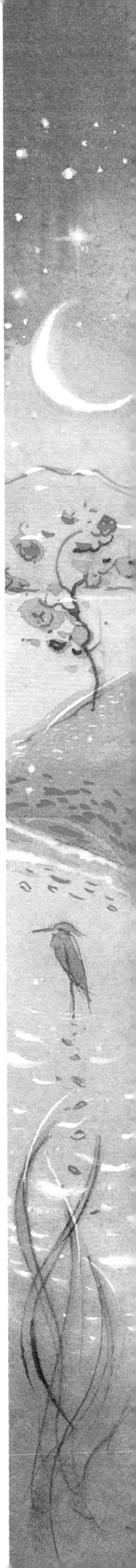

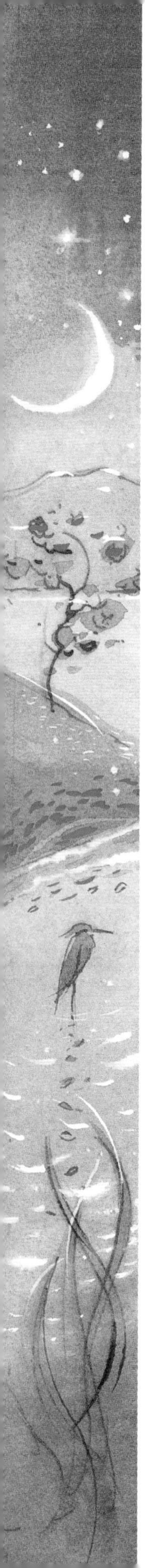

Hardly a word was said during the next three-quarters of an hour. Now the raft was passing before the distant town. Two or three glimmering lights showed where it lay, peacefully sleeping, beyond the vague vast sweep of star-gemmed water, unconscious of the tremendous event that was happening. The Black Avenger stood still with folded arms, "looking his last" upon the scene of his former joys and his later sufferings, and wishing "she" could see him, now abroad on the wild sea, facing peril and death with dauntless heart, going to his doom with a grim smile on his lips. It was but a small strain on his imagination to remove Jackson's Island beyond eyeshot of the village, and so he "looked his last" with a broken and satisfied heart. The other pirates were looking their last, too; and they all looked so long that they came near letting the current drift them out of the range of the island. But they discovered the danger in time, and made shift to avert it. About two o'clock in the morning the raft grounded on the bar two hundred yards above the head of the island, and they waded back and forth until they had landed their freight. Part of the little raft's belongings consisted of an old sail, and this they spread over a nook in the bushes for a tent to shelter their provisions; but they themselves would sleep in the open air in good weather, as became outlaws.

They built a fire against the side of a great log twenty or thirty steps within the sombre depths of the forest, and then cooked some bacon in the frying-pan for supper, and used up half of the corn "pone" stock they had brought. It seemed glorious sport to be feasting in that wild free way in the virgin forest of an unexplored and uninhabited island, far from the haunts of men, and they said they would never return to civilization. The climbing fire lit up their faces and threw

its ruddy glare upon the pillared tree-trunks of their forest temple, and upon the varnished foliage and festooning vines. When the last crisp slice of bacon was gone, and the last allowance of corn pone devoured, the boys stretched themselves out on the grass, filled with contentment. They could have found a cooler place, but they would not deny themselves such a romantic feature as the roasting camp-fire.

"*Ain't* it jolly?" said Joe.

"It's *nuts*," said Tom. "What would the boys say if they could see us?"

"Say? Well, they'd just die to be here – hey, Hucky?"

"I reckon so," said Huckleberry; "anyways *I'm* suited. I don't want nothing better'n this. I don't ever get enough to eat gen'ally – and here they can't come and kick at a feller and bullyrag him so."

"It's just the life for me," said Tom. "You don't have to get up, mornings, and you don't have to go to school, and wash, and all that blame foolishness. You see a pirate don't have to do *anything*, Joe, when he's ashore, but a hermit *he* has to be praying considerable, and then he don't have any fun, anyway, all by himself that way."

"Oh yes, that's so," said Joe, "but I hadn't thought much about it, you know. I'd a good deal ruther be a pirate now that I've tried it."

"You see," said Tom, "people don't go much on hermits, now-a-days, like they used to in old times, but a pirate's always respected. And a hermit's got to sleep on the hardest place he can find, and put sackcloth and ashes on his head, and stand out in the rain, and –"

"What does he put sackcloth and ashes on his head for?" inquired Huck.

"*I* dunno. But they've *got* to do it. Hermits always do. You'd have to do that if you was a hermit."

"Dern'd if I would," said Huck.

"Well, what would you do?"

"I dunno. But I wouldn't do that."

"Why, Huck, you'd *have* to. How'd you get around it?"

"Why, I just wouldn't stand it. I'd run away."

"Run away! Well, you *would* be a nice old slouch of a hermit. You'd be a disgrace."

The Red-handed made no response, being better employed. He had finished gouging out a cob, and now he fitted a weed stem to it, loaded it with tobacco, and was pressing a coal to the charge and blowing a cloud of fragrant smoke; he was in the full bloom of luxurious contentment. The other pirates envied him this majestic vice, and secretly resolved to acquire it shortly. Presently Huck said:

"What do pirates have to do?"

Tom said:

"Oh, they have just a bully time – take ships, and burn them, and get the money and bury it in awful places in their island where there's ghosts and things to watch it, and kill everybody in the ships – make 'em walk a plank."

"And they carry the women to the island," said Joe; "they don't kill the women."

"No," assented Tom, "they don't kill the women – they're too noble. And the women's always beautiful, too."

"And don't they wear the bulliest clothes! Oh, no! All gold and silver and di'monds," said Joe with enthusiasm.

"Who?" said Huck.

"Why, the pirates."

Huck scanned his own clothing forlornly.

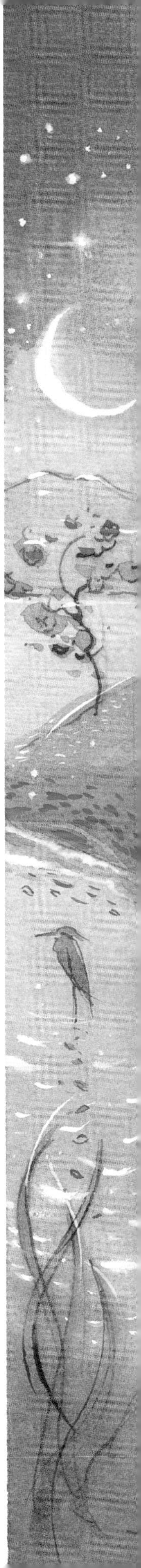

"I reckon I ain't dressed fit for a pirate," said he, with a regretful pathos in his voice; "but I ain't got none but these."

But the other boys told him the fine clothes would come fast enough after they should have begun their adventures. They made him understand that his poor rags would do to begin with, though it was customary for wealthy pirates to start with a proper wardrobe.

Gradually their talk died out and drowsiness began to steal upon the eyelids of the little waifs. The pipe dropped from the fingers of the Red-handed, and he slept the sleep of the conscience-free and the weary. The Terror of the Seas and the Black Avenger of the Spanish Main had more difficulty in getting to sleep. They said their prayers inwardly, and lying down, since there was nobody there with authority to make them kneel and recite aloud; in truth they had a mind not to say them at all, but they were afraid to proceed to such lengths as that, lest they might call down a sudden and special thunder-bolt from heaven. Then at once they reached and hovered upon the imminent verge of sleep – but an intruder came now that would not "down". It was conscience. They began to feel a vague fear that they had been doing wrong to run away; and next they thought of the stolen meat, and then the real torture came. They tried to argue it away by reminding conscience that they had purloined sweetmeats and apples scores of times; but conscience was not to be appeased by such thin plausibilities. It seemed to them, in the end, that there was no getting around the stubborn fact that taking sweetmeats was only "hooking" while taking bacon and ham and such valuables was plain, simple stealing – and there was a command against that in the Bible. So they inwardly resolved that so long as they remained in the business, their piracies should not again be sullied with the crime of stealing. Then conscience granted a truce, and these curiously inconsistent pirates fell peacefully to sleep.

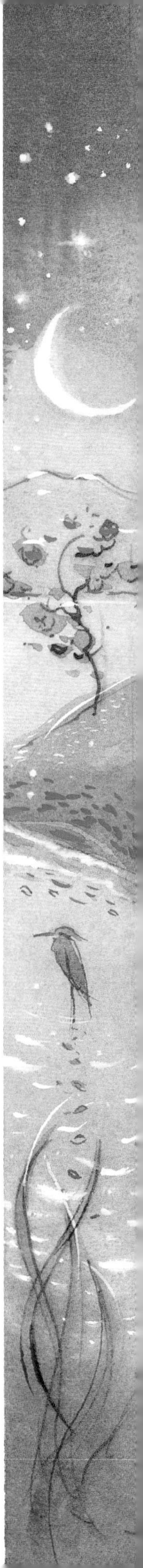

Introduction

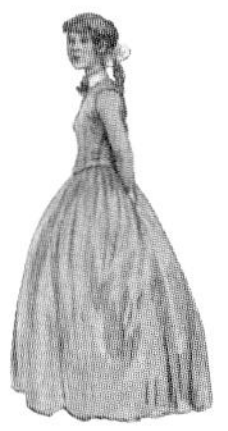

Of the four March girls, it is fifteen-year-old Jo who likes to act the head of the family now that their father is away fighting in the Civil War. In his letters home, he calls his daughters "Little Women" because they help their mother around the house during these difficult war years. Meg, the eldest, is sweet and patient but sometimes in a muddle. Beth is shy and gentle. Amy, the baby of the family, is just a little self-important, but means well. Jo, a real tomboy, always wants to be doing something interesting or going somewhere exciting. She loves to act and to dress up, often taking the male role. Like the time at Christmas when they put on a very special play for their friends. After the show, they tuck into the most splendid feast, provided by their neighbour, old Mr Laurence, and delivered by his grandson, "the Laurence boy". Jo would like to know the Laurence boy better. Perhaps there will be an opportunity in the not too distant future . . .

R. S.

LITTLE WOMEN

LOUISA MAY ALCOTT

The Laurence Boy

"Jo! Jo! Where are you?" cried Meg, at the foot of the garret stairs.

"Here!" answered a husky voice from above; and running up, Meg found her sister eating apples and crying over the *Heir of Redcliffe,* wrapped up in a comforter on an old three-legged sofa by the sunny window. This was Jo's favourite refuge; and here she loved to retire with half-a-dozen russets and a nice book, to enjoy the quiet and the society of a pet rat who lived nearby, and didn't mind her a particle. As Meg appeared, Scrabble whisked into his hole. Jo shook the tears off her cheeks, and waited to hear the news.

"Such fun! Only see! A regular note of invitation from Mrs Gardiner for tomorrow night!" cried Meg, waving the precious paper, and then proceeding to read it, with girlish delight.

"'Mrs Gardiner would be happy to see Miss March and Miss Josephine at a little dance on New Year's Eve.' Marmee is willing we should go; now what *shall* we wear?"

"What's the use of asking that, when you know we shall wear our poplins, because we haven't got anything else?" answered Jo, with her mouth full.

"If I only had a silk!" sighed Meg. "Mother says I may when I'm eighteen, perhaps; but two years is an everlasting time to wait."

"I'm sure our pops look like silk, and they are nice enough for us. Yours is as good as new, but I forgot the burn and the tear in mine. Whatever shall I do? The burn shows badly, and I can't take any out."

"You must sit still all you can, and keep your back out of sight; the front is all right. I shall have a new ribbon in my hair, and Marmee will lend me her little pearl pin, and my new slippers are lovely, and my gloves will do, though they aren't as nice as I'd like."

"Mine are spoilt with lemonade, and I can't get any new ones, so I shall have to go without," said Jo, who never troubled herself much about dress.

"You *must* have gloves, or I won't go," cried Meg decidedly. "Gloves are more important than anything else; you can't dance without them, and if you don't I should be *so* mortified."

"Then I'll stay still. I don't care much for company dancing; it's no fun to go sailing round; I like to fly about and cut capers."

"You can't ask mother for new ones, they are so expensive, and you are so careless. She said, when you spoilt the others, that she shouldn't get you any more this winter. Can't you make them do?" asked Meg anxiously.

"I can hold them crumpled up in my hand, so no one will know how stained they are; that's all I can do. No! I'll tell you how we can manage – each wear one good one and carry a bad one; don't you see?"

"Your hands are bigger than mine, and you will stretch my glove dreadfully," began Meg, whose gloves were a tender point with her.

"Then I'll go without. I don't care what people say!" cried Jo, taking up her book.

"You may have it, you may! Only don't stain it, and do behave nicely. Don't put your hands behind you, or stare, or say 'Christopher Columbus!' will you?"

"Don't worry about me; I'll be as prim as I can, and not get into any scrapes, if I can help it. Now go and answer your note, and let me finish this splendid story."

So Meg went away to "accept with thanks", look over her dress, and sing blithely as she did up her one real lace frill; while Jo finished her story, her four apples, and had a game of romps with Scrabble.

On New Year's Eve the parlour was deserted, for the two younger girls played dressing-maids, and the two elder were absorbed in the all-important business of "getting ready for the party". Simple as the toilets were, there was a great deal of running up and down, laughing and talking, and at one time a strong smell of burnt hair pervaded the house. Meg wanted a few curls about her face, and Jo undertook to pinch the papered locks with a pair of hot tongs.

"Ought they to smoke like that?" asked Beth, from her perch on the bed.

"It's the dampness drying," replied Jo.

"What a queer smell! It's like burnt feathers," observed Amy, smoothing her own pretty curls with a superior air.

"There, now I'll take off the papers and you'll see a cloud of little ringlets," said Jo, putting down the tongs.

She did take off the papers, but no cloud of ringlets appeared, for the hair came with the papers, and the horrified hairdresser laid a row of little scorched bundles on the bureau before her victim.

"Oh, oh, oh! What *have* you done? I'm spoilt! I can't go! My hair, oh, my hair!" wailed Meg, looking with despair at the uneven frizzle on her forehead.

"Just my luck! You shouldn't have asked me to do it; I always spoil everything. I'm so sorry, but the tongs were too hot, and so I've made a mess," groaned poor Jo, regarding the black pancakes with tears of regret.

"It isn't spoilt; just frizzle it, and tie your ribbon so the ends come on your forehead a bit, and it will look like the last fashion. I've seen many girls do it so," said Amy consolingly.

"Serves me right for trying to be fine. I wish I'd let my hair alone," cried Meg petulantly.

"So do I, it was so smooth and pretty. But it will soon grow out again," said Beth, coming to kiss and comfort the shorn sheep.

After various lesser mishaps, Meg was finished at last, and by the united exertions of the family, Jo's hair was got up, and her dress on. They looked very well in their simple suits – Meg in silvery drab, with a blue velvet snood, lace frills, and the pearl pin; Jo in maroon, with a stiff, gentlemanly linen collar, and a white chrysanthemum or two for her only ornament. Each put on one nice light glove, and carried one soiled one, and all pronounced the effect "quite easy and fine", Meg's high-heeled slippers were very tight, and hurt her, though she would not own it, and Jo's nineteen hair pins all seemed stuck straight into her head, which was not exactly comfortable; but, dear me, let us be elegant or die!

"Have a good time, dearies," said Mrs March, as the sisters went daintily down the walk. "Don't eat much supper, and come away at eleven, when I send Hannah for you." As the gate clashed behind them, a voice cried from a window, –

"Girls, girls! *have* you both got nice pocket-handkerchiefs?"

"Yes, yes, spandy nice, and Meg has cologne on hers," cried Jo, adding, with a laugh, as they went on, "I do believe Marmee would ask that if we were all running away from an earthquake."

"It is one of her aristocratic tastes, and quite proper, for a real lady is always known by neat boots, gloves, and handkerchief," replied Meg, who had a good many little "aristocratic tastes" of her own.

"Now don't forget to keep the bad breadth out of sight, Jo. Is my sash right? And does my hair look *very* bad?" said Meg, as she turned from the glass in Mrs Gardiner's dressing-room, after a prolonged prink.

"I know I shall forget. If you see me doing anything wrong, just remind me by a wink, will you?" returned Jo, giving her collar a twitch, and her head a hasty brush.

"No, winking isn't ladylike; I'll lift my eyebrows if anything is wrong, and nod if you are all right. Now hold your shoulders straight, and take short steps, and don't shake hands if you are introduced to any one, it isn't the thing."

"How *do* you learn all the proper ways? I never can. Isn't that music gay?"

Down they went, feeling a trifle timid, for they seldom went to parties, and, informal as this little gathering was, it was an event to them. Mrs Gardiner, a stately old lady, greeted them kindly, and handed them over to the eldest of her six daughters. Meg knew Sallie, and was at her ease very soon; but Jo, who didn't care much for girls or girlish gossip, stood about with her back carefully against the wall, and felt as much out of place as a colt in a flower-garden. Half-a-dozen jovial lads were talking about skates in another part of the room, and she longed to go and join them, for skating was one of the joys of her life. She telegraphed her wish to Meg, but the eyebrows went up so alarmingly that she dared not stir. No one came to talk to her, and one by one the group near her dwindled away, till she was left alone. She could not roam about and amuse herself for the burnt breadth would show, so she stared at people rather forlornly till the dancing began. Meg was asked at once, and the tight slippers tripped about so briskly that none would have guessed the pain their wearer suffered smilingly. Jo saw a big, red-headed youth approaching her corner, and fearing he meant to engage her, she slipped into a curtained recess, intending to peep and enjoy herself in peace. Unfortunately another bashful person had chosen the same refuge; for, as the curtain fell behind her, she found herself face to face with the "Laurence boy".

"Dear me, I didn't know any one was here!" stammered Jo, preparing to back out as speedily as she had bounced in.

But the boy laughed, and said pleasantly, though he looked a little startled, –

"Don't mind me; stay if you like."

"Shan't I disturb you?"

"Not a bit; I only came here because I don't know many people, and felt rather strange at first, you know."

"So did I. Don't go away, please, unless you'd rather."

The boy sat down again and looked at his pumps, till Jo said, trying to be polite and easy, –

"I think I've had the pleasure of seeing you before; you live near us, don't you?"

"Next door;" and he looked up and laughed outright, for Jo's prim manner was rather funny when he remembered how they had chatted about cricket when he brought the cat home.

That put Jo at her ease; and she laughed too, as she said, in her heartiest way, –

"We did have such a good time over your nice Christmas present."

"Grandpa sent it."

"But you put it into his head, didn't you, now?"

"How is your cat, Miss March?" asked the boy, trying to look sober, while his black eyes shone with fun.

"Nicely, thank you, Mr Laurence; but I am not Miss March, I'm only Jo," returned the young lady.

"I'm not Mr Laurence; I'm only Laurie."

"Laurie Laurence – what an odd name."

"My first name is Theodore, but I don't like it, for the fellows called me Dora, so I made them say Laurie instead."

"I hate my name, too – so sentimental! I wish every one would say Jo, instead of Josephine. How did you make the boys stop calling you Dora?"

"I thrashed 'em."

"I can't thrash Aunt March, so I suppose I shall have to bear it;" and Jo resigned herself with a sigh.

"Don't you like to dance, Miss Jo?" asked Laurie, as if he thought the name suited her.

"I like it well enough if there is plenty of room, and everyone is lively. In a place like this, I'm sure to upset something, tread on people's toes, or do something dreadful, so I keep out of mischief, and let Meg sail about. Don't you dance?"

"Sometimes; you see I've been abroad a good many years, and haven't been into company enough yet to know how you do things here."

"Abroad!" cried Jo. "Oh, tell me about it! I love to hear people describe their travels."

Laurie didn't seem to know where to begin; but Jo's eager

questions soon set him going, and he told her how he had been at school in Vevey, where the boys never wore hats, and had a fleet of boats on the lake, and for holiday fun went on walking trips about Switzerland with their teachers.

"Don't I wish I'd been there!" cried Jo. "Did you go to Paris?"

"We spent last winter there."

"Can you talk French?"

"We were not allowed to speak anything else at Vevey."

"Do say some. I can read it, but can't pronounce."

"*Quel nom a cette jeune demoiselle en les pantoufles jolis?*" said Laurie good-naturedly.

"How nicely you do it! Let me see – you said, 'Who is the young lady in the pretty slippers?', didn't you?"

"*Oui, mademoiselle.*"

"It's my sister Margaret, and you knew it was! Do you think she is pretty?"

"Yes; she makes me think of the German girls, she looks so fresh and quiet, and dances like a lady."

Jo quite glowed with pleasure at this boyish praise of her sister, and stored it up to repeat to Meg. Both peeped and criticized and chatted, till they felt like old acquaintances. Laurie's bashfulness soon wore off, for Jo's gentlemanly demeanour amused and set him at his ease, and Jo was her merry self again, because her dress was forgotten, and nobody lifted their eyebrows at her. She liked the "Laurence boy" better than ever, and took several good looks at him, so that she might describe him to the girls; for they had no brothers, very few male cousins, and boys were almost unknown creatures to them.

"Curly black hair, brown skin, big black eyes, handsome nose, fine teeth, small hands and feet, taller than I am; very polite for a boy, and altogether jolly. Wonder how old he is?"

It was on the tip of Jo's tongue to ask; but she checked herself in time, and, with unusual tact, tried to find out in a roundabout way.

"I suppose you are going to college soon? I see you pegging away at your books – no, I mean studying hard;" and Jo blushed at the dreadful "pegging" which had escaped her.

Laurie smiled, but didn't seem shocked, and answered with a shrug, –

"Not for a year or two; I won't go before seventeen, anyway."

"Aren't you but fifteen?" asked Jo, looking at the tall lad whom she had imagined seventeen already.

"Sixteen next month."

"How I wish I was going to college! You don't look as if you liked it."

"I hate it! Nothing but grinding or skylarking. And I don't like the way fellows do either, in this country."

"What do you like?"

"To live in Italy, and to enjoy myself in my own way."

Jo wanted very much to ask what his own way was; but his black brows looked rather threatening as he knit them, so she changed the subject by saying, as her foot kept time, "That's a splendid polka! Why don't you go and try it?"

"If you come too," he answered, with a gallant little bow.

"I can't; for I told Meg I wouldn't, because" – There Jo stopped, and looked undecided whether to tell or to laugh.

"Because what?" asked Laurie curiously.

"You won't tell?"

"Never!"

"Well, I have a bad trick of standing before the fire, and so I burn my frocks, and I scorched this one; and, though it's nicely mended, it shows, and Meg told me to keep still, so no one would see it. You may laugh if you want to; it is funny, I know."

But Laurie didn't laugh; he only looked down a minute, and the expression of his face puzzled Jo, when he said very gently, –

"Never mind that; I'll tell you how we can manage: there's a long hall out there, and we can dance grandly, and no one will see us. Please come?"

Jo thanked him, and gladly went, wishing she had two neat gloves, when she saw the nice pearl-coloured ones her partner wore. The hall was empty, and they had a grand polka, for Laurie danced well, and taught her the German step, which delighted Jo, being full of swing and spring.

Notes on the Authors

Louisa May Alcott (1832–88) was born in Pennsylvania, USA. She worked as a teacher, seamstress and domestic servant, and as an army nurse during the American Civil War. She also edited a children's magazine. Her most famous novel, *Little Women*, was published in 1868 and is regarded as the first family story written for children. A sequel, *Good Wives*, followed in 1869. The character of Jo is based largely on Louisa May Alcott herself, and the author's sisters served as models for the other March girls.

Sir J(ames) M(atthew) Barrie (1860–1937) was born in Kirriemuir, Scotland, the ninth child in a weaver's family. When a young man, he worked in London as a journalist and he quickly became successful as a playwright and novelist. Now he is remembered best for *Peter Pan*, written first as a play in 1904 and only later (in 1911) as a story. It is dedicated to "the Five" – the orphaned sons of Sylvia Llewellyn Davies, with whom Barrie played at pirates in Kensington Gardens.

L(yman) Frank Baum (1856–1919) was born in Chittenago, New York, USA. During his varied career he worked as a newspaper reporter, a poultry farmer, a comic actor and a travelling salesman (with Baum's Ever-Ready Castorine axle grease). He was also a founding director of the Oz Film Manufacturing Company in Los Angeles. He wrote nearly one hundred books (some published under pseudonyms), but it is for the enduringly popular *The Wonderful Wizard of Oz* (published in 1900) that he is best remembered. It was followed by over twenty more books about the land of Oz – which got its name from the letters O–Z on his filing cabinet drawer!

Joyce Lankester Brisley (1896–1978) was born in Sussex, England. She began writing and illustrating at an early age, and when she was thirteen had her first story published in a children's magazine. She studied at Lambeth Art School for two years and at the age of twenty had pictures exhibited at the Royal Academy in London. Her most famous character, Milly-Molly-Mandy, first appeared in *The Christian Science Monitor* in 1925, and she went on to write and illustrate many popular stories about the little girl in the pink and white striped dress.

Frances Hodgson Burnett (1849–1924) was born in Manchester, England, but emigrated with her mother to Tennessee, USA, at the age of sixteen. Her first stories were published three years later and she became a prolific writer for both adults and children. Sara Crewe first appeared in a story in 1888 which became a play in 1902, and finally a full-length novel, *A Little Princess*, in 1905. It is for this book, together with two of her other children's novels, *Little Lord Fauntleroy* (1886) and *The Secret Garden* (1911), that she is best remembered.

Lewis Carroll (1832–98) was the pseudonym of Charles Lutwidge Dodgson, who was born in Cheshire, England. The eldest of a family of eleven, as a child he edited his own magazines. *Alice's Adventures in Wonderland* began as a story to entertain Alice Liddell, one of the daughters of the Dean of Oxford University's Christ Church, where Charles Dodgson was a lecturer in mathematics. The book was published in 1865 and was followed in 1871 by *Through the Looking-Glass and What Alice Found There.*

Beverly Cleary was born in 1916 in Oregon, USA. Of her many successful books, those featuring the exploits of Ramona Quimby, her sister Beezus, their friend Henry and his dog Ribsy are probably the most popular. Ramona herself first appeared in 1950 in *Henry Huggins* and there are now over a dozen titles in the series. *Ramona the Pest* was published in 1968. Beverly Cleary has received many awards for her writing, including the American Library Association's Laura Ingalls Wilder Award (for *Ramona the Brave* in 1975) and the Newbery Medal (for *Ramona Forever* in 1984).

Carlo Collodi (1826–90) was the pseudonym of Carlo Lorenzini, who was born into a poor family in Florence, Italy. He was, in turn, a student at a seminary, a part-time soldier, a librarian, and a civil servant, until, aged fifty, he found his true vocation as a writer and translator of Perrault's fairy tales. The first story about Pinocchio appeared in a children's newspaper and was immediately popular. A collection of the stories was published in 1883 and first appeared in English translation in 1892.

Susan Coolidge (1835–1905) was the pseudonym of Sarah Chauncy Woolsey, who was born in Ohio, USA. During the American Civil War she worked in hospitals and helped to organize a national nursing service. Later she became a literary critic and worked as a consultant for a Boston publisher. She is best known for creating the character of Katy Carr, the feisty heroine of *What Katy Did*, published in 1872 and the first of five Katy novels.

Richmal Crompton (1890–1969) was the pseudonym of Richmal Crompton Lamburn, who was born in Lancashire, England. She taught Classics at a girls' school until an attack of polio in 1923 crippled her, forcing her to give up her job. She had already started to write stories about William Brown for adult readers of *Home Magazine*. These became popular with children, too, following their first publication in book form in 1922. In all, over forty books were published about William, who is said to share many characteristics with the author's own brother.

Roald Dahl (1916–90) was born in South Wales to Norwegian parents. In his autobiography, *Boy* (1984), he describes how he turned down university in favour of a job that would take him to "wonderful faraway places". After working in East Africa he became an RAF fighter pilot during World War II, and it was while he was stationed in Washington, USA, as Assistant Air Attaché that he began to write. *Charlie and the Chocolate Factory*, published in 1964, was a major success and many more books for children followed. The illustrations of Quentin Blake (the UK's first Children's Laureate) have become synonymous with Roald Dahl's stories.

Charles Dickens (1812–70) was born in Portsmouth, England. He never forgot the family's misery when his father was sent to prison for debt and he himself went to work in a blacking factory, aged just twelve. With great determination he became a shorthand reporter in the House of Commons and went on to write novels that made him immensely popular in both the UK and the USA. First appearing in short parts in the monthly magazine *Bentley's Miscellany*, *Oliver Twist* was published in book form in 1838.

Jean Craighead George was born in 1919 in Washington, DC, USA. She learned about living off the land when her father took her and her brothers exploring along the Potomac River. She even planned to run away from home (as Sam Gribley does) but was back within the hour! She has written many more stories about animals and nature, including *Julie of the Wolves*, which won the American Library Association Newbery Medal. *My Side of the Mountain* was published in 1959.

Kenneth Grahame (1859–1932) was born in Edinburgh, Scotland and grew up in the English village of Cookham Dene, the main setting of *The Wind in the Willows*. He worked for the Bank of England and originally created the adventures of Ratty, Mole, Toad and friends for his young son Alistair, only later turning the stories into a book. A stage version, *Toad of Toad Hall*, was produced in 1930, dramatized by A. A. Milne. He wrote several other books for children, including *The Golden Age* and *Dream Days*.

Ted Hughes (1930–98) was born in Yorkshire, England. On leaving university, he worked at a number of jobs (rose gardener, night watchman, zoo attendant) until his writing brought him recognition as a poet and playwright of great power and accomplishment. In 1984 he became the UK's Poet Laureate. *The Iron Man* (retitled *The Iron Giant* in the USA) was published in 1968, and made into an animated film in 1999.

Rudyard Kipling (1865–1936) was born in Bombay, India. Sent home to England to go to school, he was wretchedly unhappy, but returned to India in 1882 as a journalist, which proved the start of his career as an author and poet. He wrote the first Mowgli story while living with his American wife in Vermont, USA, and it was published in the children's magazine *St Nicholas* in 1894. The six stories that make up the first *Jungle Book* appeared in book form later that year.

C(live) S(taples) Lewis (1898–1963) was born in Belfast, Northern Ireland. He had a lonely childhood and found his chief pleasure in reading. He grew up to become a scholar of English Literature, teaching at the universities of both Oxford and Cambridge. He wrote books of literary criticism and religious study,

as well as science fiction novels and stories for children. *The Lion, the Witch and the Wardrobe*, published in 1950, was the first of seven *Chronicles of Narnia*, which were, he said, "the books I should have liked to read . . . that's always been my reason for writing."

Astrid Lindgren (1907–2002) was born in Vimmerby, Sweden. She began her writing career by winning a children's book competition in 1944 and later became a children's book editor. She published over forty novels and received numerous accolades, including the International Hans Christian Andersen Award and the International Book Award. Her most famous character, the irrepressible Pippi Longstocking, first appeared in 1950, and the series of books about her continue to be hugely popular throughout the world.

Jack London (1876–1916) was born in California, USA. By the time he was eighteen he had worked in a factory, become an oyster pirate, sailed with a sealing ship, and marched with two thousand unemployed men across the US to demand work. In 1897 he joined the Klondike gold rush in northern Canada, an event that inspired his most famous stories, including *The Call of the Wild* and *White Fang*. By the time of his early death he was one of America's most celebrated authors.

A(lan) A(lexander) Milne (1882–1956) was born in London, England. He was a journalist and assistant editor of the humorous magazine *Punch* before becoming a successful playwright in the 1920s. His first book of verse for children, *When We Were Very Young*, published in 1924, sold so many copies that his publishers begged for more. *Winnie-the-Pooh* (1926) was written for and about his son, Christopher Robin, and the animals are based on the toys in his nursery. They can still be seen in the New York Public Library. "The Forest", too, is a real place: Ashdown Forest in Sussex, England, to which Milne took the artist, Ernest H. Shepard, when the illustrations were planned.

L(ucy) M(aud) Montgomery (1874–1942) was born on Prince Edward Island, Canada. She became a schoolteacher and later a postmistress, and worked as a journalist as well as a novelist. She was the author of many novels, most notably *Anne of Green Gables*, published in 1908 and the first of six books about the lively red-haired heroine. These were followed by other books such as *Rainbow Valley* and *Rilla of Ingleside* in which Anne also appears. Other popular L. M. Montgomery heroines include Emily Byrd Starr, whose trilogy began with *Emily of New Moon*, published in 1923.

Michael Morpurgo was born in 1943 in St Alban's, England. Like Bertie in *The Butterfly Lion*, which was published in 1996, he was very homesick when sent away to boarding school. He took refuge in reading, particularly poetry, and Stevenson's *Treasure Island* became, and remains, his favourite book. He has written many books for children, including *The Wreck of the Zanzibar*, which won the Whitbread Children's Novel Award.

Jill Murphy was born in 1949 in London, England. She has been writing stories since she was four years old, and drawing for as long as she can remember. She is the creator of many popular picture books, including *Five Minutes' Peace* (winner of the Best Books for Babies Award) and *The Last Noo-Noo* (winner of the Smarties Prize). Her series of novels about Mildred Hubble began in 1974 with the publication of *The Worst Witch*. There are now four titles in the series, all of them illustrated by the author.

Katherine Paterson was born in 1932 in China, where she lived until the age of eight when her family returned to the United States. She has worked as both a missionary and a teacher and is the author of many books for children. She has received several major awards for her writing, including the American Library Association's Newbery Medal in 1978 for *Bridge to Terabithia* and in 1981 for *Jacob Have I Loved*. *The Great Gilly Hopkins* was published in 1978.

(Ann) Philippa Pearce was born in 1920 in Cambridgeshire, England. She grew up in the mill-house that is the setting for *Tom's Midnight Garden*, and still lives nearby. The book, published in 1958, won the Library Association Carnegie Medal. Philippa Pearce has written many other books for children, notably *A Dog So Small* and *The Way to Sattin Shore*.

Eleanor H(odgman) Porter (1868-1920) was born in New Hampshire, USA. A choir and concert singer, she trained at the prestigious New England Conservatory of Music in Boston.

She wrote many books and became an overnight success with *Pollyanna*, published in 1913. Together with its sequel, *Pollyanna Grows Up*, it has maintained its popularity ever since. In fact such was Pollyanna's success that after the author's death, other writers were commissioned to continue her story. In all, a further ten books by four other writers were published.

Anna Sewell (1820–78) was born in Norfolk, England and moved with her parents to London when she was a child. Disabled through illness, she grew to rely on a horse and trap for mobility. *Black Beauty* was inspired by her experience. She died a few months after the book's publication, never to know of its profound success. The story was instrumental in changing attitudes to the treatment of horses and remains today one of the world's favourite animal stories.

Johanna Spyri (1827–1901) was born in Switzerland, in a village overlooking Lake Zurich and with glorious views of the Alps. Her father was a local doctor. Although very little is known of her life, she became the author of almost fifty novels. The story of Heidi first appeared in 1880 and was an immediate success. It was published in two volumes, as *Heidi's Years of Wandering and Learning* and, a year later, *Heidi Makes Use of What She Has Learned. Heidi*, the title by which the book is now known the world over, remains her most popular book.

Robert Louis Stevenson (1850–94) was born in Edinburgh, Scotland, and spent much of his short life travelling in search of a climate that might cure what is now thought to have been tuberculosis. In 1881, on a rainy day in Braemar, he drew a map of an imaginary island to entertain his American stepson, Lloyd Osbourne. This was the inspiration for *Treasure Island*, which appeared first as a serial called *The Sea Cook*. When published in book form in 1883, it established Stevenson as a master of the adventure story.

Rosemary Sutcliff (1920–92) was born in Surrey, England. As she tells us in her autobiography, *Blue Remembered Hills* (1983), she was a solitary child, being afflicted with Still's Disease at the age of two. This prevented her from pursuing her first love, painting (she could neither stand at an easel nor reach a broad canvas), so she turned her powerful imagination to writing historical novels. It also meant that her mother taught her at home, reading to her legends, history, and the story of Beowulf – which later inspired her own retelling, published in 1961.

Ethel Turner (1870–1958) was born in Yorkshire, England, and emigrated to Australia at the age of ten. As a young girl she had a great ambition to be a famous author. Her dream was realized with the publication of *Seven Little Australians* in 1894, the first realistic Australian family story. Ethel Turner went on to write over forty books, including three more – *The Family at Misrule, Little Mother Meg* and *Judy and Punch* – which follow the lives of the Woolcot family as they grow up.

Mark Twain (1835–1910) was the pseudonym of Samuel Langhorne Clemens, who was born in Missouri, USA, and grew up in Hannibal, a town on the Mississippi River. He travelled widely as a printer, river-boat pilot, prospector and journalist before becoming the most popular writer in the US. Based on his own boyhood memories, *The Adventures of Tom Sawyer* was published in 1876 and was followed by a sequel, *The Adventures of Huckleberry Finn* in 1884.

T(erence) H(anbury) White (1906–64) was born in Bombay, India, and brought home to England when he was five. He was a teacher before becoming a full-time writer, and spent his later years living in the Channel Islands. *The Sword in the Stone* was published in 1938 but twenty years later White revised it for inclusion in *The Once and Future King*, his retelling of the complete Arthurian epic. He was profoundly influenced by Sir Thomas Malory's *Morte D'Arthur*, saying, "I have tried to look at it through the innocent eyes of young people."

Laura Ingalls Wilder (1867–1957) was born in Wisconsin, USA. Her family were pioneers, living an isolated life of self-sufficiency in a log cabin built by Laura's father, and always ready to move on in their covered wagon. Laura became a schoolteacher and did not begin writing down her vivid childhood memories until she was in her sixties. *Little House in the Big Woods* was published in 1932, the first in a series of nine absorbing books about her life.

ACKNOWLEDGEMENTS

The publisher would like to thank the copyright holders for permission to reproduce the following copyright material:

J. M. Barrie: Great Ormond Street Children's Hospital for "The Flight" from *Peter Pan* by J. M. Barrie, Hodder & Stoughton 1911. Copyright © J. M. Barrie 1911. **Pauline Baynes**: Illustrations by Pauline Baynes from *The Lion, the Witch and the Wardrobe* by C. S. Lewis copyright © C. S. Lewis Pte. Ltd 1950, reprinted by permission. **Christian Birmingham**: The Artworks for illustration on p.106 by Christian Birmingham and HarperCollins Publishers Ltd for all other illustrations by Christian Birmingham from *The Butterfly Lion* by Michael Morpurgo, CollinsChildren's Books 1996. Copyright © Christian Birmingham 1996. **Quentin Blake**: A. P. Watt Ltd. for illustrations by Quentin Blake from *Charlie and the Chocolate Factory* by Roald Dahl, from *The Roald Dahl Treasury*, Jonathan Cape Ltd. 1997. Copyright © Quentin Blake 1997. Penguin Books Ltd. for illustration on p.87 by Quentin Blake from *Charlie and the Chocolate Factory* by Roald Dahl, Viking 1997. Copyright © Quentin Blake 1995, 1997. **Joyce Lankester Brisley**: Kingfisher Publications Plc. for text and illustrations from "Milly-Molly-Mandy Gives a Party" from *Milly-Molly-Mandy Stories* by Joyce Lankester Brisley, George G. Harrap & Co. Ltd. 1928. Copyright © 1928 Joyce Lankester Brisley. **Beverly Cleary**: HarperCollins Publishers Inc. for "The Baddest Witch in the World" from *Ramona the Pest* by Beverly Cleary, Avon Books 1968. Copyright © 1968 Beverly Cleary. **Carlo Collodi**: Penguin Books Ltd. for extract from *Pinocchio* by Carlo Collodi translated by E. Harden, Puffin 1974, 1996. Translation copyright © The Estate of E. Harden 1974, 1996. **Richmal Crompton**: Macmillan Children's Books, London for "The Fall of the Idol" from *Just William* by Richmal Crompton. Copyright © Richmal C. Ashbee. **Roald Dahl**: David Higham Associates Ltd. for extract from *Charlie and the Chocolate Factory* by Roald Dahl, George Allen & Unwin 1967. Copyright © Roald Dahl Nominee Ltd. 1964. **Andrew Davidson**: The Artworks for illustrations by Andrew Davidson from *The Iron Man* by Ted Hughes, Faber and Faber Ltd. 1968. Copyright © Andrew Davidson 1985. Kingfisher Publications Plc. for illustrations by Andrew Davidson from *The Call of the Wild* by Jack London, Kingfisher 2002. Copyright © Andrew Davidson 2002. **Jean Craighead George**: The Random House Group Ltd. for extract from *My Side of the Mountain* by Jean Craighead George, The Bodley Head 1962. Copyright © Jean Craighead George 1959. **Ted Hughes**: Faber and Faber Ltd. for "The Return of the Iron Man" from *The Iron Man* by Ted Hughes, Faber and Faber Ltd. 1968. Copyright © Ted Hughes 1968. **Rudyard Kipling**: A. P. Watt Ltd. on behalf of The National Trust for Places of Historic Interest or Natural Beauty for extract from *The Jungle Book* by Rudyard Kipling. Macmillan 1894. **C. S. Lewis**: *The Lion, the Witch and the Wardrobe* by C. S. Lewis copyright © C. S. Lewis Pte. Ltd. 1950. Extract reprinted by permission. **Astrid Lindgren**: Kerstin Kvint Literary & Co-Production Agency for "Pippi Goes to the Circus" from *Pippi Longstocking* by Astrid Lindgren, Rabén & Sjogren 1945. Copyright © Astrid Lindgren 1945. Viking Penguin, an imprint of Penguin Putnam Books for Young Readers, a division of Penguin Putnam, Inc. for translation by Florence Lamborn, copyright © 1950 Viking Press, Inc. Copyright renewed © 1978 Viking Putnam Inc. **A. A. Milne**: Egmont Children's Books Limited, London for "In Which Pooh Goes Visiting and Gets into a Tight Place" from *Winnie-the-Pooh* by A. A. Milne, Methuen & Co. Ltd. 1926. Copyright © A. A. Milne. Copyright under the Berne Convention. **L. M. Montgomery**: David Macdonald, trustee, and Ruth Macdonald, heirs of L. M. Montgomery for "Anne's Confession" from *Anne of Green Gables* by L. M. Montgomery, Boston and Toronto, Page, and London, Pitman 1908. Entered at Stationer's Hall. Copyright © 1984 David Macdonald, trustee, and Ruth Macdonald. "Anne of Green Gables" is a trademark of the Anne of Green Gables Licensing Authority Inc., used under licence by Kingfisher Publications Plc. "L. M. Montgomery" is a trademark of the Heirs of L. M. Montgomery Inc. **Michael Morpurgo**: HarperCollins Publishers Ltd. for "Bertie and the Lion" from *The Butterfly Lion* by Michael Morpurgo, CollinsChildren's Books 1996. Copyright © Michael Morpurgo 1996. **Jill Murphy**: Penguin Books UK Ltd. for Chapter 4 and illustrations from *The Worst Witch* by Jill Murphy, Puffin 1978. Copyright © Jill Murphy 1974. Title page illustration by Jill Murphy from *The Puffin Treasury of Children's Stories*. Puffin Books 1996. Copyright © Jill Murphy 1974, 1996. **Katherine Paterson**: Penguin Books UK Ltd. for "Pow" from *The Great Gilly Hopkins* by Katherine Paterson, Victor Gollancz/Hamish Hamilton 1979. Copyright © Katherine Paterson 1978. **Philippa Pearce**: Oxford University Press for Chapter 5 from *Tom's Midnight Garden*, Oxford University Press 1958. Copyright © Oxford University Press 1958. **Angelo Rinaldi**: Kingfisher Publications Plc. for border illustration and illustration on p.288 by

Angelo Rinaldi from *Black Beauty* by Anna Sewell, Kingfisher 2001. Copyright © Angelo Rinaldi 2001. **E. H. Shepard**: Curtis Brown Ltd., London for line illustrations by E. H. Shepard from *Winnie-the-Pooh* by A. A. Milne. Copyright under the Berne Convention, colouring copyright © 1970, 1973 by E. H. Shepard and Methuen Children's Books. **Johanna Spyri**: "A Day with the Goats" from *Heidi* by Johanna Spyri, translated by Eileen Hall, Puffin 1956. **Rosemary Sutcliff**: The Random House Group Ltd. for extract from *Beowulf: Dragonslayer* by Rosemary Sutcliff, The Bodley Head 1961. Copyright © Rosemary Sutcliff 1961. **Sir John Tenniel**: Macmillan Children's Books for original illustrations by Sir John Tenniel coloured by Harry Theaker and Diz Wallis from *Alice's Adventures in Wonderland* by Lewis Carroll, Macmillan Children's Books 1995. Illustrations coloured by Harry Theaker, copyright © 1911 Macmillan Publishers Ltd. Illustrations coloured by Diz Wallis, copyright © 1995 Macmillan Publishers Ltd. **Ethel Turner**: Penguin Books Australia Ltd. for "The General Sees Active Service" from *Seven Little Australians* by Ethel Turner, Puffin 1994. First published by Ward Lock 1894. Copyright © 1988 Philippa Poole. **T. H. White**: David Higham Associates Ltd. for extract from *The Sword in the Stone* by T. H. White, William Collins Sons & Co. Ltd. 1938. Copyright © T. H. White 1938. **Laura Ingalls Wilder**: HarperCollins Publishers, Inc. for "Christmas" from *Little House in the Big Woods* by Laura Ingalls Wilder, Harper 1932. Copyright © 1932 Laura Ingalls Wilder. Copyright renewed © 1959 Roger Lea MacBride. "Little House" ® is a registered trademark of HarperCollins Publishers, Inc.

Every effort has been made to obtain permission to reproduce copyright material but there may be cases where we have been unable to trace a copyright holder. The publisher will be happy to correct any omissions in future printings.

The publisher would like to thank the artists for their original illustrations as follows:

Ian Andrew: illustrations for *The Jungle Book* copyright © Ian Andrew 2000. **Peter Bailey**: illustrations for *Pinocchio* copyright © Peter Bailey 2000. **Ian Beck**: illustrations for *The Wizard of Oz* copyright © Ian Beck 1999. **Christian Birmingham**: border illustration for *The Butterfly Lion* copyright © Christian Birmingham 2000. **Mick Brownfield**: illustrations for *The Great Gilly Hopkins* copyright © Mick Brownfield 1999. **Emma Chichester Clark**: illustrations for *A Little Princess* copyright © Emma Chichester Clark 1999. Illustrations for *Peter Pan* copyright © Emma Chichester Clark 2000. **Robin Bell Corfield**: illustrations for *The Adventures of Tom Sawyer* copyright © Robin Bell Corfield 2000. **Kady MacDonald Denton**: illustrations for *Little House in the Big Woods* copyright © Kady MacDonald Denton 1999. **Mark Edwards**: illustrations for *Anne of Green Gables* copyright © Mark Edwards 1999. **Chris Fisher**: illustrations for *The Sword in the Stone* copyright © Chris Fisher 2000. Illustrations for *The Wind in the Willows* © Chris Fisher 2002. **Michael Foreman**: illustrations for *Beowulf: Dragonslayer* copyright © Michael Foreman 2000. **Anne Yvonne Gilbert**: illustrations for *Little Women* copyright © Anne Yvonne Gilbert 1999. **Felicity Gill**: illustrations for *Heidi* copyright © Felicity Gill 1999. Illustrations for *My Side of the Mountain* copyright © Felicity Gill 2000. **Rob Hefferan**: illustrations for *Seven Little Australians* copyright © Rob Hefferan 1999. **Alison Jay**: illustrations for *What Katy Did* copyright © Alison Jay 1999. **Susie Jenkin-Pearce**: illustrations for *Pollyanna* copyright © Susie Jenkin-Pearce 1999. **Richard Jones**: illustrations for *Oliver Twist* copyright © Richard Jones 2000. **Stephen Lambert**: illustrations for *Tom's Midnight Garden* copyright © Stephen Lambert 2000. **John Lawrence**: illustrations for *Treasure Island* copyright © John Lawrence 2000. **Chris Riddell**: illustrations for *Pippi Longstocking* copyright © Chris Riddell 1999. **Angelo Rinaldi**: illustrations for pp. 284, 285 of *Black Beauty* copyright © Angelo Rinaldi 2002. **Tony Ross**: illustrations for *Just William* copyright © Tony Ross 2000. Illustrations for *Ramona the Pest* copyright © Tony Ross 1999.